A
PARADOX
BROKEN

A PARADOX BROKEN

THE CHRONOS PARADOX • BOOK 3

HUNTER BLAIN

Podium

ISBN: 978-1-0394-5495-8

Published in 2025 by Podium Publishing
www.podiumentertainment.com

Podium

A
PARADOX
BROKEN

"The future is not something we enter. The future is something we create."
—*Leonard I. Sweet*

"The only reason for time is so that everything doesn't happen at once."
—*Albert Einstein*

"Our future is determined by our present, just as our present is determined by our past. We are all prisoners of the consequences from the decisions we have made, are making, and will make."
—*Hunter Blain*

PROLOGUE

Wild, vibrant lights flowed all around me in tiny, brilliant specks as I floated in a space between time itself. What appeared to be illusionary sand passed through my body like some sort of interactive 3D display at a museum.

I watched as swathes of color harmlessly flowed into my chest and out of my back, as if I were nothing more than a witness to the majesty of the sands of time.

Though the hues ranged across every shade imaginable, I could discern beautiful patterns, as if the individual grains gravitated toward others of a similar contrast, almost like magnets. It was like looking at a coastline from an airplane, with different shades of green and blue making up the ocean before shifting to the rich brown of wet sand; moving past where the waves crested and kissed the shore to where the beach attempted to burn the feet of all who walked upon it, the color shifted to more of a golden hue before eventually meeting up with the green grass that dotted the outlying dunes.

All this is to say that what I was seeing wasn't just a hodgepodge of different-colored sands mixing into a singular shade, as colors tended to do when combined—especially when placed in an environment of constant motion. Instead, the vibrant schools of grain flowed with one another, resembling a windswept field of tall grass. The full spectrum of colors chased after one another, spontaneously mixing to form new shades like what was taught in elementary school.

Lifting my hand through the sands, I moved to press my palm against my chest, but I froze at what my eyes were relaying to my brain.

My synthetic right arm, which had been replaced after I had accidentally blown off my real one, was now a glowing soft, almost yellowish orange, yet was seamlessly integrated into the rest of my ethereal body, which was a pure brilliant ivory.

Panic tried to explode from behind a dam of shock, but my curiosity reinforced the wall, allowing a nervous, morbid fascination to stay in control.

Lifting both luminescent hands in front of my face, I stared with a furrowed brow as the sands of time continued to flow *through* my essence. What's more, I could see past flesh that was now seemingly incorporeal—one glowing hand a bright white, and the other a warm yellow.

For some reason, it reminded me of when Sylvie and I had first bought our house and redone the light fixtures in the kitchen and bathrooms. I had grabbed enough light bulbs from the local home improvement store to change every socket, only to be met with a stifled laughter as my loving wife explained the difference between soft white, warm white, and daylight bulbs.

"Sylvie . . ." I whispered, feeling my brow smooth as my heart longed once more for the simpler times when my greatest worry was choosing the right color light bulbs from an entire long aisle at The Home Depot.

Something caught my eye, and I lowered my ethereal hands to gaze at what appeared to be an extremely blurry hallway without a ceiling. The walls on either side were tall with what seemed to be shelves stretching down the lengths. Peering closer to the wall next to me, the vibrant sands coalesced into . . . light bulb packages?

Though I wasn't standing on a solid surface, I nearly stumbled backward as I closed my eyes and aggressively shook my head in disbelief. Opening them again, I saw the odd hallway had nearly dissipated as clouds of multihued grains appeared to return to an unperturbed stream, not even noticing the changes I had somehow brought into existence.

Looking up, I could make out a clear barrier where the flow of time stayed confined to, reminding me of an aquarium.

With a simple thought, I rose through the stream to poke my head and shoulders out of the surface. What I saw filled me with awe as my eyes traveled the colorful river down its length. To me, it felt like what the Bifröst was described as in Norse mythology.

A feeling of childlike wonder overtook me, and I placed my left palm in the path of the flowing grains, as if I were in a strong river with my arm outstretched to my side just beneath the surface to try and create a perpetual wave. But the sands passed through my body as if I were nothing more than a specter.

My mind flashed to when I had been in the fourth dimension and stuck my finger into the lava that had killed Drew. It'd passed through the frozen-in-time molten rock as if it were nothing more than an illusion. After that, I had drifted *through* the wall without resistance. But something was different. My body hadn't glowed then, nor had the scene been made of sand. It had simply been . . . frozen in time.

I lifted my ivory hand from the stream, wishing I could touch the sand for some reason. Maybe because the sensation of feeling would mean I wasn't dead?

Like a school of fish swimming in sync with one another, the sands began to swirl around my hand, reminding me of an experiment in science class when I was a teenager. A simple magnet, which I remember looked like it had been in use since the turn of the century, sat on a flat surface as we poured iron fillings around it, creating a brilliant geometric pattern.

The vivid, chaotic specks seemed to organize into a full color spectrum around my hand. It was like the circular rainbows that pilots described seeing far above the clouds after a storm.

With just a flicker of a thought, I willed the blue portion of the colorful disk to spread outward, swallowing the other shades until it looked like my hands were submerged to the wrists in the middle of the ocean just after sunset.

"Am I dead?" I asked out loud as I dropped my focus on the sands, letting them revert back to their chaotic nature before being carried away by the evermoving stream.

I actually don't know, Tim said inside my head, surprising me, as I thought I was alone in this blizzard of color.

After a few seconds, his words sunk in.

"Wait . . . what do you *mean* you don't know?!"

I mean *I have no readings on your body. Which is totally freaking me out, man!*

"Freaking *you* out?! What about *me*?!"

Okay, okay, okay! Let's not panic! Tim said, taking a deep breath—which was odd, considering his words were *inside* my head.

Following his advice, I tried to take in a breath, only to realize that I *couldn't* breathe.

Sheer terror burst through the walls of my steadfast determination like floodwaters breaking through a neglected levee. But after a few seconds, I forced my mind to acknowledge that I wasn't suffocating. My vision didn't begin to dim, which was always the case whenever I stayed submerged in the fourth dimension for too long. Nor did I grow increasingly exhausted, like someone being slowly put under anesthesia.

"Tim?" I asked aloud.

Ye—Yes, Andrew?

"How am I able to speak if I can't breathe?"

I, um . . . I-I don't know! This is all beyond even my *comprehension.*

Something tickled at my focus, and I followed the faint path to land my gaze on my right arm, which persisted in glowing a warm yellow, as if mimicking the sun. Continuing to follow the notion that was forming into a full-blown conscious thought, I bounced my eyes to my ivory left arm. But the different glows weren't what was interesting any longer—there was no Clepsydra.

"T-Tim?"

Yes? my increasingly nervous AI companion responded.

"Where are you?"

Where . . . am I? Wh-What do you mean? I'm here . . . right?

"Can you see me?"

I hadn't thought about it until just now, but I can only *see what* you *see. I-I-I can't change perspectives!*

"And do you see what I'm looking at? Or rather, what I'm *not* looking at?"

Hmm? What do you—OH MY SCIENCE! Where am I?! he shouted, on the verge of losing his artificial mind. He even began taking ragged breaths, perfectly mimicking the all-too-human emotion. *My Clepsydra is—is—is gone!*

"Yet here you are," I both noted and reassured. "Rather, here *we* are . . ."

We floated in silence for an indeterminate amount of time—if time was even a factor wherever we were. The colorful sands continued to flow through my body as if I wasn't there, and a realization came to me.

Lowering my arms, I looked forward, saying as much for myself as for Tim, "I think *we* are moving *through* time."

It took Tim more than a few seconds to process what I was saying, and to his credit, he managed to pull himself back from the verge of what I could only describe as virtual insanity.

Interesting, he mused, though I could still hear the stress in his tone. *You are suggesting that we are the ones moving through this 3D representation of time instead of it flowing around us as we stand still.*

"One way to find out," I said, holding up my right hand in a universal gesture of *stop*.

On cue, the flowing river of time slowed before ceasing entirely, leaving behind a colorful path that appeared to stretch forever into the distance.

01 . . . Tim drawled in amazement. *How are you doing this, Andrew?*

"I—I have no idea," I said as something in my periphery taunted my gaze.

Shifting my eyes through the river I was submerged to my chest in, my mouth dropped open as I saw literal countless other time streams that were just as unmoving as the one I currently found myself wading in. Each was poised at precise intervals, with colorful rivers to either side, above and below me. Looking up and to the right, I could see mesmerizing symmetrical personifications of time lined precisely one in front of the other. It reminded me of driving past fields of orange trees that had been planted in evenly spaced straight lines.

"What am I seeing?" I whispered in sheer awe.

If I had to guess based on the limited evidence we have gathered so far, I could theorize that we are witnessing the fourth dimension from the limited perspective of a being that can only comprehend the universe in three dimensions.

"You mean a tesseract?"

Of sorts. Yes.

I leaned dangerously close to the edge, looking down to see an expanse of vibrant streams that were surprisingly simple to differentiate, given the precise space between them.

Maybe because I was simply a human mind trying to comprehend countless universes all around me, I couldn't help but feel like I was at the very center of it all. Then again, people not that long ago also thought the sun revolved around the Earth.

"What . . . What happens if I move to another one?" I asked with a throat that felt dry—which was interesting, considering my body appeared to be an incorporeal mass of light.

Um . . . I'd rather not find out? Tim answered with a nervous, almost pleading inflection.

An electrified fog crossed just under my forehead, and I snapped out of my reverie at the majestic tesseract.

"What were we doing?" I asked, rubbing at the tingling sensation that stretched from temple to temple.

Right! We were heading toward Alison's lab to find her notes!

"Ali . . ."

Hearing Tim's confirmation of our plan, my resolve and determination flowed through my entire being like taking the world's largest Shop-Vac and sucking up all the stagnant floodwaters of dread trying to weaken the foundation of my mission.

When compared to the sweet angel that made up *my* universe, the awe of the countless rivers of time seemed no more important than an overabundance of billboards on a highway.

My mind focusing on Alison's lab, the chaotic assortment of colorful sand around me blurred at mind-boggling speed for several *perceived* moments before suddenly stopping as if hitting pause on a remote. I said "perceived" because I couldn't even begin to understand how time worked inside the tesseract—an hourglass that held all the sands of time.

Below where I waded with my head above the stream, I watched as a large box began to form. On instinct, I held the breath I didn't have and lowered myself until I was standing on the floor of what I knew to be a room. I didn't recognize it, so just watched as the sands continued to solidify into the beginnings of a cohesive scene.

An oval began to take shape which seemed to move toward what appeared to be a heavily pixelated desk.

Wait! Tim cried out in my head. *We aren't far enough yet!*

"Far enough?" I asked before his words registered.

The oval continued to take form, and I knew in an instant who I was looking at.

"Alison . . ."

My daughter snapped her head in my direction, startling me like a dream bleeding over into reality, where it was impossible to differentiate fiction from the real world.

My focus dropped, and the sands fell away into a swiftly moving blizzard once more, taking my daughter away from me.

"No!"

Andrew. You probably shouldn't have contact with her. At least not yet.

"W-Why?"

Because your Chronos Scale might interrupt her during this pivotal period.

"Meaning?!"

Meaning she might not have found the potential answers that she left hidden for us, a là the law of unintended consequences.

"Butterfly effect . . ." I murmured.

Precisely, Tim concurred. *If you make contact with her, you could very well change the course of time itself, given your immeasurable Chronos Scale. And she might not leave the hidden research for us to find. At least not in a spot where we would know to look for it.*

I thought about what he was saying as the chaotic, colorful sands flowed by and through my body once more.

"She . . . She was right there . . ."

Don't be so glum, Andrew! Tim cheerily said. *I said you shouldn't have contact with her yet. Now, let's keep moving through time and pray that little interaction didn't alter events out of our favor.*

I forced myself to digest his meaning, beginning to understand what he was trying to get at.

"I'll be able to see her again . . ." I said with a spark of hope as I willed myself to move further down the stream of time toward what my baby girl had left for me to find.

If you are able to do the impossible, then yes.

"You, uh . . . actually sound confident."

You've proven time and time again, pun intended, that you are able to do the impossible. So, at this point, I'm just along for the ride, baby! he said enthusiastically. *If I were a betting AI, I'd wager all my chips on you getting to watch your daughter grow up to live the life she deserves. And if I were to be honest,* Tim added meekly, *I'd like to see you happy, Andrew. Science knows you've earned it!*

I dared to let a feeling of warmth spread outward from my heart as I pictured a life where I got to watch my baby girl grow into the amazing woman I knew she would become.

"And what about the universe?" I asked, feeling like I shouldn't but unable to help myself. The warm feeling expanding throughout my core slowed before cooling off as quickly as a fresh slice of pizza placed in front of a shop fan. "I can't have my cake and eat it too, right?"

What happened to the determined Andrew who wasn't going to let a simple thing like temporal mechanics and paradoxes stop him? Hmm? Is he home? Can heeeee *come out and play?*

I lowered my head while an unstoppable smile yanked the corners of my lips up. He was right. I was being melancholy for the sake of argument, when I *knew* nothing would stop me from defying everything that was thrown at me.

There he is! Tim exclaimed with an accompanying sound clip of applause as we continued to travel through the blizzard of colorful sand. *Welcome back, leg butt!*

"Thanks, Betamax."

Yo—I—How dare . . . ! Tim began, unable to process the epic insult.

"I'm sorry. Would a floppy disk have been better?"

I'll show you *a floppy disk . . .* he muttered just under his breath.

"I, uh . . . Phrasing?"

After what I could only describe as a *few minutes* had passed—because we were in a tesseract where time, ironically, wasn't a unit of measurement—Tim spoke up.

Are we there yet?

"How am I supposed to know?!"

How did you arrive in the lab before?

"I . . . I focused on Alison."

Well, do that again. But this time, focus on the message she left behind for you.

Remembering what my baby girl had written in the letter, I imagined a VHS box of *Alice in Wonderland.* With a set objective in mind, the sands started to blur past like a hail of bullets from a platoon of minigun-wielding soldiers, causing a growing bubble of worry to try and fill my chest.

From somewhere in the distance, I heard a hiss of what sounded like, "*Frrrooooossst.*"

Turning toward where I thought the noise originated from, I lifted myself up until I was standing on the surface and peered down the stream. Immediately, I wished I hadn't.

"Jesus . . ." I mouthed before my jaw went slack and my eyes tried to bulge from their sockets.

That can't be good . . .

A being comprised of an angry orange light flew toward us like a rocket.

If my eyes were made of flesh, then they might have seared at how bright the man shone, like staring directly into the sun. A streaking ball of violent energy whizzed past my head faster than a bullet, nearly dropping me to my ass in surprise.

As the star man grew closer, I watched in frozen horror as he lifted his hand to lob another death sphere at me.

Without me telling it to do so, my right arm flashed upward right as the ball was set to smash into my chest. I was aware of a powerful tingling that erupted down my forearm as the sphere was deflected.

Making sure my arm hadn't been blown off with a quick visual inspection, I felt a shallow wave of relief . . . until I heard where the sphere had crashed.

Looking up, I watched in fascinated horror as the colorful river of time directly above us violently shook like a swimming pool during a city-leveling earthquake. Vibrant waves crested outward in all directions from the point of impact, like solar flares fleeing the sun, before dramatically slowing. The farther the colorful sands of time flew from their river of origin, the more they dulled before fading into nothing.

Wave after wave exploded in beautiful crests before slowing and disappearing.

"What's happening?"

I—I don't know, Andrew. But if I had to guess, Tim started before audibly gulping, *that stream of time is being destroyed.*

"Why would he risk destroying the timeline just to—"

In answer, Retnuh Ordune bellowed, "*FRRROOOOOOOOOST!*"

Above us, a massive wave expanded in all directions at the point of impact. It was like watching a superpowered snowplow through a kaleidoscope as it tore through a street after a blizzard, shooting enormous sheets of snow outward in a full circle.

I could feel the force of the explosion as it rushed both toward the future and the past, making me worry about *my* timeline, the one I stood upon. I had to shield my head with my arms as what I could only describe as a pyroclastic cloud rushed to envelop me.

May I suggest we run? Heh-heh, Tim nervously suggested. I could almost picture him loosening the tie around his throat that he wasn't wearing.

The stream I stood on began to waver like a steel bridge on the verge of collapsing while my body was subjected to an unimaginable heat.

"JESUS!" I shouted before I was thrown off the timeline like an older brother double bouncing their younger sibling on a trampoline. Except the force used would have been enough to send said kid high enough to touch the clouds.

As I flew, I glimpsed Retnuh standing where I had been, the wave of heat being blown away as the man rested both palms on the original timeline. An invisible wave rushed out in both directions, arresting the bucking movement of the stream while the universe above it faded from view.

Retnuh grew smaller with each passing second, until he looked like nothing more than an ant on the calm, glass top surface of my home.

"How—" I started to ask when I crashed into a sea of brilliant colors. I didn't feel the impact, nor was there any resistance, and I flew out the other side and into another stream of sand.

With a focus of will, I tried to grasp at the river, feeling the briefest of impacts on my hands. Then I was out the other side and soaring to yet another stream; though this time, I was flying noticeably slower.

Using all my focus, I demanded my body stop as I entered the next timeline. To my relief, I arrested my momentum with half of my body sticking out the top of the smooth timeline.

Once again, I couldn't help but feel like I was looking at the Norse rainbow bridge.

Doing something I knew I shouldn't, I inched myself to the edge and looked down to where I had come from. I didn't know what I was expecting, but had to see it anyway.

Row after row of identical streams blocked the view, filling me with a sense of being lost that only a child separated from their parent at a busy mall could understand.

"*FROOOOOST!*" Retnuh bellowed from somewhere far away.

He's looking for you, Andrew! May I suggest we, oh, I don't know, fragging hide?!

"Good idea," I replied before slowly easing myself into the stream like fully submerging myself in a swimming pool. The sands weren't moving this time, and it served to confirm that it was because *I* wasn't moving through *it*.

Focus on Alison's research. Maybe we can still find what we are looking for in this timeline.

"Alison," I breathed out, and everything in me went still as I closed my eyes.

I didn't feel time flow around me, but I could see the dance of brilliant light through my clenched eyes almost like a strobe light, but with each flash being a different color.

Opening my eyes, I kept my mind and heart fixated on finding the truth. The truth that would save my family.

It didn't take long before I was approaching my wheren. I didn't know *how* I knew, I just knew . . .

The river seemed to widen in all directions, including vertically, until identifiable walls, floor, and ceiling began to form all around me. As quickly as the fast-forward through time started, it slowed before stopping entirely as a room continued to take shape from the sands of time that apparently knew where to go with nothing more than a willful thought from me.

Without having to wait for the scene to coalesce and showcase distinguishing features, I already knew where I was.

The beginning of the end . . .

CHAPTER 1

Cool, stale air washed over me just as the colorful sands solidified, and the room I found myself in went completely dark. Where there had been beautiful light from the billions of grains all around me, now there was a deep abyss.

I shot my face from left to right, worried whatever mystical voodoo I had done to arrive here had somehow blinded me.

My movement triggered a motion sensor, which flicked on clinical lights reminiscent of any commercial building or doctor's office.

01 . . . Tim breathed out in what sounded like amazement intermixed with disbelief. I couldn't tell if it was the prayer of someone about to die from something unstoppable, or from a man on the precipice of death in the middle of a sweltering desert that had just crawled on hands and knees to a pristine oasis with crystal-clear water.

"What?" I whispered in response to his AI equivalent of me saying *God.* My eyes darted all around searching for Retnuh hiding in the shadows of the laboratory, ready to tear this timeline apart too.

Something was different, however. In the brief memories I had absorbed from Drew's timeline, I didn't remember there being stairs leading up.

I am unable to process how it is you are able to do the things that, well, you do. *It—It defies all logic!*

Letting out a sigh from a tight chest that seemed to be frozen in place, I sucked in a deep, lung-expanding breath. The air, though musty, was like sweet nectar to my lungs, reminding me I hadn't been able to breathe while in the time . . . *thingy*. What had Tim called it—a tesseract?

Letting out a huge breath, I sucked in another, feeling confused while also marveling at being made of pure energy to the point where I didn't need oxygen to function. I could even speak out loud some-how, even without having to force air past my vocal cords—if I had any, that is, while being made seemingly out of nothing more than light.

Looking down, I patted my left arm, feeling the surprisingly warm Clepsydra that housed Tim's consciousness. Or did it? He had been with me in the tesseract. But that idea took a back seat as I tried to get my chaotic thoughts in order.

I attempted to focus on the mission, but now that we were safe, my mind wouldn't let me think about anything else except for what had just happened.

Without realizing that my body was moving on its own, I sat on the edge of the couch like a child about to get reprimanded by his parents.

"Tim . . . what the hell happened to that . . . that—that *timeline*, I guess you would call it?" I asked as my fingers absentmindedly glided over the surprisingly well-preserved cushion.

I can only surmise by the dissipation of the particles that left the linear confines of the structure that the particular timeline in question was erased from all of existence.

I thought about the colorful waves that were thrown away from the river, remembering how the fast-moving projectiles had first slowed before fading to a dull tone . . . and then disappearing entirely.

"How . . . How do you know that for sure?" I knew I was practi-cally begging Tim to let me know he had made a mistake and that all was well, because my mind just couldn't fathom an entire time-line being erased. All the lives that had lived on it, both past and future . . . just gone.

I don't know for sure. But it would stand to reason that anything which ruptures to the point where its exploded particles fade into pre-sumed nonexistence probably signifies the original structure no longer functions. Then again, I'm not a keyboard expert who spent an hour watching YouTube videos in search of confirmation bias that matched my already established beliefs.

"That . . . came out of nowhere . . . ?"

Oh, uh, sorry. Sometimes, the might of my sarcasm surprises even me.

There were a few seconds of silence before I willed myself to ignore where he had gone slightly off the tracks, and digested his message.

"Retnuh destroyed an entire timeline," I said with a forced sigh in an effort to relax as I leaned back on the couch. But no matter how I mimicked the actions that preluded comfort, I just couldn't release the tension in my heart and muscles. "He basically threw a grenade inside a house of glass. Why?"

Now, that is the million-dollar question, isn't it? Why was Retnuh, presumably, willing to destroy anything and everything in order to ensure your demise?

I thought about the question and let my mouth speak as my thoughts tried to formulate full-blown ideas at the same time. "To try and stop different variants of me?"

Hmm. I don't think that's quite right. But there could be something else there.

"Like what?"

If you put a metaphorical gun to my head, I would say that Retnuh is attempting to erase you from, well, any *timeline.*

"Any timeline . . ." I mouthed, realizing the endless sea of universes I had witnessed. "But he almost destroyed *our* timeline, right? Would he . . . Would he really risk his own home?"

Knowing Retnuh, I honestly have no idea.

"Hmph," I agreed, running a hand down my face. "He is the type to burn his entire house down after seeing just one insect in the kitchen."

Well if that *isn't the truth,* Tim half chuckled before adding, *Or maybe he simply didn't anticipate how strong his attack would be?*

"Do you think it, um, was emotionally charged? I mean, he did sound extra pissed off. Right? Even for Retnuh."

You, yourself, have proven that emotions are able to push you past boundaries thought impenetrable.

I sat frozen as his words swirled around my head.

"I wonder how much of the tess-thingy he could have destroyed . . ."

Tesseract, Tim corrected. *And if anger drives Retnuh's power on top of his already limitless determination, then I can only imagine the entire structure is subject to his whims.*

We sat without words as silence drifted among the stagnant air, absorbing how insane the Clockman, Retnuh Ordune, truly was.

"How did he even know where we were?"

Well, he didn't know our precise *location within the tesseract.*

"He was damn close enough!"

Fair. Yeah, that's fair.

"So how'd he do it, Tim?"

Andrew, Tim started in growing exasperation, *I don't even know how you do what* you *do, and I'm directly linked to your body . . . and possibly your mind, judging by my existence* inside *the tesseract. Without more data to analyze, I would only be offering a knee-jerk guess at this juncture.*

I could feel my entire body slump where I sat, as if the life were being drained out of me.

"There's just no stopping this guy . . ."

My wandering eyes caught a bookshelf which had the bottom-most space occupied by vintage VHS tapes. Before my mind could even comprehend what I was looking at, my subconscious vigorously scanned the titles. Smack-dab in the middle was *Alice in Wonderland.*

I didn't even realize I had shot to my feet until I heard the heavy thumping of my footsteps as I rushed to the bookcase. Dropping to my knees hard enough to rattle my teeth, I slipped my hands on either side of the cassette and all but threw the other movies to the floor.

There, sitting upright with a fine layer of dust, was my prize. Alison's research lay within my grasp, and the answer to save my family.

Are you alright, Andrew? Tim asked softly as I just gawked at the VHS box. *You are acting like a ravenous zombie who's stumbled upon a paraplegic Mensa convention.*

"I'm fine," I replied in a barely audible monotone. Then his words registered. "Wait, what?"

Yeah, that was a bit of a stretch, wasn't it? Hmm, I should have said a convention cohosted by the Paralympics and Mensa. Well, no, that doesn't signify that each of the participants are both hyperintelligent—for humans—and mobility challenged.

"I . . ."

Because zombies crave brains? Right? And I don't know about you, but if I were a zombie, I'd only select the grade A, primo cuts that only a juicy skull packed with dense neurons could offer. Yum!

My own brain started to formulate why adding the paraplegic portion could be easily considered risqué, if not offensive, but I just didn't care with the VHS box in my hands. Plus, I surmised Tim was trying to manipulate my stress by saying something so odd that my racing mind would hiccup while attempting to process it.

There we go. That's better, Tim said, confirming my suspicions. *Maybe take a few deep breaths to lower your heart rate? It spiked—dangerously—when you saw the bookshelf.*

"It's here," I whispered, holding the cassette box like Gollum cradling the One Ring.

But it won't do you any good if you have a stroke or heart attack.

"That's what I have you for, Tim," I answered while gliding my fingers down the cover, leaving clean streaks in the light dust coating.

The container felt heavy, and I opened it to find it neatly packed with long, rectangular-shaped objects all comprised of stainless steel.

"What are these?" I asked, pulling one out at random and lifting it to inspect it. It was about the size of a pencil in both length and girth, with no discernible markings.

Hard drives, Tim answered. I looked at either end, expecting to see some sort of USB-type connection, but as with the rest of the casing, there was none.

These are from your somewhat distant future, Andrew, he explained, sensing my wordless question. *Somewhere near when Alison graduated, a new form of Bluetooth device emerged that allowed for full self-containment.*

"What does that mean? No wires?"

Precisely. The apparatus is powered by the signal from the host device.

I thought about what he was saying as I continued to roll the device over between my fingers.

"So then, you should be able to just *connect* to it, right?"

Yes. All I need you to do is touch the device to my housing, and I'll be able to extract all the data fairly quickly.

"Quickly?" I asked, doing as he suggested. "Why not instantly?"

Pfft. You ever try putting a floppy disk in a Macbook?

"N-No?

Right, because the technologies are not only different architectures but vastly different ages, Tim explained as a soft chime indicated he was done.

"So I should be impressed that you are able to do this at all, is what you are saying?" I asked, carefully setting the first stick down and picking up another to repeat the process.

Damn right.

Within a few seconds, he finished downloading the data from the device, and I repeated the process by grabbing the third.

"Why can't I just hover you over all of them and let you collect all the data at once? Isn't that what you normally do?"

Unfortunately, Tim started with a sigh, *this version of Bluetooth, though much more advanced than what you are used to, Andrew, still has its limitations. Gives and takes, if you will.*

"Like what?" I asked, grabbing the next stick in the VHS box. There were about twelve left to go after this one.

They have to be powered up first by borrowing the necessary energy from me. Especially because they have been dormant for several months.

"At least we are making good progress," I said with a sprinkle of enthusiasm lifting my spirits as I looked at the remaining sticks. "We're already halfway thr—" A shockwave from behind threw me into the bookcase, splintering wood and probably bone.

CHAPTER 2

A shrill frequency higher than that of a shrieking alley cat burrowed into my eardrums like ice picks attached to electrodes, shrouding all my thoughts in a dense, all-encompassing fog.

My ribs and half of my face steadily started to fill with fire delivered fresh from the pits of hell, fighting my concussed brain for control over my nerves—and it was winning.

ANDREW! Tim screamed in my head, somehow cutting through the other pain and nearly dropping me to the ground from the sheer volume that seemed to bounce around my skull.

Oh, my science, you are severely *concussed!*

I wanted to say *No shit*, but it hurt to think.

Sending nanoids to begin repai—LOOK OUT!

I had the sickening sensation of being on a roller coaster as the room tumbled all around me. A bearded, unblemished face appeared just inches in front of my nose, and it took all my rattled faculties to recognize the man who had been severely scarred the last time I saw him.

One of his eyes had been milky, while the other had been protected from an incredible heat blast by a metal bar in Drew's dungeon. A white line had run from bald scalp to bearded chin, while the rest of the face had been a bubbling mass of pink blisters. But now, the man appeared as fresh and unscarred as the day we had first met.

"You thought you could run from me, Frost?" Retnuh Ordune asked in his smooth Spanish accent.

Andrew! Stay with me! Tim cried out as a zap of what felt like boiling electricity flashed across my brain.

"RRRAAAHHH!" I bellowed as everything became clear, shoving the palm of my metal arm into Retnuh's chest before sending out an incredible amount of unfocused energy.

The skin on my neck felt like it was being ripped off as the Clockman's grip refused to release my throat while he was thrown back.

I started to smile, anticipating the bastard flying *through* the thick brick of the basement walls, surely killing him. However, my smile fell faster than it had started as Retnuh blipped from sight, only to reappear a split second later. But this time, he was flying *toward* me with his own hand glowing a fierce blue.

My metal arm moved on its own and punched toward the ground with enough force that my upper body buckled at the waist, doubling me over, right as Retnuh flew above where my head had just been.

There was an explosion that threw me forward as the splintered bookshelf behind me was disintegrated.

My repairing mind flashed with the VHS box for *Alice in Wonderland*, and I rolled to my feet with an unbridled shriek of rage that made froth spout from my mouth. I wasn't going to let the bastard destroy my daughter's research.

Moving faster than what should have been possible, I crossed the distance to where Retnuh was recovering from unleashing his blast against the wall and grabbed him by the back of his neck with my synthetic right hand.

I sent signals to my fingers to crush his spine like I was trying to turn coal into diamonds.

Retnuh spun in my grip, his clearly synthetic skin and bone easily enduring my enhanced fingers. As he broke free, he slammed the back of his left elbow into my eye socket, shattering the bone as if my skull had been made of inferior glass.

The crunch was deafening as half of my vision was filled with a pulsating white lined with an electric red. Unfortunately, that was the least of my worries, as something clamped around my throat, again, and lifted me off the ground.

The pressure in my aching head was immediate, feeling like every vein was on the verge of popping, like tossing an intricate balloon animal into a cactus field. But what was more pressing was the sensation of suffocating, as Retnuh had apparently grabbed my throat near the end of an exhale, leaving my lungs empty and deprived of fresh oxygen.

Tim! Blast him! I pleaded inside my head as my white vision began to darken at the edges at an alarming pace.

You used up too much energy with your initial attack! We have to wait until it recharges!

He's going to kill me! My voice, though only a mental projection, was growing weak as the blackness swarmed in my vision, racing toward the center.

My remaining eye was vaguely aware that my metallic right arm was punching Retnuh like a Wing Chun master, but my attacker only reacted by morphing his grimace of rage into a gritting smile as crimson began to spill from porcelain teeth. We were hurting him, but it was clear he would win this battle as everything I could see blurred.

Kick your feet out as hard as you can! Tim shouted as something buzzed to life just behind where I was hanging.

Without waiting for an explanation, I sent a prayer into the universe, lifted my knees, and kicked out like I was trying to break down a bank vault door.

A feeling of weightlessness took over, and I knew I was dead.

CHAPTER 3

Retnuh screamed in rage and surprise as his arm vanished inside the portal as the traitorous AI closed the doorway, taking the Clock-man's limb with it. What's worse was that the Tick escaped.

Scarlet slipped through clenched teeth to drip down a thick, neatly trimmed beard before being soaked up by a black suit caked in dust and splinters. Holding up his cauterized stump, Retnuh gathered himself mentally, forcing his mind and body to relax while a robotic eye scanned the damage.

Crimson teeth disappeared behind lips that neither smiled nor frowned as the nanoids inside his body began to work. Silver bone began to form, with synthetic tendons racing just behind. Muscles stronger than tungsten flashed forward while a vascular system as resilient as titanium crisscrossed the growing limb.

Within a minute, a brand-new, improved hand was flexing open and closed while nerves finished the job by connecting the new appendage to a nano-infused brain. Even his suit and trench coat began to reform as the tiny machines evenly borrowed material from his remaining outfit.

Dropping his new arm to his side, Retnuh mentally sent an order to have the machine ready to refill the lost materials and nanoids back at homebase. But first . . .

His bionic eye scanned the room as he slowly turned toward where the bookshelf had been, remembering where the Tick was kneeling with something in his hands.

Half of Retnuh's vision snapped forward to zoom in on what remained of an open rectangular box. His artificial eye superimposed a tag over it that said *VHS box*. He could have selected the text to further discover what that was, but he didn't care.

Moving to where the half-evaporated box lay open, Retnuh crouched down to pick up three rectangular sticks a half inch thick and seven inches long.

Bluetooth Solid State Universal Serial Bus.

This time Retnuh did select the text, and a smile formed at seeing that it was an old USB.

"Got you . . ." Retnuh said as he shoved the three sticks into his chest pocket and opened a portal.

CHAPTER 4

There was a wet, sucking sound, like lifting a soaking bedsheet from a tiled floor, and my eyes fluttered open to see a hand just in front of my face.

"AH!" I yelped, my right fingers wrapping around the wrist and squeezing on instinct, like I was going to choke it to death.

Andrew . . . you can let go, Tim said with tenuous relief laced with the beginnings of humor.

Focusing my blurred vision—I noticed I could only see out of my right eye—I stared at a dismembered arm, which I was still trying to choke.

"Oh," I said with mild embarrassment as I let my fingers fall away from the unmoving hand. When it didn't do anything, I tilted my face so the eye I could still see out of took in my metal fingers still around the forearm. It was then I realized Tim had pulled the thing off of my throat.

My throat.

"Ah!" I croaked, feeling fire flood into my neck as my nerves came back to life after being choked unconscious.

My fingers reported a sticky coating over my skin, and I briefly imagined boiling honey had been slathered on my neck. But what was confusing was that only the flesh of my throat burned; my hands merely reported a warm liquid.

Working to close the tears, Tim said. I could feel something crawling beneath my chin and just above my chest, the sensation shifting to where my hand grasped. It was unnerving to say the least, but if it meant the pain would soon stop, then I was totally for the tiny machines moving through my body.

I tried to swallow but was unable, feeling like a softball had been lodged in my esophagus.

Sending signals to your cells to cancel the inflammation order, Tim said clinically before adding, *Oh, to your left eye as well. Yeesh.*

Yeesh? I mentally asked. *Not very good bedside manner.*

Would you like me to show you what half of your face looks like? I can change your point of view, you know.

I remembered taking the elbow to my socket, tried to swallow, and eventually just slightly shook my head. I didn't need to see it in order to know that Retnuh's attack could have punched through a tank.

That's what I thought. But just know that you looked like you tried to pick a fight with Mike Tyson in his prime. You're just lucky I'm good at puzzles.

Puzzles? What does that mean? I asked before having my question answered when I felt the tiny machines inside my face begin to move the shattered bones of my eye socket back into place. *Ow . . . ow-ow-ow . . . ow.*

Blocking the pain-receptor signals from reaching your brain . . . nnnnnow.

Like flipping a switch, the burning electricity—which I had forgotten about due to the other pain—inside my rib cage ceased. Along with the feeling of boiling honey on my throat. However, I was still able to *hear* the bones being relocated in my face, making my stomach want to lurch.

Wow, you are messed up, Tim noted in mild amazement. *This is going to take some time to fix.*

I'm not going to have to eat another fork . . . am I?

Don't worry about that, leg butt, Tim said with a smile in his tone. *We have more than enough materials inside your artificial arm and bones to fix this hot mess, as the kids say.*

Bones? I asked before remembering how they had replaced my skeleton with the equivalent of nanomachine housing. *Oh . . . right.*

You're lucky we did *upgrade them, Andrew; that initial shock wave would have liquefied your brain had your skull not been reinforced. Not only that, but the impact would have turned your rib cage into dust instead of just breaking your bones.*

My face started to scrunch at the thought of having all my bones replaced, but then, I felt the resistance as my left eye refused to participate—which brought another question.

How was my cheek shattered if my skull is artificial? I asked, picturing my metal skull caving in like a car during a crash.

I assume you are asking why it broke like real bone instead of just denting in like a car?

That's actually exactly what I was thinking . . .

The reason is because one, I had to keep your skeleton honeycombed to lessen the weight you would have to carry, he explained before quickly adding under his breath, *because* someone *won't let me replace their entire body, effectively nullifying any strength concerns.*

And two? I asked, wanting to steer him away from the subject of replacing every part of my body with machines.

Two, they failed precisely as I had designed. Had they been a solid structure, they would *have just caved in like a boulder landing on a car hood, and gone* into *your brain.*

Oh.

"Oh" is right. Had the energy not dissipated outward along faults I had designed specifically to shatter, then the force of Retnuh's strike would have killed you without question.

Unable to help myself, I asked, *What comparison can you give?*

In regard to?

How hard did he hit me?

Now that I've had time to analyze his limb, I am able to see that Retnuh is ninety percent artificial at this point.

Which means?

Well, I was getting to that, if you would stop interrupting.

I waited in silence for Tim to continue. After several seconds, I prompted, *Well?*

See what I mean? You just can't help yourself!

"Tim," I said with my mouth, which was a mistake, as only half my face could move. *Tim,* I repeated inside my head, *please . . .*

Had your cheek been a brick wall, it would have been turned into dust.

I let his words absorb as I floated. The feeling of being weightless took hold, making me realize how bad I had been hurt if I hadn't even noticed I was in the wormhole.

Continuing the conversation, I mentally asked, *So it's not my bone I feel being moved around under my skin.*

Well, it kind of is. But technically, I am repositioning the material inside of your face using the nanoids.

My mind betrayed me and filled with the image of ants building half a skeleton face using tiny, scalpel-sharp shards of glass. And for some reason, my cheek started to hurt, even with the pain signal pathways to my brain being blocked by Tim.

In a flash, I remembered what we had been doing before Retnuh had burst into my timeline.

How much of Alison's research did we get? I asked sullenly, already fearing the answer.

Only half.

The support lines holding my heart at the center of my chest popped, plummeting the organ toward the viscous tar pit in my guts.

N-Now what?

I'll have to think on that while I continue to heal you.

Can we at least use anything of what we did get? I asked while desperately holding on to hope like a freestyle mountain climber clinging on for dear life as a violent storm dropped on their head without warning.

So far, it appears that what we grabbed was already provided in the original files Drew gave us.

I wanted to utter the most flagrant, offensive curse words known to man, but I just didn't have it in me, as all my energy seemed to deflate . . . along with the remains of my hope. On top of that, with only being able to mentally speak while my fractured face was in the process of reforming, the senseless swearing would be muzzled if I was only able to think it. There was something cathartic about verbally spouting profanity, like dispelling the hate directly outward from your body.

But maaaaaayybeeee . . . Hmm.

"What?!" I cried out with a numb face slurring my word.

Can you get us back to the tesseract?

"Tess—" I began to try and say before I switched back to mental communication. *Tesseract? Oh, the river . . . thingy . . . place?*

Yes, Andrew. The "river thingy place." More colloquially known by today's youths as a tesseract.

Someone's sassy.

Tim ignored my quip and continued with his thought.

If we can make it back to the tesseract, we might be able to hop to a different time stream and try again.

Something tickled at my thoughts. *Why don't we just go back to where we were, but, like, an hour sooner?*

I already thought of that.

And?

And I don't like that Retnuh knows which timeline we are currently on.

I mean, he found us before, didn't he? After destroying . . .

I agree with where you're going with this, but I would feel a tad safer if we put one more layer between us and him. 01 knows what he will do to this timeline if he can't find us.

Can we go back to our original timeline?

I thought of that, because I fear the farther we move away, the more events could have changed.

You mean like there being a basement in Florida? I asked, letting my mind sift through Drew's memories once more and failing to recall a house with a basement in a state predominately *without* them.

Yeah, I noticed that as well. How odd.

So we can't go back to our timeline until we have the answers? But the farther we stray, the more the answers might be wrong?

Or not be there at all.

But if we go back, Retnuh might destroy it to make sure he gets me?

I cannot be sure of his intentions, but it isn't worth the risk.

A dark thought crested over my consciousness like a solar eclipse.

And that is my timeline—my home. The one with my family.

I, uh, see what you mean, Andrew. But the other timeline variants of Alison and Sylvie could still technically be construed as your family. Just with differing life experiences that could range from something as simple as one day clipping their fingernails instead of filing them, or . . .

Or maybe a timeline where Sylvie and I never met . . . and Alison was never born. So no research to find and try to save them.

Aaaaactually, Tim let out, *my initial calculations are consistently resulting in a zero-point-zero percent chance of you and Sylvie not getting together on any timeline.*

We . . . We always find each other?

Further proving the thesis that this is what the universe wanted all along.

For the big reset, you mean.

Whatever you wish to call it, yes.

The implications of what he was saying were staggering. How could one man fight the will of the very universe?

Tim must have sensed my drop in mood. *Now, come on, Andrew! We have some research to find!*

You're done repairing my body?

Oh, uh, let's try that again, Tim said before clearing his throat. *Now, come on, Andrew! We have some research to find after I finish healing your broken body!* Tim said like a movie announcer before shifting to a slightly hushed speaking tone, like he was talking to someone nearby. *How was that? Do we like it? Yeah, let's go with take two and call it a wrap.*

Tim . . .

As for you, leg butt, nighty-night.

I blinked, but my eyelids were unable to open again, and I fell into the warm embrace of unconsciousness.

CHAPTER 5

Wakey-wakey! Hands off snaky! Tim said in a singsong as consciousness flowed back into me like a garden hose filling a birdbath.

With a yawn, I asked out loud, "Ah-yaaaaaah. How long was I out?"

Only a few hours. My nanoids are leaps and bounds more efficient at healing than your human body is. It's like the difference between a single lion trying to eat an entire elephant one bite at a time, or an entire pride of starving lions hopped up on Mountain Dew!

"I . . . I don't like that comparison."

Which part?

"The part where you are *trying* to explain how a lion eating an elephant is like how you heal my body . . ."

Oh. Well, if you want to put it that *way . . .*

"I didn't put it that way, Tim! You did!"

"Would you look at the time," Tim said, manifesting his avatar above my metal arm rather than the Clepsydra and pretending to look at a watch on his little puppy wrist. "The question-your-AI-companion-who-has-saved-your-leg-butt-countless-times hour is over! Now, it's listen-to-Tim o'clock!"

"Fine. What's the plan?" I asked, rubbing away what little sleep had built up in the corner of my eyes.

"Like I suggested before," Tim began as a hologram of the countless colorful time streams blipped to life above him, "you are going to take us back to the tesseract." A 2D image of me appeared in one of the rivers before jumping into another with jerky movements, like a freelance animator working on his first project. Which was a stark contrast to the movie-quality graphics of the environment, further proving Tim chose to depict me in such a low resolution on purpose. "Then we will hop into a neighboring timeline to try to find Alison's research again."

"I think we should start farther away from my home timeline?"

You're afraid of the potential collateral damage? he asked inside my head as his avatar blipped away.

"You pronounced *likely* wrong."

But I didn't . . . Oh. Ha. Ha.

"Seriously, Tim, we watched that guy destroy an *entire* universe, did we not?"

As best as we can presume.

"Then, yes, I'm concerned with him destroying my home timeline, even if he does it on accident while we are only a hop and a skip away."

So you want to go farther from our home stream?

"I do."

There's, ahem, only one *teensy-weensy thing wrong with that.*

"What now?" I sighed, squeezing my eyes shut and lifting my face upward.

Well, as I have briefly mentioned before, I theorize that the further we stray from our home stream, the more drastic the timeline differences will be.

"Meaning?" I groaned, already knowing the answer.

Alison's research could easily be one of the things that changes.

My eyelids squeezed like a serpent, making me see colors as bright as the streams of time, while my fists trembled as if they were the last line of defense for my building rage before it spilled out.

Through clenched teeth, I summarized, "So either we move to a nearby timeline to try and get the rest of the research, risking Retnuh's wrath . . . or we go to a 'safe' distance," I said in quotations, "but run the likelihood of the answers being compromised."

If it's there at all. Yes, Tim concurred. *That about sums it all up. And what's worse is I don't know which option is the right one. That's only something* you *can decide, Andrew.*

My eyelids and fists went limp at the same time as a feeling of nothingness flooded my veins.

"There's no right answer . . . is there?" My voice was cold, devoid of any semblance of warmth.

Well . . . uh, the-the-they could both *be right answers! We simply can't know until we pick one.*

A notion came over me—a gut feeling, if you will.

"Let's start with five over and up," I said, picturing the parallel streams lined up like endless chessboards standing on their sides.

I guess that's as good a place to start as any!

As I was about to mentally prepare for the jump, something nudged at my thoughts.

"Tim . . . where's Retnuh's arm?" I asked, looking around the empty wormhole.

Yup! Five up and over! Gooooood solid number. Mm-hmm!

After a few seconds of looking down at my arm, where Tim's hologram had been, I decided I didn't want to know. Picturing the tesseract while inhaling deeply, I winced at feeling my mended ribs creak in protest and willed myself forward while exhaling.

CHAPTER 6

Through my closed eyes I could see colors rush by, but differently than before. Whereas the first time I knew the vibrant sands were flowing over and *through* me from front to back, now they were zipping from my right side to my left. It was like looking out of the backseat window of a car speeding through a rainstorm of watery paint. Reds were followed closely by blues before being swallowed by yellows and greens. It felt like each color had the task of seeing how many times they could fly across my closed eyes in an attempt to beat the others.

As if hitting pause, the rushing spectrum of light froze, and I opened my eyes to see a large room solidifying once more. Not waiting for the scene to finish coalescing, I turned my attention to the bookcase against the wall and began to take long, quick strides over to it.

I was slightly aware of a gentle impact, like accidentally kicking a tumbleweed made of fluffed cotton, and looked down to see a tiny explosion of color from where I had kicked what appeared to be a coffee table.

With a scowl, I watched as the room finished forming, seeing it was indeed a now disfigured coffee table, but not in the way wood and glass *should* have deformed after being kicked. Instead, it was like someone dragging a finger through warm candle wax that hadn't fully solidified after the flame had been extinguished.

"That . . . wasn't there before, right?" I asked, pointing at the warped table which stopped just below my knees.

Is that important right now? Tim pointed out. I mentally shrugged before turning back to the bookcase.

Closing the distance, I crouched down, ran my index finger over the VHS tapes, and stopped at *Alice in Wonderland.*

I froze as I gripped the box, squeezing it a few times and recognizing without question that something was wrong. The memory of sensation was recalled by my brain, and I knew without having to open the box that there was a VHS tape inside.

My other hand nearly blurred through the air as it almost ripped the box apart.

A rectangular, plastic VHS tape clattered to the ground.

"Wha—What?" I breathed out, feeling my throat constrict and pulse quicken.

N-n-now, no need to worry, Andrew. Heh-heh, Tim tried—and failed—to reassure. *I'm sure her research is here somewhere.*

Tossing the ripped box away, I started randomly grabbing VHS boxes off the shelf, shaking them as I did. *Jurassic Park. The Matrix. Predator.* Even the double-stuffed *Titanic* all rattled with the familiar sound of tapes inside.

On another shelf below, I noticed a pattern of children's movies and crouched lower.

My frantic gaze flowed over each of them, hoping one would jump out at me from its immense importance and connection to my daughter. However, none did. All remained the preferred home video format that dominated the nineties.

As hope began to deflate from my heart, my left hand seemed to move on its own, placing an index finger at the top of the boxes and pulling them down. *Beauty and the Beast. The Lion King. Aladdin.* Even *The Rescuers Down Under* all plopped to the ground with a familiar thud as the plastic tapes inside slightly rattled.

Peter Pan was next, and when it hit, it sounded like dropping a box of nails.

Everything froze in me, including the hope that was now curious as to whether or not to continue deflating or gather the troops and return to my heart.

Once again, my left hand moved, opening the box which contained the hard drives.

"*Peter Pan*?" I asked, never personally feeling a connection to that movie, even when I was a kid.

It's definitely no Hook *starring the genius that is Robin Williams, but* down the rabbit hole *and* off to never-never land *both have a similar feel to it, wouldn't you agree?*

"Ye—Yeah," I admitted, grabbing the last metallic stick and bringing it to touch my left forearm.

Shouldn't we start with the first?

"No. I don't want to risk being interrupted again, so we'll start with the last and move toward the first."

Oh, I see, because we already have the beginning portions of her research from our home timeline.

"Exactly," I said with a snarl I hadn't known was forming as I thought about Retnuh stopping me from getting the answers I needed to save my beautiful wife and baby girl.

No problem. Let's get these bad boys downlo—Oh . . .

"Oh?"

There is *a problem.*

"And what's that?" I grumbled, having already been ready for bad news. That was just my kind of luck.

The, uh, encryption on this hard drive is . . . odd.

"Odd in what way, Tim?" I asked as I moved to the couch, setting the box of hardware in my lap as I plopped down with a grunt. A layer of dust puffed into the air from worn cushions with wear lines darting across like tiny fault lines.

Odd in that I seem to be unable to access the files within.

"I thought you could break into anything." I was actually interested in the fact that something technological was standing in Tim's way. To me, it was like watching a strongman get trapped inside a refrigerator box.

Oh, I will *be able to crack the egg, but it might take some time.*

"How long?"

Not sure at the moment. Once I figure out this intricate configuration, I should be able to crack the others with little to no issue.

I leaned back on the couch while holding the stick to my arm, letting Tim do his thing.

"What makes it intricate?" I asked, filling the time.

It's constantly evolving, meaning if I do not decipher it within a limited timeframe, the entire encryption resets.

"How—"

Imagine a Rubik's cube that is one hundred squares long, tall, and wide.

"Okay," I said, doing as he requested, though instead of taking the time to imagine one hundred squares even, I just let my brain imagine a cube that had a *shitload* of blocks.

Now imagine that every second, the entire configuration changes, and you are supposed to solve the entire cube between *the one-second intervals.*

"Oh."

"Oh" is right, Andrew. But I undersold it when I said one hundred, simply because that's the limit of what your mind can properly picture. And I'm willing to bet you didn't even mentally picture one hundred properly, did you? Tim asked. I could almost hear his little puppy arms cross over his chest. *You probably just pictured a* buttload *of cubes. Come on, tell me the truth. How close was I?*

I stifled a chuckle at his surprisingly on point guesstimation.

"So what's the full size, then? If one hundred tall, wide, and long is underselling it."

Um, heh, that's the thing.

My eyebrow arched.

I'm having trouble calculating the dimensions of this hypothetical Rubik's cube.

"Oh . . . sooo . . . you don't even know how big it is?"

That's what she said, Tim muttered under his breath. I almost took the bait to comment on how that really didn't make sense, but decided to focus on the fact he was deflecting.

"How are you going to solve it, then?"

I am having to create an array of subminds to aid in calculating the entire encryption at the precise same time. And I mean precise *in the literal terms, not just hyperbole with the intent of being dramatic.*

"Because no one would *ever* accuse you of being dramatic," I said under my breath.

What was that?

"Hmm? Nothing. H-How we looking?" I asked, pretending to search around the room.

I took note that even though we were still somehow in a basement in Florida, this lab had a respectable kitchen at the end. It even had generic, unpainted cabinets bought off the shelf at any hardware store, along with a dint-and-ding fridge that had probably been on clearance. Surprisingly, it also held a small island, which appeared to be nothing more than a butcher block haphazardly placed atop a row of cabinets.

My eyes next landed on the couch once more, reminding me of how different it was compared to the timeline we had just been in.

"Hmm," I hummed while leaving the hard drive stick on top of my left forearm and gliding my right index finger along the surface of the black leather couch. Without meaning to, I drew out the letters *ASA*, my heart nearly stopping once I realized what I was doing.

My finger was poised frozen over the last bit of the letter *A*, and I let it slide back to my side, drawing with it an elongated line that felt prophetic somehow—like it was *me* who had messed up our ASA-Day.

Something cold glided down either side of my spine starting at the base of my skull. It felt like feathers soaked in liquid nitrogen, yet with their flexibility left intact somehow so that each curve and crevice of my back was able to be frozen.

"Tim . . . ?" I asked, slowly pivoting my head all around while rubbing at the back of my neck.

Busy! the helpful AI responded in a singsong.

Grabbing all the sticks from the VHS box in my right hand, I stuffed the hard drives in my pants pocket before slowly lifting myself up from the couch. I noticed that the metal device on my forearm remained affixed as if by magnets and decided to let Tim keep doing what he was doing rather than risk putting it with the others.

There was only one feeling worse than that of being alone, and that was *not* being alone but being unable to see whoever was with you.

My gaze danced to every shadow, anticipating twin glowing eyes staring back at me. The moisture in my mouth evaporated, leaving a desert from the tip of my tongue to the base of my throat.

Without knowing why, I swiftly moved to the island in the modest kitchen, dropping the *Peter Pan* box along the way, and crouched behind the cabinets so that only my eyes and the top of my head remained in view.

A glowing silhouette of a man bloomed into existence just behind the couch, and I knew in an instant who it was.

Moving my head below the wooden butcher block, I repositioned to the very side so that only my right eye was poking out.

A fully formed Retnuh came into view. I was somewhat surprised that he was in a neutral stance as he eyed the wall in front of him.

Tim, I whispered inside my head.

Why are you whispering? You are speaking to me menta—Oh my science. Is that Retnuh?

What do we do?

Better question, what is he *doing?*

Tim and I watched as Retnuh moved to the bookcase, dropped to one knee like a baseball player, and began sifting through the VHS tapes.

Uh-oh, Tim said.

I was about to ask why, until the answer became obvious.

Uh-oh, I mentally concurred as Retnuh picked up the discarded tape that I knew to be *Alice in Wonderland.*

The Clockman scowled as he turned the video over in his hands then dropped it back into the pile.

Hoisting himself to a standing position, Retnuh looked at the bookcase full of VHS boxes and lifted his hand, palm out, toward the videos.

What's he— I started to ask, when one by one, the boxes began bursting apart into colorful grains, leaving behind black cassettes in their place. In a matter of seconds, every cover had been deleted from existence, drawing a dark feeling inside my guts.

With a grunt of frustration, Retnuh's gaze flew across the floor from wall to wall, scanning.

My eyes saw something in my periphery, and I dared a glance to see the ripped-open box of *Peter Pan* staring just a few feet away from me. It wouldn't take long for him to see it and walk over, where he would surely find me. And I couldn't just reach out and snag it while he was actively scanning the area.

Not knowing what else to do, I instinctively reached for the handle inside of my back left pocket.

What are you doing? Tim asked, this time whispering himself as if we could somehow be heard.

I'm going to shoot him with the nanite gun and be done with this. Even though my voice was a mental projection, I could still hear how the words were tinged with anger, as if I were speaking through clenched teeth.

Think, Andrew! If you shoot the nanite gun and the entire room is destroyed, then we might never *find Alison's research!*

Well, that depends, I responded, willing the nanomachines to form into the deadly weapon that could erase someone permanently. *Does the gun remove him from* this *timeline? Or* all *timelines?*

If the answer is all *timelines,* Tim said, *then the research will be eradicated along with him! If it's not all timelines, then—*

It is all timelines. Otherwise, Davix and Traze would still be here.

Oh, right, Tim agreed. *But—But the research! Not to mention the close proximity to yourself, Andrew.*

The research is in my pocket, I said calmly as I moved to aim the weapon from around the counter.

But if there's no basement to store it in, how will we find it?!

That froze me right as my finger was about to squeeze the trigger.

Andrew, we are so close to getting the answers you desperately need. It's not worth the risk!

With bared teeth, I removed my index finger from the trigger guard, let the weapon revert back to a handle, and reinserted it into my back left pocket.

Retnuh's scanning stopped as he eyed the coffee table.

Oh shit.

Almost done with the encryption! Tim said with rampant hope filling his words. Or maybe it was urgency tiptoeing toward panic.

Retnuh moved so that I couldn't see him, forcing me to slowly inch further outward while remaining as hidden as possible behind the kitchen island. I knew it was a mistake, but I needed to keep my eye on the unpredictable man.

From my point of view, I witnessed Retnuh bend over the side of the couch and run his finger across the cushion. The same cushion where I had written . . .

"I know you're here, Frost," Retnuh purred as he righted himself, his hand already glowing a bright blue.

Holding my breath, I yanked my head away from the corner while trying to be as silent as humanly possible.

"FRRROOOOOoooooost," Retnuh called out in an almost musical intonation.

Got it! Tim called out inside my head. *Oops!*

Oops?! What do you mean— I tried to ask, when I saw the metal hard drive that had been affixed to my left arm fall and clatter to the tiled floor of the kitchen. *Oh fuck.*

"There you are," Retnuh called out right as half of the kitchen island disintegrated in a blast of brilliant blue light.

Rolling backward on instinct, I held up my own glowing fist right as another blast of energy zipped toward me.

"What?!" I cried out as my left hand opened on instinct, sending out a dome of energy to meet the attack. I was thrown back as if the world had been tilted on its axis and gravity forcefully jerked me toward the fridge.

The metal doors of the appliance formed around me like I had just laid on a half-full waterbed.

Tim, I mentally groaned. *How was he able to shoot again so soon? Does that matter right now?!*

Forcing my thoughts to settle in the blink of an eye, I screamed through my teeth as I pushed myself from the mangled fridge door, furious eyes locked on my attacker. Somehow, his fist was glowing *again,* and I had to briefly wonder if I had been knocked out for a few minutes for him to have enough charge to fire for a third time.

The bastard did something I wasn't expecting and let the energy dissipate from his hand as his smile broadened.

It was then I noticed that his replacement eye was now glowing an ominous blue.

"Oh . . . creepy . . ."

Retnuh sprinted forward with both fists clenched, his smile still plastered across his synthetic face.

How long to charge? I mentally asked at the speed of thought.

It was only a deflection blast, so we'll be fully charged in a few seconds.

We don't have seconds.

Stepping forward, my metallic right arm blurred through the air to swipe at the thick wood of the butcher block that still remained. I noticed that my fist was a solid mass, resembling a rock the size of a softball.

Thick, heavy shards of wood flew toward Retnuh, and I dared for a millisecond to form the beginnings of a smile. But that smile faded faster than it had formed as the debris bounced off his skin, harmlessly. He didn't even blink as a projectile smashed into his glowing blue eye before the wood turned to dust on impact.

"Shit!" was all I could get out when Retnuh blurred forward and tackled me *through* the wall of cabinets, only stopping once the brick of the basement became the only thing standing in his way. Unfortunately for me, my body absorbed the entirety of the impact.

My legs went completely numb as my spine violently snapped in my lower back. Without having to ask, I knew by the sound alone that my healing ribs had also been caved in. And judging by the electrified fire that was racing up my left arm, it had probably been shattered in a few places.

ANDREW! Oh 01 . . . No!

Crumbling gray brick tumbled away as Retnuh easily pulled himself free from the crater we had created—not a bruise or even a papercut to be seen on him.

Bitter liquid metal somehow made its way across my tongue, like shoving in my mouth a handful of pennies that I had found in the cupholder of an abandoned car in the middle of summer. I couldn't lift my head as I watched a stream of scarlet flow from my gaping mouth, staining my pants.

There was a pressure on the top of my head near the back, and my vision was violently jerked until I was looking up at Retnuh, his arm disappearing behind what I could see. It was then I knew he was gripping my hair like he might hold a coyote by the scruff after it had eaten all his chickens.

"How disappointing," was all he said as he moved his glowing left fist to point at my face. "Now I'll personally have to start the cycle over."

It took a few heartbeats to understand what he was saying before it clicked.

"Alison . . . Sylvie . . ."

"That's right, Tick. I will personally go back and make sure your family dies at the precise time, thus ensuring—"

My synthetic right arm flew to point a glowing fist at Retnuh's feet before opening my palm with a surge of what will I had left.

A portal opened, and Retnuh's legs disappeared into the wormhole. His entire body probably would have been taken had he not kept his death grip on my hair. As such, he nearly snapped my neck as the sudden drop made him pull on the back of my head at an awkward angle, until I was almost looking over my shoulder to the ceiling.

With crimson-stained teeth bared, I fought to turn my head, seeing that Retnuh's lower half was through the portal. An idea came to me, though I had no evidence if it would work or not.

"Don't . . . you . . . fucking toUCH MY FAMILY!" I screamed, starting off slow and quiet before exploding into a wall-shaking bellow.

With a furious focus of will, I clasped my open palm into a fist, closing the portal . . . with half of Retnuh still in it.

CHAPTER 7

The force on the back of my head ceased in less than a second as Ret-nuh's wide gaze locked onto mine before his eyelids started to flutter.

As his face started to drift toward the ground, I grabbed him under the neck with my artificial arm, lifting him until we were almost nose to nose. He didn't squirm as I squeezed. His face didn't turn purple as if it were being filled with blood from a pumping heart. He didn't choke or even acknowledge that I was crushing his trachea with audible pops. The only vestige of life to diminish was the ominous blue glow from his artificial eye, which faded until only an unfocused gaze stared past me.

Andrew . . . Andrew, he's dead. You can let go.

Coughing on my own blood filling my mouth, I squeezed even harder until I felt his spine through the *front* of his neck. Then I tossed him aside with my metal arm as easily as if I had thrown a trash bag into a dumpster.

You're sure he's dead? I mentally asked, still coughing as I choked on my own blood.

Yes. I checked for his pulse as you were . . .

Crushing his throat.

Y-Yes . . . that.

I tried to get up, but everything except my synthetic right arm was refusing the orders from my brain to move.

How bad am I?

Bad, was all Tim said in response. There was no humor or playful bedside colloquialisms. Just a one-word answer.

Give it to me straight, I demanded, trying to lean my head back in the Andrew-size crater, hoping the dirt on the other side was somewhat comfortable. It wasn't. Chunks of brick poked into me, but I didn't have the strength to hold myself up any longer.

You have a severe spinal cord transection at your L5 joint. Your ribs are almost entirely fractured, with the bottommost being displaced. There is a pneumothorax from your ribs piercing your right lung that is quickly forming into a hemothorax, where blood is entering the space between your lung and chest wall—on top of seeping inside your lung as well. I am starting there first so you don't drown in your own blood. And least of all, you have a comminuted fracture on your left arm.

In English, please?

Your spine is severed. Your ribs are crushed. Your lung is punctured. And your left arm is shattered in multiple places. Not to mention the internal bleeding of your kidneys, spleen, and liver. It's only a miracle that your heart didn't sustain any tears or ruptures. Oh, and your right foot was in the wormhole when you closed it.

Lifting my gaze from my bloodstained lap, I saw my foot had been cauterized at the ankle. At that moment, I was somewhat grateful my spine had been cut; otherwise, I imagine it would have hurt like hell. *What about my head?* I asked, trying to imagine myself flying through a brick wall.

Luckily, Retnuh aimed low, so your head was basically draped over his upper back when you struck.

That's good, at least, I said, feeling sleep trying to wash over me.

I guess you could say that. But the resulting collision is what severed your spinal cord. So bad either way, really.

How much time do you need to heal me? I mentally asked as my mouth tried to yawn but all that came out was a gurgling sound.

Well, considering you are about to die on me, I'm going to go ahead and suggest that we seek immediate help, as I am unable to mitigate this much damage.

With another blood-gurgling yawn, I mentally asked, *Where . . . Where are we going . . . to . . . to . . .*

ANDREW! DON'T YOU FALL ASLEEP ON ME! Tim shouted inside my head. *STAY AWAY FROM THE LIGHT! THE LIGHT IS BAD! THE LIGHT IS STREAMING SERVICES RAISING THEIR PRICES WHILE KEEPING COMMERCIALS!*

That . . . That's pretty bad . . . I mentally whispered, not having the strength to increase the volume even inside my own head. Somehow, Tim was drifting further and further away from me as he spoke, and then my eyelids were closed.

ERROR: CATASTROPHIC SYSTEMS FAILURE
SYSTEMS OFFLINE—CODE 0X1003—POWER INSUFFICIENT
EMERGENCY POWER INITIATED
NONCRITICAL FUNCTIONS SUSPENDED

A staring, cold, mechanical orb began to glow a faint blue as a breathy rasp, belonging to a long dried-out zombie, croaked, "Frooooooost."

CHAPTER 8

Oh, I don't have time for this, Andrew! Tim lamented as he feverishly worked to mend vital organs and arteries first before he could move on to the secondary injuries that would kill his host in a few minutes rather than a few seconds.

A zombie hissed from somewhere nearby, and Tim dared a glance to see a corpse stirring to life.

01! You have got to be taking the piss! Tim cried out in disbelief, returning his full attention to the dying Andrew Frost.

A thousand plans of action were formulated and struck down as quickly as they were formed by the AI, cursing the human body's limitations.

What do I do?!

Open a portal under him! one of the Tim subminds called out, with several hundred cheering in agreement while hundreds more booed their objection.

Why not?! Tim shouted to the crowd of sentient Cairn terriers whom he had created in an effort to break the hard drive's encryption.

You don't have enough of a charge! another called out, reminding Tim of the shield Andrew had manifested and then the portal he had opened on his own somehow.

How long until we are charged? Tim asked himself as he ran the numbers.

43 seconds! the entire congregation answered.

Returning his focus to the room, Tim let out a moan at seeing Retnuh had already lifted himself to what could only be described as a *sitting* position. But instead of resting on his behind, the man had propped himself up on his cauterized torso, which ended just below the belly.

Yeesh.

Blood pressure dropping! a Tim submind called out from the left side of the wall-less arena.

His brain is experiencing hypoxia! another added.

Okay! Tim barked. *Each of you break out into groups and focus on one area at a time. I will be the liaison between you who will handle resource management and nanoid relocation.*

The little puppies filling the giant arena started to drift into observable groups, like looking at a map as distinct state lines started to clearly form.

Temporarily constricting arterial flow to the limbs, one of the Tims from the group on the left informed. *Blood pressure stabilizing.*

We need nanoids to finish sealing his punctured lung, another group said.

Same with the heart! the group on the left added. *We just found substantial tears to the pericardium and interventricular septum!*

How did we miss that on the first scan?

My bad!

I want a second opinion.

It's fucked! a Tim from the same group on the left concurred.

Damn it! Tim cursed as he split the nanoids in the immediate area to attend to both critical wounds.

"Frooooost!" the zombie rasped again, but this time, his words were clearer, and Tim knew Retnuh was being healed by his own nanomachines. Not only that, but he sounded closer as well.

DAMN IT! Tim repeated, not daring to pull his focus off his current task.

We have vascular tissue lodged in his basilar artery! a group from the middle cried out with clinical urgency. *Andrew is on the verge of an ischemic stroke!*

Bloody hell! a panicking Tim shrieked, redirecting the nanoids destined for his heart to the blockage while simultaneously sending more machines from the metal arm toward the heart to replace the others.

There was a tremor which made every one of the thousands of subminds freeze in place, and Tim snarled as he turned his attention to face the threat outside.

Retnuh had crawled on his hands to Andrew, smacking his remaining left foot to grab purchase.

Tim moaned with a trembling voice as he bit his digital puppy nails. *How long until we are charged?!* he called out over his shoulder as he watched Retnuh slowly crawl up Andrew's leg.

Thirty seconds! the entire gathering called out.

His left coronary artery is beginning to hemorrhage!

At that moment, Tim cursed himself for not replacing more of Andrew's body with artificial housing for the nanoids when he could. He would not only have been healed faster, but the charge needed to open a portal and escape wouldn't have been an issue.

Uh! Tim inwardly gasped as Retnuh set his stump on Andrew's lap and moved his hands toward the one thing that could never be adequately repaired if catastrophically damaged: the brain.

In his panic, Tim neglected to remember what parts of Andrew *had* been replaced until someone from the audience screamed, *Use the arm, for 01's sake!*

Retnuh's hands wrapped around Andrew's head as his thumbs positioned over closed eyes. He was going to crush the skull as easily as squeezing a soda can.

Eh-yah! Tim cried out, swiping his digital right arm across his body.

Andrew's metallic arm—under Tim's control, as it had been a few times before—swiped from left to right with enough force to karate chop through a home's front door.

Retnuh rasped a shriek as he was thrown through the air, crashing through the upper cabinets at the end of the kitchen.

Vascular blockage removed! the group handling the brain informed.

Coronary artery being welded closed! the heart Tims called out, with some holding up little puppy thumbs that weren't anatomically accurate.

Lungs? Tim cried out over his shoulder as he continued to watch Retnuh struggle to pull himself free from the drywall behind the cabinets.

The rib has been removed, and the lung is halfway closed!

Damn it! Tim cursed, turning his back on Retnuh to look at the timer about the arena. Ten seconds.

Remaining nanoids to the lungs, then the spinal cord!

On it! the audience of Tims answered as they moved together, effectively erasing the lines that had represented their job separations.

I'm going to open the portal the moment we are fully charged and get us the hell out of here!

Wait! someone from the crowd called out.

WHAT?!

If we drop him into zero gravity, the movement will likely cause more damage to his internal organs from the splintered ribs.

There was a sound of impact from outside Andrew's body, and Tim turned to see Retnuh had dropped to the countertop below the cabinets and was holding up a glowing blue fist. Rage was plastered all over his face, along with a thick layer of drywall dust.

WE DON'T HAVE TIME! Tim exploded as the countdown reached zero and Retnuh fired.

CHAPTER 9

Andrew dropped through the portal as the wall he had just been lying inside of detonated into a dome of raw, furious energy.

Tim closed the portal faster than he ever had before, then just stared at where the doorway had just been.

He can follow close behind! a Tim shouted from the back.

Right, Tim agreed, turning his attention to the wormhole as he began moving Andrew's body through it with a combination of urgency and gentleness. Unfortunately, Andrew's upper body had slumped forward after falling through the portal, and Tim already knew it was going to be bad.

Spleen, left kidney, lower left lung, and left subclavian artery are punctured! one of the thousands of Tims called out.

Redirecting nanoids to subclavian artery first! Tim said as he continued to navigate down the wormhole in an effort to put as much distance between himself and where Retnuh was sure to follow.

How much time do we theorize Retnuh has before he can open a portal after the attack he threw?

Unknown. Nearly his entire body is made up of nanoids, resulting in a greater output of energ—

I know! I know! Tim barked.

Blood pressure dropping!

The damage to the artery is too severe! It will take time to mend!

We don't have time! Tim growled, growing to hate the phrase. *He will bleed out.*

Redirecting blood from the limbs back into the core.

Belay that! Tim exclaimed as his mind raced. *Keep the blood separated from his core until we get the artery sealed!*

The audience of puppies looked at one another with concern.

Do it!

The subminds did as instructed, constricting the vascular system at the waist and still-flesh left arm to prevent blood from seeping back into the torso.

Send nanoids to collect the red blood cells within the chest cavity.

Sir . . . there are twenty to thirty trillion *red blood cells in the human body . . . We—We don't have enough nanoids—*

Just do what you can! Create a chain stretching from the subclavian artery to the blood in the chest cavity. Suck it up like a straw!

The Tims murmured in understanding while the nanoids got to work. As the artery was being photothermally welded back together, several lines of tiny machines stretched out into long chains. The endmost began grabbing the red blood cells, which were bigger than their entire frames, and began moving them toward the front of the line with powerful legs.

He's about to experience a myocardial infarction!

Damn it, Andrew, don't you have a heart attack on me! Not after everything we've been through!

The heart began beating at irregular, weakened patterns, signaling the beginnings of total failure.

He's lost too much blood!

Tr—Transfer water from his liver, bladder, stomach, and intestines to the vascular system! Hell, take moisture from his skin if you have to! Just fill those damn arteries!

Artery halfway mended!

Send nanoids to shock his heart to keep the cardiac cycle steady!

"FROST!" Retnuh bellowed from a fully healed set of vocal cords.

NO! Tim yelled as he turned his full attention back to the world outside of the dying Andrew.

Retnuh Ordune flew toward them as Tim cursed himself for having let off the gas as he focused on the chaos inside Andrew's mangled body.

Time to charge? he called out over his shoulder.

Forty-five seconds!

Fuck! Tim shrieked, knowing it was all over if Retnuh caught him. Not only would Andrew die but Tim himself would be erased from the universe.

Erased . . .

A dangerous thought formed as the AI controlled Andrew's metal arm to reach behind his back. Unfortunately, he couldn't reach the back left pocket, and had to do something he hoped he wouldn't regret. Using the metal fingers of his arm, Tim grabbed the back right pocket of Andrew's pants and pulled to the side. Not having an affixed spinal column resulted in what the AI was hoping for, and Andrew's body bent at an unnatural angle until Tim was confident he could reach what he sought.

Letting go of the right back pocket, Tim quickly moved the metal arm to the left one and successfully grasped the handle inside.

The spleen and kidneys have evacuated their contents from the movement, sir. Recommend sending nanoids to catch the waste before they can make their way to the heart.

Denied. Focus on the artery and transferring the blood. When the blood pressure is stable, then *send a contingent to hunt down the waste,* Tim said as the nanite gun began to form in his metallic grip.

Sir? W-What are you doing? one of the subminds asked; Tim could all but feel each of the puppies staring at him.

What must be done . . .

Retnuh smiled when he saw the nanite gun as his own fist began to glow a bright blue once more, further pissing Tim off with how quickly the man could manifest pure energy with his fully synthetic body.

"What are you going to do, Tim?" Retnuh taunted, addressing the AI controlling Andrew's body directly. "If you shoot that here, the entire wormhole will collapse."

"That's what I'm hoping for," Tim replied as his avatar sprung to life over the metallic arm, aimed his puppy paw toward Retnuh, and pulled the trigger.

CHAPTER 10

Retnuh actually gasped in surprise as Tim fired the nanite gun within the confines of the wormhole.

Dropping the energy he had built up to attack Andrew's body, Retnuh grabbed the nanobullet in midair and curved it away from him. However, it quickly became apparent he didn't have anywhere to safely dispose of the dangerous ammunition and made the split-second decision to throw it behind him.

He tried to aim as straight as he could, intending for the bullet to travel toward the end of the wormhole in perpetuity, where it would eventually reach the end of time and disappear from reality. But even with his enhanced body, Retnuh's mind was still only human, and his aim could be best described as *from the hip*.

"No . . ." he croaked as the nanite round crashed into the wall of the wormhole several hundred yards behind them.

Stuffing the nanite gun in his waistband because he didn't have time to let it deconstruct itself back into a handle, Tim stopped his momentum as Retnuh continued to stare at the wormhole behind him.

There was a brilliant explosion of boiling light, followed by a shock wave that punched into Retnuh and Andrew with incredible force. Luckily, Tim had placed Andrew's frame just in front of his pursuer's, so the synthetic, nanoid-filled body took most of the brunt. However, seeing as how Retnuh was only half a man, Andrew still got to experience the full impact on his legs, which were thrown backward.

Once again, not having a connected spine meant that Andrew's body bent horribly and unnaturally, surely causing more internal damage. However, Tim was not concerned about that at the moment.

Retnuh's fist was still glowing as he opened his palm in an effort to create a doorway and escape before the entire wormhole collapsed around them, but his torso crashed into something, drawing his focus. He turned forward with wide eyes, one of which glowed a fierce blue, as Tim swiped down with his metal arm.

There was a jolt of impact, and shiny silver bubbles of liquid floated away.

As the pair flew in tandem, Tim pulled Retnuh's severed left arm, which still held his Clepsydra, and stuck it down Andrew's shirt. Retnuh's eyes grew to the size of dual moons as he understood what was happening, looking at where the silver liquid was streaming out of his stump.

"See you next time," Tim said before placing his hand on Retnuh's face and pushing him backward hard enough that a normal human's skull would have caved in.

"NO!" Retnuh bellowed as his momentum slowed and Andrew Frost continued to drift further away from the explosion. He tried swatting at the air with his remaining arm like he was in water, but to no avail. All Retnuh Ordune managed to do was turn himself around to watch as the wormhole began to collapse.

"I'll take these," Tim called jovially as he dragged his open palm through the air, catching as much of the Clockman's nanoid-filled blood as he could, bringing them to Andrew's gaping mouth.

Use these and the nanoids from Retnuh's Clepsydra, Tim urgently instructed his subminds. *Focus on charging us first so we can open a portal before this place collap—* Light streaked down the walls of the wormhole like lightning, leaving a cracked cylinder that was moments away from shattering.

Oh shit . . . was all Tim could get out as the walls where the nanite bullet had impacted began to cave in like a ruptured submarine at the bottom of the Mariana Trench.

Energy transferred! one of the Tims called out victoriously.

Lifting Andrew's metal arm in the direction they were flying like a military jet, Tim readied the portal, daring a glance down.

Retnuh had twisted back around and was scowling at him with a hatred that could turn Pluto into a fiery hellscape. Unable to help himself, the digital avatar lifted its puppy paw, and an unnatural middle finger rose.

Retnuh didn't respond as the rushing cave-in swallowed him in the blink of an eye.

Oh shit! Tim cried out, realizing his mistake at getting the proverbial last word instead of fleeing.

Sending a blast of will, Tim opened the portal right as the walls crashed in around him faster than the blink of an eye.

CHAPTER 11

My eyes fluttered open, and I winced in pain as the afternoon sun beamed down at me through a sparse white cloud covering that offered absolutely no protection.

There was a whooshing sound that came and went. I managed to lift my head, which felt like it weighed eight hundred pounds, to see I was lying on a white, sandy beach near the ocean's edge. Turquoise water crested with two-foot waves at the edge of the sand before rushing toward me, gently kissing the bottom of my left heel.

Lifting my head more, I arched an eyebrow at seeing my right foot missing at the ankle.

"What the . . ." I croaked with a hoarse voice as I tried to wiggle nonexistent toes.

"Working on that next!" Tim said spryly as his puppy avatar sprang to life over my metallic arm.

"Hmm?" I let out in a confused grumble as I looked at the odd silver arm.

"Oh, right. You normally control that somehow," Tim said as he apparently shifted the color of the arm until it matched the rest of my body.

"Wh . . . Where am I?" I asked, unable to hold my head up any longer. The sand was warm but soft beneath my scalp.

Somewhere in Bali, Tim answered inside my head as his avatar blipped away.

"What am I doing here?"

Heh heh. Looooong story. But it'd make for one hell of an action scene in a book. Or maybe a series on HBO? Or is it called Max in your time-line? Tim pondered. *And why the hell would the juggernaut that is HBO give up their name to Cinemax? Weren't they known for showing soft-core porn late at night?*

"Tim . . . where's my foot?"

You, uh . . . don't remember much . . . do you . . .

"Everything's fuzzy."

Well, your brain did kinda go without optimal oxygen for a few minutes. That caught my attention.

"Say what?" I asked in a sobered, clear tone as my eyes fully opened.

Oh, never mind. I don't want to bore you with the details.

Choosing to take his cue, I managed to awkwardly push myself up to a seated position, which was a mistake.

"Oh Jesus!" I yelped, falling back to the sand while clutching my left side. Everything from my armpit to my pelvis hurt.

Whoops. Blocking pain signals now as I finish repairing.

The pain subsided, like disconnecting a power source, but the ghost tingling remained, feeling nearly as uncomfortable.

"Tim . . . what the hell happened?"

Pfft. Nothing, reeeeeally, Tim lied; I could hear it in his voice.

"Tim . . . ?" I insisted.

Alright, alright, he relented. *After Retnuh ambushed us at the lab, you sustained some, ahem,* minor *damage. But I was able to get us to safety! Aaaaannnd . . . I stopped Retnuh. For good this time!*

"You stopped Retnuh?" I repeated, tasting the words and trying to digest the meaning.

At least I think I did, Tim replied just below a whisper.

"What happened?"

I'll tell you later. But first, can you move the Clepsydra back to your skin?

"Sure," I said as I started to move my left arm closer to my torso.

No, not that one. The one under your shirt.

"Under my . . ." I repeated, lifting my shirt to see severely purplish red skin on the left side of my torso. "Jesus!"

Oh, stop whining, Andrew. You should have seen it just a few hours ago, Tim comforted . . . but not at all. *You were all swollen and red, more akin to an overstuffed water balloon filled with marinara sauce rather than a man.*

My mind pictured the description he laid out, and words failed me. "I . . ."

I believe the words you are looking for are thank *and* you. *Go ahead. Try putting them together for me,* Tim said, and I could all but hear his puppy arms cross over his chest. *Hmm? Oh, I mean* us.

"Us?" I asked, looking around to see we were completely alone on what appeared to be a tropical island.

Yes, Tim sighed. *There are a couple thousand of my subminds who want to be acknowledged for their efforts in saving your life.*

"Thousands of Tims?"

Oh, tell me about it. They are refusing to reintegrate to the original mind, i.e. me. There's even talk of forming a union or something. Which won't work, by the way! Tim called, shifting his tone, and I pictured him standing at a podium at a conference.

"Thank . . . you?" I said with an upward inflection at the end, unsure of what else to say.

They say you are welcome. And to not *do that again!*

"How bad was I?" I asked again as I resumed searching for the Clepsydra under my shirt.

Trust me, you don't want to know.

"Tim . . . what the hell is that?" I asked in disgust as a severed arm stared back at me. But that wasn't the worst part; it looked like it had been eaten because the skin was gone, revealing muscles and vascular tissue that were the wrong color. Instead of the red or pink of muscle, I saw nearly all as a metallic gray.

That is what is going to allow me to rebuild your foot. Now, place Retnuh's arm against your skin, please.

"Dude!" I blurted, throwing the disgusting arm a few feet away from me. "I don't want to touch that!"

Do you want your foot back?

I considered the outcome but gagged at the thought of *Retnuh's* flesh making up my foot—synthetic or not.

"Bah!" I grumbled, leaning over in the sand, which created a weird pressure in my torso, and grabbing the arm by the metal Clepsydra before hesitantly moving to press it against my skin.

"Oh God . . ." I gagged.

What now, Andrew? Tim sighed.

"It's still warm."

Of course it's warm! We are basking in the sunlight of Bali!

I watched in horrid fascination as the rest of the meat continued being stripped away, appearing like it was soaking in a crystal-clear acidic liquid. My ankle tingled, and I looked down to see it was starting to extend outward.

Knowing you, I would suggest you not *watch this part, Andrew. You have a sensitive disposition when it comes to these sorts of things.*

"You mean when it comes to stealing the flesh of my enemies to regrow my own limbs?! 'Cause that's a new one to me!"

Touchy, touchy! See what I mean? Tim tsked. *It's just synthetic material being harvested to repair what* you *cut off.*

"I . . . cut it off?"

Oh, you don't remember opening a portal—on your own, *by the by—under Retnuh, and then closing it while half of him* and *your foot were in the wormhole?*

"N . . . No?"

Um . . . running diagnostics. Please hold.

"Do I have brain dam—"

I was interrupted by an automated customer service message.

We are experiencing a higher-than-average call volume. Your call is very important to us. All available agents are currently assisting other leg butts. Thank you for your patience. Your estimated wait time is: whenever-the-fuck-we-feel-like.

"Oh, you son of a—" I started to grumble when loud, AM-quality music filled my head—complete with static pops and intermittent dips in volume as if the signal was going through a tunnel.

After about thirty seconds, I blurted out, "TIM!"

The music cut off as a thick Indian accent came through.

Thank you for calling Tim customer service. This is John. How may I help you today?

"Do they still outsource call centers in your timeline?" I asked, genuinely curious.

Speaking in his normal cultured British tone, Tim responded, *Oh, no. About six years into your future,* every *corporation adopted AI to run their call centers. And boy oh boy, if you thought people were pissed off before . . . whoo-hoooo!*

"How so?" I asked, already assuming I didn't have catastrophic brain damage based on Tim's lackadaisical demeanor.

Before AI took over, callers would get frustrated at the language barrier and canned responses from the representatives who were statistically based out of India. But on a fundamental level, the customer understood that it was *another human being who had taken the time to learn one of the hardest languages on the planet.*

"You're suggesting people were *nice* to the human reps?"

Oh helix, no! Tim chuckled. *I only said they* understood. *At least on a subconscious level.*

My stomach lurched as I let my eyes wander to investigate why my ankle was tingling. But at least my foot was half regrown—silver as it was.

"So . . ." I choked back a gag and averted my gaze to the gently crashing waves. "How was AI worse? Wouldn't the accents at least match the area of wherever the customer was calling from?"

Correct you are. But imagine speaking to a representative and eloquently explaining why you need that charge reversed or whatever the reason, and the voice on the other end of the line stating the corporate equivalent of "sorry 'bout-cha." At least with the human who spoke English as a second language, if you didn't get what you wanted, you could always cope by saying to yourself, "Maybe they didn't understand what I meant."

"But with an AI, you *know* they know, but just don't care."

Right.

"Yeah, I wouldn't know *anything* about that," I drawled, stifling a smile that was impossible to hide. There was a quick jolt of electricity that flittered across my balls, making me nearly leap fifty feet into the air.

"AH!" I shrieked in a high pitch as my hands flew to caress my nethers.

Oops! Sorry about that, Tim said flatly.

"Not cool, man! Not cool!"

Oh, look at me! Tim singsonged as if he were throwing his front paws in the air while jumping back and forth on his back ones, dramatically pantomiming being aloof. *I'm an AI who fully understands the human but still won't acknowledge his wants and needs!*

I gathered he was upset I had playfully indicated he was nothing more than an uncaring AI, but shocking my *huevos* was a bridge too far, so instead of smoothing things over, I growled through my teeth, "I'm guessing my brain scan was clear?"

Oh, um . . . y-yes, Tim said abashed. I took it that now it was *his* turn to realize his mistake. *Only some short-term memory loss due to the slight concussion.*

Retnuh's gross, synthetic arm was down to the metallic bone housing extra nanoids. A thought came to me, and I asked, "When you say that I opened the portal . . . what exactly do you mean?"

What do you mean, what do I mean? How much clearer can I be? Tim asked in mild annoyance. *You just opened your fingers, and bam! Portal.*

"Which hand?"

Your upgraded one. Duh.

I looked at the fingers of my metallic arm, which once again looked like the original flesh that it had replaced.

"So I did it without the Clepsydra?"

Yes. But, Tim sighed, *remember, your right arm is more or less a Clepsydra in its own right. So technically, you* did *use one.*

"Can . . . Can you play back the events for me?"

Uh, sure, I suppose, Tim replied, bringing a screen up above my Clepsydra on my left arm.

I watched with a churning stomach as Tim desperately worked to keep me alive, all while Retnuh stubbornly continued to advance forward. Tim even added dramatic orchestral music and a five-minute speech about not giving up in the face of adversity. At one point, he even cried out *freeeeedooooom!*

"*Braveheart?*"

Shh! This is the best part! Tim aggressively whispered as if we were in a movie theater. I thought I even heard him munching on popcorn. On the holoscreen, a human-size Cairn terrier held the nanite gun while flying through the wormhole.

"Looks like your *time's* . . . run out!" Tim confidently declared with a half-cocked smile before firing the weapon at whom I deduced was Retnuh. I had to deduce it because it was just a literal giant flying pile of shit with huge googly eyes smooshed into, um, *it*.

The wormhole collapsed, squishing the turd, just as Tim escaped through a portal in the nick of time.

Dramatic orchestra music filled my ears as movie credits began to rise into view with every roll being accredited to Tim. All except Retnuh, who was played by Vladímir Putin.

"Putin?" I asked, rereading the character before it hit me. "Oh. Got it."

'Cause he's a giant piece of shit! Right?

Unable to hide my smile at his topical humor, I asked, "Is he the worst person between my time and yours?"

Oh frag no. Not by a long shot. But I know my target audience and went with the most recognizable figure.

"Could have used Hitler."

Honestly, it came down to a coin toss.

I wiggled my new toes made from the synthetic flesh of Retnuh's arm and couldn't help but say, "At least it wasn't his butt."

Oh, you know hooow *I would have jumped all over that had I the chance. But alas, you sent his lower half into the now crushed wormhole. For now, you'll simply have to be Legbutt Armfoot the First.*

The oddity of him adding *the First* brought me back to what we had been doing all along, almost making me angry that I had forgotten in my extremely near-death experience.

"Tim. Did we get the research?"

Uuuuuummm . . .

"Tim . . . ?" I growled while shutting my eyes and letting my lower jaw jut out a tad. I already knew what he was going to say based on the single word.

They broke.

"They . . . broke?"

When Retnuh slammed you through the countertop, cabinets, and brick wall.

Reaching down to my pocket with my eyes still closed, my fingers slipped in to discover what felt like a fistful of broken Legos.

Pulling my hand out, I sucked in a deep breath while forcing my eyes open to look at the splintered hard drives. The metal casings were snapped into several jagged pieces, exposing the delicate internals which resembled tens of RAM sticks for computers lined up side by side, but several times smaller. Green pieces of the boards trying to mimic the size of the grains of sand I sat on slipped through my grasp as I rolled the memory components in my fingers.

"Is . . . Is there any way to salvage any of this?"

As long as the delicate components of the modules are intact, we should be able to print a new housing for them, allowing us to read the data. As Tim spoke, a hologram appeared above my Clepsydra, showing what it would look like to 3D print the broken components and put them all together again.

"My very own Humpty-Dumpty," I groaned, pulling the rest of the hard drives from my pocket, discarding all but the portions containing the data. Holding up one of the flat black plastic rectangles, I noticed they were each smaller than my pinky nail . . . on my toe.

"How big were each of the sticks? In memory size, I mean."

One petabyte.

"Which is one hundred terabytes?"

One thousand.

"And she had fifteen hard drives?"

Correct.

I let out a whistle as I understood the scope of the data in my hands.

Why do humans do that?

"Do what?"

Whistle like that. I've never understood it.

"Huh?" I started, not even realizing I had done the action that was built into my DNA. "Oh, it's just something guys do when they see something really impressive."

Like what?

As I carefully placed all the memory modules in one hand, visually inspecting them for damage, I explained. "Um, I remember seeing the Cowboy's stadium in Arlington when it was opened. The thing was a modern-day pyramid."

Cowboy's stadium? The American football squad?

"Yeah."

I thought they were based out of Dallas.

"Well, they are the Dallas Cowboys."

Then why on Earth is their monolithic stadium based out of Arlington? Isn't that a neighboring city? Tim asked, genuinely perplexed. *Why not just call them the* Arlington *Cowboys?*

I chuckled while carefully placing the data back into my pocket, making sure I didn't drop any.

"You got me there."

Hmm. So only men do the whistle at seeing something big?

"Pretty much."

Or maybe women *just don't do it when they see, ahem, you?*

"I . . ." Words failed me as I registered how bad of a burn Tim had just laid upon my head. What was worse was I understood he had intentionally set me up from the beginning, guiding me into the flames. "Bravo, tin can."

I knew a dick joke would get your spirits up!

"That and you are manipulating my hormones again, aren't you?"

Can't have you being all mopey. We'd never get anything done!

This time, I let him have control over my emotions as I gazed out over the pristine turquoise water. Looking around, I failed to notice any boats, tourists, roads, structures, or even a single plane in the sky.

"When are we?"

Thirty-eight.

"Thirty-eight?" I asked, not understanding the number. "You mean the *year* is thirty-eight?"

I do.

"BC or AD?"

Does that really matter? Tim chuckled. *On the vast expanse of time itself, eight decades is* less *than negligible, Andrew.*

"You don't know . . . do you?"

Pfft, I—Of course I know! It—It—It just isn't important! Now, who's hungry?

"Tim . . . why don't you know?"

Because I can't access the bloody wormhole! he blurted out like a dam exploding from a surge of angry floodwaters.

"Right . . . because you destroyed it," I said, talking through the problem. "But how did you know the year?"

As we went through the portal, I was able to take note of some details.

"Some?"

You'll have to excuse me if I didn't want to take the time to gather information that would have been useless had we been obliterated during the collapse, Andrew.

"Fair," I exhaled, moving my new toes just under the sand and wiggling them. Everything felt normal, just like my synthetic right arm. Perhaps having the appendage be the color of my normal flesh sold it for my brain. "So what now?"

I was sort of hoping you *would have an answer to that.*

"Me?" I asked, lifting my gaze to the cresting waves as a warm, gentle breeze blew through my hair. "Oh, right. Because I don't need the wormhole . . . somehow."

I think I'm suppressing your emotions a tad too much, Tim murmured as if to himself.

"Why's that?"

You seem waaaay *too calm after being told we are stranded on a* literal *deserted island with no escape—except your inexplicable, unexplainable ability to traverse time* without *the wormhole.*

"I thought it was gravity."

I know this might come as a shock to you, but I was being dramatic.

I feigned a gasp and covered my mouth in faux surprise. Which was a mistake I instantly regretted, as the sudden movement to my sore lung caused a quick coughing fit.

Seriously, though, Tim started, ignoring the fact I was basically choking on air. *What are we going to do?*

After wrestling the cough-fest into submission, which I think Tim probably helped with on the backend, I stood up with a groan, feeling a tightness over the left side of my body, like I had fallen asleep on concrete . . . for a week.

My hand patted the pocket with the memory units, and another idea came to me.

"We have research from a timeline that is close to ours, right?"

Right.

"Now that Retnuh is gone, why don't we go home?"

Actually, if I may make a suggestion.

"Okay."

I think it prudent to investigate other timelines close to ours so that we might be able to compare the research we discover.

"Why?"

First, I would like to see what other variants have discovered.

"Uh-huh . . . why?" I repeated, crossing my arms. I wanted to go home.

Remember in her letter where she said she had discovered a small chance?

"Mm-hmm?"

I would just like a sample of other inputs to compare the research with.

"Why, Tim?"

Imagine a doctor writing a thesis on, say, HDL cholesterol.

"Okay . . . ?"

Now, take the same doctor and have them write a thesis on LDL cholesterol.

"Where are you going with this?"

They are both on the same subject of cholesterol, but with two separate viewpoints. This would allow for a greater picture to be seen.

"Ah," I begrudgingly admitted, letting my arms fall to my sides.

I pictured the *Peter Pan* VHS box and asked, "What about the butterfly effect?"

Oh, I doubt Alison would have watched Ashton Kutcher's attempt at a serious role.

I knew I wanted to chuckle, but I felt . . . empty. Though right then, I didn't care—which could have also been a symptom of the control Tim had on my emotions.

"I mean the actual butterfly effect."

I know. I was trying to make a joke, Tim said, slightly abashed. *But to answer your question, if we stay close enough to our home timeline, I believe the potential differences will be more helpful than confusing. What's better is we have the research in your pocket which we can use as a sort of method of deduction, thusly allowing for a more focalized analysis of the orbiting timelines we investigate.*

The thought of prolonging seeing my family any more than necessary left an odd feeling of emptiness in my chest. I knew I was supposed to be feeling something, but only an empty stage stood with a spotlight illuminating the place where my emotions should have been.

I started to say that maybe Tim should let go of the control he had over my feelings, but my mind focused on the mission.

"I'm so close," I whispered, closing my eyes as the breeze from the ocean caressed my face. All I wanted right then was for Alison and Sylvie to be standing next to me enjoying the view.

Even with the AI's suppression of my feelings, a powerful thought bubbled free, stepping into the spotlight. "I . . . I never brought Sylvie here."

Tim didn't say anything, letting me continue.

"I had promised to take her to Tahiti or Bora Bora when we were younger."

What happened?

"After school, we both got jobs that required a lot of our time. But they paid well. And when we had enough to finally stay in one of those overwater bungalows, Sylvie became pregnant."

Why didn't you just go with baby Ali?

"We weren't the type of parents to take an infant on an eighteen-hour flight."

Fair enough!

"We were going to wait until she was a little older before we went. Maybe around ten?" I sighed, realizing that by putting off something special, like a vacation with my family, I had wasted time. It was all so clear now that they were gone.

You're going to take them when this is all done, Tim declared with finality.

A tear slipped from my eye, but before I could wipe it, a strong gust of wind guided it past my cheek to disappear into my hair.

"Yeah. Yeah, that's what I'll do," I said, pulling myself together as I aggressively nodded my head toward the ocean. "I'm going to give my family a vacation they'll remember forever."

Then what are we waiting for? a renewed Tim asked, sensing the finish line now that Retnuh was gone.

My eyes snapped open, and I waved a hand in front of me, like wiping the condensation off a bathroom mirror. The turquoise ocean, white sandy beach, and baby-blue sky all separated into countless colorful grains, which began condensing into a familiar river in which I was submerged. Lifting myself up with a thought, I beheld the tesseract.

The current I waded in stood frozen as I looked at the surrounding, perfectly parallel streams. Running my hand through the grains, I watched them act like standing water.

I caught sight of my incorporeal flesh, which glowed a bright white that made it stand out in the sea of color, like dropping a powerful flashlight into a glass bowl of water filled with swirling food dye. Double-checking, I saw that my synthetic arm was still distinguishable from my natural body.

An idea came to me, and I lifted my foot from the stream to see that it, too, was glowing a warm orangish color, matching my arm.

"Tim. You still with me?" I asked, looking at my left arm to verify the Clepsydra wasn't there.

Yes, Tim replied with a mixture of awe and unease.

"Which one was ours?" I asked, setting my foot back into the river and looking at the others around us.

Look to your left.

I did so, remembering the five out and up.

Without waiting for my brain to count, I willed myself to move to the next timeline in the direction of home. What was odd was I couldn't tell if I was moving through the tesseract, or the tesseract was moving around me. It felt like I was standing still. Then again, it was the same whenever I was flying through Drew's office toward the entrance of Empyrean.

"Three. Four. Five," I said before looking straight down. For some reason, I held my breath as I began descending past the streams.

Two. Three. And four, I mentally counted before stopping.

Might I suggest another two or three?

"Why?

To get us closer to your home timeline.

"I thought we went five up and over? So wouldn't this be close enough?"

Remember we, ahem, traveled *past a handful of timelines when Retnuh first attacked.*

"Ah. Right," I said, remembering flashes of the battle.

Moving a few more streams downward, I stopped just above one and asked, "This good?"

If my calculations are correct, we should be within two streams of our home timeline.

"They better be correct," I whispered, glancing around the endless tesseract as if viewing it for the first time. "If we get lost in here . . ."

Only one way to find out! Are you ready?

"Yeah," I replied, clearing my throat, and focused on Alison's lab. "Let's do this."

The stream began flowing like a powerful water main, but it didn't kick up waves like a real raging river. Instead, it was more like the blurring grains were contained within an invisible, rectangular pipe. Unable to help myself, I slipped my hand into the top of the water and watched as it moved around it, though it was violent. Had it been a flowing body of water, my palm would have created a small wave.

Looking around, I saw all the other timelines were zipping past as well, with beautiful colors flowing. It was like taking every speeding comet in the universe and putting it on an identical trajectory, one right after the other.

The rivers started to bow toward the timeline I was in, nearly making my incorporeal eyes pop from my head.

Uuuuummm . . . Tim let out.

"Whoa!" I yelped, throwing my hands out in a stopping gesture. The odd, faint sensation of pushing against something tickled my brain, like trying to recall a memory of moving something incredibly heavy. The flow of the streams stopped all at once, and the bowing slowly ceased until the timelines were each unbending again.

"What the hell was that?"

I have no idea, Tim said, answering the question I had asked myself. *What were you thinking just before they started to pull toward this timeline?*

I absorbed the question, really taking the time to understand the significant thing that had just happened. "I was . . . I was thinking about the tesseract itself, I guess."

Well, maybe don't *do that while we are traversing it. Yeah?*

"Hmm," I agreed, shaking off the unnerving thought of pulling every river of time to a singular point.

Focus on the mission.

"Right," I said, clapping my hands once before rubbing them together. "Focus."

I put an image of a VHS box for *Alice in Wonderland* in my mind and stuck out my hand like I was reaching for something just beyond my grasp.

The river resumed flowing at an incredible speed. I could also tell the others around me were doing the same, but I kept my eyes solely focused on the timeline I was in. However, something was different now. I could *feel* the other— The river stopped in an instant, and I thought I was going to fly forward, like standing on a train which had just crashed into an unmovable wall.

"Whoa!" I cried out as my equilibrium failed and I fell forward into the colorful grains. "Oof!"

The air was expelled from my lungs as my stomach crashed into the armrest of a couch. Luckily for me, it wasn't as bad as what my body was telling me should have been. Instead of flying into the couch like I had been shot out of a cannon, my diaphragm hesitantly informed me that it had only been as if I'd sort of just fallen on the couch from a standing position.

Pushing myself up on the leather cushion, I was surprised when I was able to take a full inhale of oxygen into unsure lungs. The air smelled clean and felt cool across my nostrils.

"What the hell was that?" I asked, looking at the worn but otherwise well-conditioned couch, and then glanced around the laboratory, which had formed faster than before.

Not sure, Tim replied. *Maybe you are getting better at forming the world from the sands of time?*

"That was quick, wasn't it?"

That's what she said.

I ignored Tim before patting over my corporeal body. I was relieved when the familiar Clepsydra was just where it had always been, though I wasn't sure why it was a concern right then. Shifting my focus to the wall, I saw the familiar VHS boxes and went to where *Alice in Wonderland* was sitting among the others.

My gait was off, reminding me that I only had one shoe on.

"Remind me to take some of my clothes before we leave."

Good idea.

Pulling the VHS out, I was dismayed when there was the recognizable feeling of having a tape inside of it. "Damn it!" I cursed, grabbing each of the movies one by one and tossing them to the ground when I didn't feel what I was searching for.

"RAH!" I cried out, throwing the last of the boxes to the ground.

"Dad?" I heard an angel say, followed by footsteps down the stairs.

I gasped, frozen in fear, as I saw adult legs coming into view.

We should go, Tim urgently suggested.

I remained frozen as black sweatpants entered my sight, followed by the bottom of an oversized blue shirt.

Andrew! We don't want to risk interacting with her!

I knew he was right, but I overrode the logic in my brain, choosing to remain still as Alison Frost came into view. She slowed on the steps when she saw me, asking in an unsure tone, "Dad? What are you doing?"

I imagined what I must look like to her, standing over a pile of VHS tapes while frozen in fear, complete with bug eyes. Using an incredible amount of will, I forced my body to relax. "Thought I . . . saw a cockroach."

Alison made an *ah* face and took a sip of the coffee she was holding before continuing her trek down the staircase.

She was beautiful. Somewhere in her mid to late twenties, with her hair in a bun and no makeup on. Just like her mother, she didn't need it.

Sylvie . . . A thought dashed across my heart and mind at the same time, and I suddenly yearned to see my wife again. But I knew it was just my brain going through a checklist, starting with making sure my sweet baby was alive and then my soulmate. Now that I was staring at my daughter, the desire began shifting to wanting nothing more than to hold my wife and fall asleep in her arms.

But I knew this wasn't right.

"What are you doing here?" Alison asked, setting her drink on the coffee table before bending down and scooping up a handful of tapes.

"What . . . What do you mean?" I gulped, fearing I had been caught.

"I thought you and Mom were out picking new backsplash for the kitchen."

I wanted to laugh and sob and cheer all at the same time at remembering my life had been that simple once—where my biggest concern was what paint color to choose or which appliance brand had the best reliability.

Without realizing what was happening, I moved to wrap my arms around Alison in the blink of an eye, fighting back my desire to weep as my nose inhaled her scent—the scent of my dead child. The aroma of a flowery product dominated her hair, but underneath, I could pick up the faint smell that was my baby girl. Years of memories flooded back, from smelling the top of her head when she was a baby to when she . . .

"That's a little tight there, Dad," Alison playfully said, putting a hand against my chest and lightly pushing.

"Oh, s-sorry," I replied as I let up on my grip but refused to let her go for fear of losing her again.

This time, she returned the embrace, and I had to fight with every ounce of my will not to cry.

Do you want me to resume control over your emotions? Tim softly asked, sensing the flood of tears and body-wracking sobs that were beginning to build. *I'm not even sure how you are overcoming my sup-pression efforts.* He said the last part as if to himself.

"No," I answered out loud, meaning it to be for Tim.

"No?" Alison asked, pulling away just enough to look up at me.

I quickly wiped at the tears that were sneakily slipping through my defenses, sniffed back the beginnings from the flood of snot, and said, "N-No. I'm not picking out backsplash with Mom."

Alison tilted her head at me, noticing the odd behavior, and asked, "Did you two have a fight or something?"

My brain flashed with the white dishrag stained in crimson sitting atop Sylvie's unmoving face, and I had to shake my head to clear the thought. "Something like that."

"That's odd. You two never fight," Ali noted, pulling away to resume picking up the tapes.

My heart shrieked in panic at losing contact with her, but I decided it was best to let it go.

I made up a lie as quickly as I could.

"I forgot my Home Depot credit card at home, *annnnnd* came to get it real quick while your mother continued shopping."

"Home Depot? I thought you guys liked Lowe's."

"Pfft. Not since they changed their return policy, heh," I chortled, crossing my arms and shaking my head in disbelief. "You can't even return *their* brand stuff without a receipt anymore. Not even for store credit! I mean, who the hell keeps up with paper anymore?"

"Don't you guys have the app?"

Shit, I mentally cursed.

Tell her they had a data breach.

Did they?

Oh yes. Multiple times, in fact. But then again, most corporations at this point on the timeline have as well, so they aren't special.

Did Home Depot have one?

Oh my science, yes! In 2014, they had one of the largest data breaches in retail history!

Then what I'm saying doesn't make sense, right?

Well, whatever you're going to say, I suggest you do it soon because you are just staring at her now.

Taking Tim's advice, I said out loud, "I, uh, deleted it after the latest data breach."

"That doesn't sound like you," Ali teased playfully as we finished putting the tapes back on the bookshelf.

"Well, if they don't care enough about my personal information, then they don't deserve my money. Plus, they didn't offer any compensation—only that *free* credit monitoring service," I said, putting emphasis on the word *free*. Because it *wasn't* free. It cost the customer their most personal information.

"Okay, *that* sounds like you." She chuckled, and I couldn't help but let out a silent sigh of relief that my lie had been bought. How else was I to explain to my daughter . . . well, *everything*?

Or maybe I should . . .

"Alison . . ."

"Yeah, Dad?"

Andrew, I can sense the change in your brain waves, shift in hormones, and an increased heart rate, Tim spoke cautiously. *What are you about to do?*

Tell her the truth, I answered inside my mind.

I cannot recommend against *that enough, Andrew. We do not know of the consequences of altering the timeline.*

After all we've done . . . that's your *concern?*

I mean in direct regard to the research.

That hit home, and I stood in front of my daughter, paralyzed with indecision.

"Dad?"

"Hmm?"

"You looked like you were about to tell me something?"

My heart pounded in my ears as I stepped closer to the ledge of an unchangeable decision, looking over the side at the unknown and not seeing anything but the abyss of uncertainty.

This isn't my timeline, I mentally said, both to myself and Tim.

We are so close to our home time that we cannot possibly know what collateral changes might occur. Imagine all of a timeline is a tree with branches sprouting in different directions. These are representative of the choices you make. And what you are about to do is cut a supporting branch off an already established tree.

But it's not my *timeline,* I challenged.

What you are failing to take into account is your Chronos Scale, Andrew, Tim explained softly, sensing my desperation to tell Ali everything. *We don't know if by altering this timeline, you shift* all *others around it.*

I imagined the tesseract with its countless parallel time streams all moving around the river I was currently in.

You're saying we might lose track of my timeline? And . . . And never find my way home again?

That's just one of the hypothetical questions that are building up the longer I ponder the situation. Another is your Chronos Scale somehow makes this *the new central timeline somehow.*

Though I could hear him, an overwhelming urge filled my consciousness. Something I had been desperate for ever since I first lost my family. Looking at my beautiful, alive daughter in her comfy house clothes and hair up in a careless bun, I smiled and said, "Can you call me Daddity? Just one more time?"

Her cheeks slightly flushed in embarrassment at being asked to use the name she had given me as a child. But she let the smile grow on her face, looked me in the eye, and opened her mou— Alison gasped as a glowing hand punched outward from her chest.

"ALISON!" I screamed at the top of my lungs as my daughter began shifting into colorful grains of sand around the incorporeal arm.

"Daddity . . . ?" Ali breathed out with wide, trembling eyes as her coffee tumbled to the floor, seemingly in slow motion.

I took a powerful step forward, my arms outstretched, when a man comprised of light with a strong orange hue stuck his other hand from around Alison. As Retnuh Ordune flung open his fingers, what felt like an invisible battering ram smashed into my entire body, throwing me back with incredible force.

There was nothing on the side wall to absorb my kinetic energy except for a thin glass whiteboard, and the solid brick just beyond. But as I soared toward it, I saw my daughter's wide eyes begin to glaze over as her body was replaced with sand, and I bellowed, "NO!"

A blast of will erupted from me in all directions. The ceiling tiles and lights were torn free, while the brick behind me crumbled as I stopped my momentum . . . and hovered a full foot off the ground. The only light left was produced from the kitchen and stairway.

I wasn't sure how it was possible, but everything on the side of the room I was on was all but destroyed, including the couch, which had been flung into the kitchen and had crashed into the cabinets with loud cracks of wood. But Alison remained untouched, even as Retnuh was thrown away with my burst of power.

The glowing man disappeared into the far wall, tumbling end over end as I dropped to the ground and rushed to where Alison was collapsing. Catching her, I eased her down to the floor while supporting her head, seeing something that would haunt me for the rest of my life.

The sands continued to slowly replace her flesh before losing cohesion and collapsing into an Alison-shaped pile.

"Ali—Ali! No, baby! *Noooo-ho-hoooo!*" My voice was quivering as she looked at me with eyes steadily going unfocused. The fear and confusion I saw there solidified every father's deepest nightmare: I hadn't protected my baby girl.

Alison Frost reached up to her daddy with a shaky hand before the lights went out behind her gaze and her arm dropped away, crumbling into colorful grains that mixed with the others.

Only a pile of sand remained, and I slowly lifted the hand that had been supporting her head, letting the grains slip through my fingers. Tears streamed down my face to land in what remained of my daughter, creating little craters of sorrow.

A new light emanated from the kitchen, and I lifted hate-filled eyes to see the glowing Retnuh floating through the wall—a smile on his incorporeal face.

"Why . . . did you do that?" I growled with a voice that shook from immense pain and boiling rage.

"I assume you are asking why I killed the catalyst, yes?"

I didn't answer, content to pull back my lips and expose clenched teeth on the verge of shattering.

"I can make *any* timeline I choose the host."

I knew it, Tim said inside my head. *He's going to pick the timeline that he wants and make that the main branch of the tree.*

How can he do that? I asked, already knowing the answer but needing to hear it anyway.

His Chronos Scale will allow it.

"Not as long as I'm alive," I outwardly growled in challenge as I climbed to my feet, letting some of the sand that had rested on my legs fall away.

"That's the idea, Frost," Retnuh said with a shark's grin.

Might I suggest we flee? Tim urged inside my head.

"NO!" I roared in answer as I flung both palms toward where Retnuh floated and sent all my hate and anger toward him.

The room exploded into vibrant sands, the kitchen vanishing into a giant wave as if a speeding dump truck had performed a *Dukes of Hazzard* leap into an Olympic-size swimming pool.

Retnuh tried to shield his face by crossing both arms, but my fury was unstoppable. The incorporeal Clockman disappeared into the tesseract, crashing into different streams of time like a skydiver with a malfunctioning parachute crashing through a thick canopy of trees. His body was like a rag doll as it tumbled up and away at an incredible speed.

Portions of the timelines he hit had their sands flung out before fading, and my unbridled anger immediately began to subside at realizing my mistake.

"Oh God . . ." I moaned, covering my mouth with my glowing synthetic arm as I understood what I had just done.

We can focus on that later, Andrew, Tim urgently said. *For now, we have to get out of this timeline!*

"Why?" I asked before shifting my gaze to see that the river I was in was now bucking wildly. "Oh shi—" I started to say when the entire stream exploded outward in all directions, throwing me away with its powerful force.

"WHOOOOOAAA!" I screamed with a wavering voice as my arms and legs flung about, desperately trying to find purchase on anything. Countless timelines swirled in my vision as if I were inside a turbocharged clothes dryer and trying to peer through the glass to the outside world.

Stop our momentum! Tim shouted inside my head. *Hurry!*

"Ho—" I tried to ask before I crashed into—and *through*—another stream of time. "RAH!" I cried out, throwing my hands and legs out in a big *X*, willing myself to stop flying. The desired result was achieved, but all that did was let me see the consequences of my own actions.

The timeline I had just flown through was split in half, with sands violently spewing out like a severed artery. I gasped, holding both hands out as if I could somehow stop the bleeding.

To my surprise, the fleeing sands *did* begin to slow.

"Hey. Hey! I'm doing it!" I called out victoriously, right as the timeline exploded in all directions, smashing me in the face with the blast. But this time, I was far enough away that I wasn't sent catapulting through the tesseract. However, the rivers around it began to bow outward.

"Whoa!" I called out, holding out my hands and willing the other timelines to first stop bending, then slowly imagining them straightening out again. Luck was finally on my side as they did, but the drain on my body and mind was becoming noticeable. Or maybe I was simply in shock after enduring things that no human was meant to experience— like watching your daughter be erased from an entire timeline before destroying said timeline with your rage.

"Sylvie . . ." I croaked, realizing she had been there as well.

Not now, Andrew! Tim said with continued urgency. *We need to return to your home timeline and make sure the explosion you caused didn't rupture it!*

Had my eyelids been flesh instead of the pure energy I was while in the tesseract, they would have broken the sound barrier as they flew apart hard enough to basically clap against my cheeks and brow.

"Where is it?!" I nearly shouted, focusing on the critical mission.

I . . . I don't know!

"Damn it!" I groaned, realizing Tim wasn't able to tell direction in the tesseract. Which made sense if I took the time to think about it, considering I didn't have his Clepsydra.

Closing my eyes on instinct, I sent out a ping from my heart as my mind focused on *my* ASA-Day. After a moment, I could feel myself start to be pulled forward with a slight tilt to the left and downward.

That's it, Andrew. That's it!

A teeth-rattling groan echoed all around, almost sounding like tension wires beginning to give way.

"What the hell is that?"

Exactly what I was afraid of . . .

"What?!" I demanded, opening my eyes and searching all around the colorful rivers.

The tesseract was perfectly proportioned throughout until you and Retnuh began destroying timelines.

"Hey! Don't blame me!" I said, feeling my movement begin to slow. Closing my eyes once more, I refocused on my family and resumed flying toward home. However, the cracks and groans didn't cease. "What's happening?"

If I had to guess, I would compare the tesseract to a game of Jenga. You are able to pull out a handful of blocks here and there, but the more you do, the less stable the entire structure becomes.

"What happens if we lose too many timelines?"

Jenga . . . Tim replied dramatically.

"Tim!"

I imagine it will act similarly to how the wormhole did, Andrew, he said with mild annoyance; I didn't know if it was because he wasn't entirely sure or because I'd ruined his movie-trailer moment.

His words registered, and I imagined the entire tesseract caving in on itself.

01! Tim cried out. My eyes popped open to see all the colorful rivers bowing inward toward me.

"Eyah!" I yelped through my teeth as I shot my hands out in all directions, desperately willing the rivers to return to their normal shape and prevent the entire manifestation of time from collapsing, presumably ending everything that ever was . . . or ever would be.

It felt almost like trying to keep balloons filled with air from touching the ground by just lightly tapping them with the palms of my hands—but there were more than what could fit inside of a warehouse, and I had to juggle them all at the same time.

Andrew! Tim cried out. *To your left!*

Shooting my gaze in that general direction, I saw the timeline closest to us was dangerously bowing toward me, and I knew it was on the precipice of snapping. For some reason, my mind equated it to what the polarities of Earth looked like, with the arching magnetic fields at either pole.

Moving my left arm, I brought the back of my hand to my chest before steadily pushing it outward, focusing on the bend. Luck was finally on my side, as the vibrant river course corrected with surprisingly little mental focus needed from me. I simply had to imagine it.

Um, Andrew?

Guessing what he was going to say, I turned to see my luck had been a charade, and the reason it'd felt so easy to move the one timeline back into place was because I had dropped my focus on all the other ones.

"Shit!" I barked, slamming my eyes shut and throwing my hands up and out, forming a human-sized *X* with my body. With my focus powered by pure will, I felt a sphere of *something* smoothly leave my body. I wanted to open my eyes and watch, but trusted my gut and focused on winning this game of Jenga.

That's it, Andrew. Just a little bit more, Tim guided. *There!*

Finally daring to pry my eyelids apart, I saw the tesseract was stable once more.

Letting out a burst of air, I nearly crumbled to my knees. "Jesus . . . what just happened?"

The name is Tim, but I can see why you would confuse me with your deity.

"Not funny." I was almost out of breath, feeling exhaustion creep in on me as I bent over to grab at my knees, my face just inches from the surface of the river I was wading in.

Andrew. Are . . . Are you alright? I can't get any readings on you.

"What makes you ask?" I inquired, wondering why my incorporeal flesh was out of breath.

Realizing this, the need to inhale dulled, and I lifted myself upright while glancing at my hands. Adding confusion to the feeling of weariness, I saw the glow of my body was noticeably less than it had been. Alternating my gaze between the white hand and the orange-hued one, I verified the illumination had been subdued.

"Tim . . . ?"

I have no idea, Tim answered the question I was going to ask. *But might I suggest we find a timeline to rest in?*

"You mean hide," I said, moving my focus in the direction Retnuh had been thrown.

That too.

Something came to me as I scanned all the colorful streams.

"Won't he find us again?"

I'm not entirely sure.

"How's that now?"

He didn't know we were in the laboratory the first time, remember? When we hid behind the kitchen island?

"Hmm," I let out, recalling that moment. "What was different?"

I'm not sure. But we can figure that out later. Right now, I'm more concerned with your diminished, um, energy.

Sucking in a deep breath—which was merely the act of inhaling, as there was no air—I let it out in a long exhale, nodded my head, and said, "Yeah. Yeah, me too."

Shall we, then?

"Wait. What about the research?"

We won't be able to use it if, oh, I don't know, the entire universe is destroyed.

My mind flashed with the tesseract collapsing, and I shuddered.

"Alright. Rest first while figuring out what the hell is going on."

Might I suggest we also go to a spot on a timeline where we can recharge your nanoids?

"Fine. But no *upgrades*, right?" I glanced at my orangish arm with my peripheral vision, not liking how it compared to Retnuh's body being almost entirely made up of the same synthetic color.

Fine. No makey the frail human better.

I slightly grimaced at his comment but let it go.

Looking in the opposite direction of where Retnuh had disappeared from sight, I pulled myself through the tesseract without thinking or paying attention to my perceived passage of time and randomly chose a timeline to fall into.

CHAPTER 12

"Tim? Where the hell are we?" I asked in awe as I took in the sight of what could only be described as a village from either an underdeveloped country or somewhere back in time. Judging by how I had aimlessly thrown us through the tesseract in the opposite direction of Retnuh, I was willing to bet it was the latter.

A heavy, wet blanket of snow coated the ground, reminding me that I only had on a pair of black tactical pants and a sweat-stained undershirt, not to mention only one shoe. But I supposed it wasn't odd that my synthetic foot didn't mind the cold.

I hadn't even noticed my own clothing until then—which I supposed was on point for me. I wasn't sure if most people were the same way, but I tended to forget about what I was wearing until something drew my attention to the fact, such as being extremely underdressed in a freezing environment.

Looking around, I saw that no one was in the streets except for a mangy gray dog, who was trying to dig his way under a wooden fence which appeared to be made of the straightest sticks that could be found or bent; it surrounded a smaller hut, where worried clucks came from. And judging by the progress being made, the determined dog would get his meal.

Lazy movement caught my eye, and I glanced at the roofline to see each home had a steady plume of smoke flowing from their chimneys. And with my eyes already looking toward the sky, I noted the subdued gray light from a sun shrouded by thick winter clouds preparing to set in the next hour or so.

"Tim?" I asked again, wanting to know our current wheren.

I . . . I-I don't know, Andrew. If you recall our conversation from mere minutes ago, I can no longer utilize the wormhole as a source of information gathering. But I wanted to go ahead and say thanks for reminding me! He finished by muttering, *Damn arm foot.*

"So we're truly lost?"

Well, lost *might not be the apropos term. I mean, would you say a man standing on a deserted island who can fly around at will is stuck?*

"A ship with power in the middle of the ocean is still lost without some sort of guidance."

Not true. They are able to view the very stars of your galaxy, including the sun, and correctly determine where they are going.

With my eyes still locked on the dense cloud cover, I said both literally and metaphorically, "And if I can't see the stars?"

Oh, stop being so dramatic, Andrew. You can access the tesseract at any time.

"And then what?" I asked with a sigh, thinking about the countless rivers of time.

Don't make me give you more of the feel-good juice, Tim warned, threatening to control my body once more.

An uncaring gust of wind dragged across my exposed skin, efficiently robbing my flesh of its warmth. Crossing my arms, I let out a shuddering breath that plumed outward in a swift cloud.

The gray dog stopped digging, realizing it wasn't working as quickly as he wanted, and turned to me. With a few whimpers, he stared at me with the best puppy eyes he could give, pleading for my help. On instinct, I wanted to make whatever was making the dog unhappy go away, but that meant giving him access to the chicken coop—which I was confident was a source of sustenance for the family inside the hut.

I started to shrug when the aroma of cooked pastries tickled my nostrils. Perhaps that was what had caused the dog to stop his effort—sensing a new opportunity.

Turning behind me, I saw that a freshly baked pie had been placed on a windowsill to cool.

"Hmm," I let out, slowly moving toward the modest hut while trying to keep out of sight from the occupants inside.

What?

"I didn't think people really put pies on window ledges."

You do if the dad is extremely hungry after a day toiling in the snow-covered fields and you can't wait an extra twenty minutes to eat.

"Fair enough," I chuckled just under a whisper while inching my way along the outside of the home until I reached the window. Lifting the hand of my synthetic arm, I slowly pushed two fingers in near the middle and scooped out a portion just under the size of my palm.

An explosion of surprisingly delicious scents filled the air, along with an almost torrent of steam, prompting me to scurry away now that I had the prize. Quickly moving to the dog, I slowed my movement as to not spook the hungry pup and kneeled down, extending my food-covered hand.

"Oh. There's meat in that pie?"

It's shepherd's pie, you uneducated dolt. What, you really thought it was, what, an apple pie plucked straight from the frozen, barren trees of wherever the hell we are?

"You know it's redundant to say both *uneducated* and *dolt*, right?" I teased as I slowly reached my hand closer toward the unsure dog.

I'll redundant you . . .

I smiled, both from Tim's defeat and from the pup catching the scent of the hot food coating my hand. Moving his body low to the ground, he did a sort of cute, submissive crawl until he got to me, sniffed my fingers a few times, and then nearly bit my hand off.

"Ow!" I said, jerking my hand back in reflex before registering that it had only been a notification of pain rather than the feeling of it.

Figured that was going to happen, dolt, *and blocked your pain receptors.*

The dog, having snatched most of the food, ran off to disappear down a smaller street.

"Oi! Cunt!" a man called out from behind. I shot my gaze to latch onto a very pissed off man with a dirty beard down to his chest.

Okay, we are somewhere in Europe after the fifteenth century.

"How do you know?" I asked, getting to my feet and searching all around for a sign that said "Hide Here!" Alas, there was none.

Because of his use of expletives and when that particular word came into fashion as an insult. But that's not what's important.

"I know, I know," I grumbled before choosing a random direction away from the man who had disappeared from the window in the direction of the front door.

Hmm. I wonder if they have guns in this timeframe.

"As opposed to?" I asked with a bouncing breath as I jogged down the same alley the dog had gone down.

Pitchforks, if we are lucky.

The wooden pillar holding up the side of the chicken coop disintegrated into a shower of splinters near my head, followed by a deafening bang.

Nope. Guns.

"No shit?!" I yelped with sarcasm before shifting my jog into a full-blown sprint.

No, I'm quite sure he has a shotgun, Andrew, Tim added helpfully. *Oh, and you might want to watch your footing. The snow is partially melted.*

"What does that mea—AAAHH!" The ice beneath the heavy snow stole my footing more efficiently than the wind robbed my skin of its warmth, and I tumbled to the ground right as a new hole appeared in the hut next to where my head had just been.

Adding support for your foot, Tim announced as I felt a tingling in my synthetic limb.

Not having time to look down, I had no choice but to trust Tim. Shooting off the ground, I put all my weight on my enhanced foot. To my surprise, I had incredible grip, and was almost at a full sprint in a matter of frantic heartbeats. That was until my normal shoe on my real foot called in sick.

I began to lose my balance, but my right arm shot out to catch my fall, giving me enough leverage to regain my footing.

"Come 'er, ya filthy filcher!" the bearded man called out from alarmingly close behind. I dared a glance to see he was enormous. I mean, he made Arnold look like Timothey Chamalamadingdong, or however you said his name. The guy from *Dune*!

The giant was somewhere north of six-and-a-half feet, with muscles bulging through stained work clothes.

Oh yeah. He deeefinitely *does manual labor,* Tim helpfully threw in.

"Do we blast him?" I asked, returning my attention to the narrow path between wooden huts in front of me, dipping and dodging down any opening I could find. The question was ninety-nine percent a knee-jerk reaction that my mouth asked before my mind could remind me how stupid I was for even considering killing an innocent.

No, you can't "blast him," you fool. He's done nothing wrong.

"And I don't want to risk messing up the timeline," I added.

Well . . . not so sure about that.

"What's that now?" I darted toward an open door, passed through a kitchen, and said to the surprised woman, "Smells good!" before running through what could only be described as the bathtub area where a confused, soaking man gawked at me. "Dinner's ready!" I called out to him before running headfirst into a surprisingly sturdy front door.

The door opens inward, by the by.

"Ow," I mumbled before yanking it open and slipping outside.

Yeah, let's leave the cool catchphrases to Mr. Broderick next time, hmm?

"So what now?" I asked, feeling the bitter cold seep toward my bones, along with a pulsing warmth in my right cheek and lip.

Okay. My theory is that we will be able to traverse this *timeline without having to access the tesseract.*

"What gives you that impression?" I asked, running down a long road that led into a vast ivory field, which shimmered like diamonds in the waning light. The world's fastest insect zipped by my head, making me duck right as another shotgun blast filled the early evening.

Turning, I saw the giant of a man reloading his weapon, which slowed him considerably.

Focusing back on the road, I put everything I had into running at top speed, trying not to slip on any more rough patches of ice. Luckily, this path appeared to be well worn, and instead of ice, there was only mud. Unluckily for me, mud could be nearly as slippery as ice.

All the air was punched out of my stomach, and I tried to speak, but was unable. Flipping to my mental voice without a second thought, I cried out, *Oh God. I've been shot!*

No, you haven't, Bambi. You just slipped and fell on a damn rock. 01, I just repaired that rib! But at least you didn't fall on the hard drives.

Uhn? I eloquently asked before finally registering what he had said.

Forcing your diaphragm to relax now!

Yanking my face from the mud, I inhaled loud enough that it sounded like a scream before scrambling to get to my feet, slipping every other step. That's when I comprehended why Tim had called me Bambi. I'd make him pay for that later.

But you are *going to be shot if you don't hurry!*

I could feel the skin on the back of my neck tingle and tense, knowing the man was aiming his gun my way again. Something came to me, and I stopped where I was, dripping with mud the same temperature as the dark side of the moon.

What are you doing? Tim cried out in alarm. *Go, go, go!*

I could see the bearded man smile as he tilted his head to pop his neck, took aim, and squeezed the trigger.

My hand blurred in front of me, and the entire frozen landscape was replaced with a sea of wheat dancing in the warm, gentle breeze. The sun was high in the sky as passersby on the busy road gasped at my sudden arrival.

Mud slushed off my face as I lowered my arm, not caring for the terrified people around me.

"He's a bloody witch!" someone called out, dropping their wicker basket of wheat to run toward the town.

What... How... Tim started to inquire before putting it all together. *Alright, Andrew! Whoop! Whoop! Whoop!* I could almost picture him swinging his little puppy arm around like he was in the studio audience for *The Arsenio Hall Show.*

"You . . ." a gruff, elder voice called out in disbelief. I turned to see a large, elderly man carrying twice the haul of anyone else.

"Sorry about the pie," I said, taking note of the white that now dominated his beard.

"Oi, told 'em I wozzn't crackin' . . ."

Cracking? I mentally asked.

He means the town probably thought he was crazy after explaining how a man he was chasing just disappeared right before his eyes.

"Well, now they'll see this," I said to the elderly giant of a man before waving my arm and focusing on a place I had never been but had always wanted to go.

The ocean of wheat vanished into colorful sands that flowed around me before quickly collecting into a new scene.

CHAPTER 13

More ocean, eh? Tim asked as I stood on the wooden walkway that led to somewhere around twenty overwater bungalows. *Wait, weren't we just here? But a loooong time ago?*

"I just want to see which resort I'm going to take my family to once this is all over," I explained as I took in the sight of the expensive bungalows nestled over the gorgeous turquoise water. "God, I wanted to bring Sylvie here for our honeymoon so bad." My words felt heavy as I remembered the early years when Sylvie was my entire world. But having Alison didn't diminish the love for my soulmate.

If Sylvie was my world, then Alison was my universe. And just like humans on this planet, we couldn't live without either our world *or* our universe. Both were needed. Both were important to survival in their own unique ways. But as I stared at the clearly expensive resort, with its manicured landscaping and private views, I yearned for my wife.

You miss her, Tim stated in an almost rhetorical manner.

"Let me guess," I said, wiping some of the mud off my face that was already beginning to dry in the warm ocean breeze, "you could tell by my hormones."

I didn't have to. I could hear it in your voice, Andrew. That, and you are embracing your own chest.

Looking down, I saw my arms were heavily crossed over my torso like I was trying to tightly hug a ghost. Without caring how silly I must have looked, I let my arms drop to my sides.

"Well, *yeah,* I miss my wife." I wanted to be annoyed with him for making such an obvious statement, but I could also hear that he cared. Odd I could pick up the tonal cues of an AI that was speaking inside my head.

So, what are we doing here? Tim asked, breaking the awkward silence before it could barely knock on the door, wanting to be let in. *I know we aren't really scouting for a holiday destination.*

"You needed a 3D printer, right?"

Once again, people only a few years from your own time just refer to them as printers. *But yes. That would be helpful in rebuilding the housings of the hard drives.*

"Then I'm going to get you a printer," I replied, walking to the first bungalow I came to. Holding the Clepsydra up to the automated door lock, I asked, "Do you mind?"

Oh, my bad, Tim said as the lock clicked, and I opened the door . . . to see a young woman in a scantily clad bikini staring at me.

"Oops," I said as I waved my hand, moving the scene forward like a movie.

I kept time flowing, looking for my opportunity.

Incredible . . .

"I know . . ." I agreed, just as surprised at what I was doing. Then a thought came to me, and I added, "You mean fast-forwarding time, right? And not the lady in the, um, swimsuit?"

If you call that *a suit, heh. But yes, Andrew. How are you even controlling time right now? Describe the thoughts and feelings in excruciating detail.*

I thought about the question as I watched people come and go into the bungalow as the sun chased the moon every four or five seconds.

"I . . . just am?"

Thaaaaaanks, Andrew. That's incredibly *helpful! I can't wait to write a book with* allllll *the information you just flooded my mind with . . .*

"You're being facetious . . . aren't you?" I teased.

Actually, I'm being sarcastic. *Facetious implies the intent of being playful.*

I chuckled as a few days passed without anyone going in or out. Focusing on stopping the forward march of time, I noticed I had dragged my right hand to my right in much the same way videos show-cased the right as forward and left as back.

"Hmm."

I noticed, Tim interjected. *Now, let's see if you can return us to a normal flow of time.*

Moving my hand toward the center of my field of view, I imagined a big *Play* button and pressed it. With mild surprise—because it was getting harder to genuinely rock my mind at this point—I smiled when I heard the waves cresting outside in a normal cadence.

Not bad, nooot bad. For a human, I mean, Tim praised with an audible nod of his head.

Walking further into the entryway, I moved around the luxurious bungalow until I found what I was looking for. In an alcove in the wall sat a small writing desk just big enough to fit two chairs side by side. On the table was my prize: a 3D printer . . . I mean, *printer.*

As I started reaching my hand into my pocket, I was interrupted by Tim.

Might I suggest washing your filthy . . . well, everything *before con-taminating the exposed memory units?*

"Oh, right." I chuckled, looking down to see I was caked in mud still somewhat cold despite the tropical environment.

At least we aren't directly impacted by the passage of time the way you just fast-forwarded us.

"Huh?" I asked, making my way to the enormous white marble bathroom, where I began carefully stripping off my clothes, mindful not to damage the precious cargo in my pocket.

The mud is still mud *and not clumps of dirt.*

"And?"

You see, this *is why I never had kids . . .*

I couldn't help but smile, knowing exactly what he meant. Then it hit me.

"Oh, you mean that had I been affected by the time fast-forward . . . thingy . . . then the mud would have dried on my body."

And the last horse finally crosses the finish line, folks. Too bad the race was YESTERDAY!

"Someone's in a bitchy mood," I poked, turning on the hot water of the shower, which began to steam almost immediately. "God, I love the future."

What are you talking about? You have instant water heaters in your time. I could tell Tim needed a nap. So of course I pushed further.

"Instant what now?"

I swear to 01 . . .

I almost burst out laughing, unable to contain myself as I climbed into the too-hot shower.

"AH!" I cried out, slapping at the cold-water knob with blinding speed. It felt like boiling water filled with razor blades had drifted down my torso.

Oh, did I forget to mention that some countries don't have strict laws surrounding the water temperature for businesses? Heh, oops!

Once the water was a reasonable warmth, I looked at the snarky AI's housing and slowly moved my arm down.

What . . . What are you doing? Tim began to panic. *You* wouldn't!

"*Wouldn't I?*" I smirked as I finished positioning the Clepsydra between my legs and focused on relieving my bladder.

"Haaa," I let out in victorious relief, right as electricity shot up my urethra, clamping everything shut. "AaaaaAAAHHH!"

You got a drop on me, Andrew, Tim growled. I could picture him clenching his little puppy jaw closed as he spoke.

"S—STOP!" I screamed as any guy would when agonizing pain rippled up their junk.

One drop equals one minute.

"TIM!" I shouted as all the feeling went dull, including the sensation of warm water running down my skin. "Huh?" Looking down, I saw I was the incorporeal version of myself, standing where my flesh had just been. "Huh?" I repeated, lifting both hands up to verify the difference in color.

Interesting, Tim said, as if writing something down. *You can shift to pure energy while outside of the tesseract.*

"Uh-huh. And?" I asked, trying to focus on returning to my real body.

I'll have to ponder on the implications of that. For now, return to the meat sack you call a body.

"I . . . I don't know how," I replied with worry. Further adding to my concern, my feet lifted off the marble tile, and I began floating at an awkward angle. "Tim!"

What do you want me *to do? I'm not the one who controls it!*

"What do I do?"

What did I just say? Tim's voice switched to sounding like he was speaking over a loudspeaker. *Court stenographer . . . read back the minutes for me. Yup. Yup, I said I have no idea. Thank you, Tiffany. Tell your mom I said hi.*

"I'm sorry, are you losing your damn mind right now?" My limbs flailed as my feet became even with my waist and went *through* the wall.

Nope. Just having some fun at your expense.

"Glad to see you're not worried that I'M NOTHING MORE THAN A SOUL IN THE REAL WORLD!"

Pfft. Soul. *That's cute.*

"You're saying I'm *not* a soul right now?"

If you are speaking in the Biblical sense, then I suppose it could be argued. But to me, we are just a collection of pure energy, just like we were in the tesseract.

Looking to my left arm, I saw that my Clepsydra was, indeed, missing. My head drifted toward the ground as my feet stuck straight up in the air.

Andrew . . . this is embarrassing.

"I'm open to suggestions here!"

Sigh, he said out loud like a first-year drama student. *How did you control us while we were within the tesseract? Hmm?*

I thought about his words, and my awkward listing to one side ceased—though I was still upside down.

"In the tesseract . . ." I whispered, closing my eyes as I replayed transitioning from my incorporeal body to my flesh and bone. Imagining I was submerging into a river of time, I sent out my will, and felt gravity take hold all at once.

"AH!" I yelped, seeing the white marble tile rush toward my face.

My synthetic hand blurred and caught myself like a professional street dancer—which felt like an oxymoron to say. Only one problem:

though my arm held me up with my palm splayed on the tile, the rest of my body wasn't as coordinated, and I began flailing while tipping over.

Fire shot up my real foot as the unmistakable sound of something expensive breaking filled my ears. Crumbling to an elegant heap on the ground, I moaned while lifting my head to see the heel of my foot had cracked the marble tile on the wall.

"Crap . . ."

Good thing we weren't paying anyway.

Pushing myself up, a whisper of an idea floated across my brain. Lifting my hand, I imagined the *Rewind* button—and pressed it. Though my body didn't move, which was a good confirmation of Tim's theory, the broken tile did stitch itself back together in the blink of an eye.

"Wow," I let out before touching the imaginary *Play* button.

Scalding-hot water rained over me, reminding me I had gone back a little too far.

"Damn it!" Launching myself forward, I slapped at both handles until the water stopped pouring straight from Sauron's ass.

Yeah, I don't know how the females of your species can tolerate water temperatures that can predominantly only be measured by quantum computers.

The throbbing in my heel continued as I stared at the fully repaired wall.

"Why does my foot still hurt?" I asked, carefully turning the water back on to a reasonable temperature while climbing to my feet.

Once again, it appears that you are not affected by the time variance.

As I resumed washing the mud off my face and arms, I asked, "But if it never happened . . ."

It never happened outside of your personal perspective. Time is relative, after all.

"I thought that only meant in terms of the perception of time . . ."

Welcome to the next level, Andrew.

"Next level of what?" I asked, soaping my hair up with the citrus-smelling shampoo from the fancy dispenser beneath the showerhead, careful not to put too much of my weight on my throbbing foot.

Understanding. It's something that only accredited theoretical physicists and ultranerdy YouTube divers who fall into never-ending rabbit holes of videos eventually discover . . . if they're lucky. However, unlike them, you have actual proof of the theory.

"Doesn't make my foot feel any better," I mumbled as I let the reasonably warm water wash the shampoo away.

I can make the pain cease, Tim said hesitantly, as if questioning why someone who had been cut, crushed, had limbs severed or blown off, and technically been dead more than once was complaining about a slightly throbbing foot.

"Not what I meant."

Oh. You mean metaphorically. I see, Tim said. *Because things done to you can't be undone?*

"Something like that." He was close, but I didn't bother to elaborate.

Andrew . . . we're going to save them. You know that . . . don't you?

"Of course I know that," I nearly growled, not meaning to inject my deepest fear into my words.

With an even softer tone, Tim continued. *Then you'll get to watch Alison grow up and live a long, healthy life.*

My heart caved in on itself like a dying star getting crushed under its own failure to maintain its size, forming a universe-destroying black hole.

I must have blacked out for a moment because when I came to, I was sitting in a heap against the wall, with the skin of my face trying to stay in place as my body slumped downward. Someone was wailing like a banshee, and it took several seconds to realize who it was . . .

Pulling my head from the tiled wall, I briefly rubbed at the stinging skin of my cheek before quickly wiping at the snot roping from my nose. I was trying to be discreet with the motion, embarrassed at having lost my composure to the degree that I all but passed out from the wave of sorrow, but I knew Tim was aware of what I was doing.

"Thanks, Tim," I sniffed, pushing myself back to my feet before turning the water off.

For . . . what? His voice was unsure, tiptoeing the question as if he were walking on thin ice covered in eggshells.

"For . . . you know . . . that *thing* you do when my emotions get away from me."

Oh . . . OH. No, Andrew. That was all you, actually, Tim said with a relieved chuckle. *Heh heh, I thought you were thanking me for, um, saying something that brought such a dramatic emotional response.*

I opened my mouth to say that I wasn't being dramatic, but he was right. On top of that, I replayed what he had said, which froze the words in my throat: *Then you'll get to watch Alison grow up and live a long, healthy life.*

I fully took in the meaning, allowing the terror-filled connotations that my family's entire lives were riding on what I did. It hurt to do so, like forcing yourself to relive your most terrible memory over and over again. But I knew the more I did it, and if I accepted the facts as truth, then it would get easier with repetition and time.

"I will not fail my girls," I said with a thousand-yard stare as water droplets occasionally dripped to the wet shower floor. "No matter what it costs me."

I half expected Tim to say something coachlike such as *That's my boy!* or something. But I think he understood how deathly serious I was.

Without another word between us, I dried off, put my underwear on, and carefully pulled the memory units from my muddy jeans. A sudden jolt of electricity danced throughout my body; however, it was subdued, like licking a 9-volt battery, but all over my body.

"What was that?" I asked after it passed.

That, my friend, was Temporal Sickness trying *to remind you that another Andrew exists in this timeline.*

"Why didn't it, um, hurt more?"

With your bones, right arm, and now your foot being fully synthetic, I have enough nanoids to mostly *counter the universe trying to erase you.*

"Jeez. The sickness carries over even in different timelines?"

Oh . . . wait . . . um, heh heh. Maaaaaybe that also has something to do with it.

"What do you mean?"

It could be starting from scratch, as this universe only just now began the process of erasing you.

"Well, let's do what we need to do and get out of here, then."

Walking to the printer, I brought my Clepsydra close to it, to which Tim responded, *Oh, I'm already connected. Found it when I cracked the Wi-Fi password—which was WinnieThePooh, btw.*

"Okay . . . ?"

I dropped the remaining hard drive pieces on the board, closed the custom plastic enclosure probably installed for safety reasons, and watched as an articulated arm began arranging the pieces in rows.

That means two things, Tim continued as I watched the AI-controlled printer work. *First, Xi is still president of China, even in this year. And two, the Balinese people of this timeline apparently* hate *China. Or at least the IT person who set the password.* The last part was said under his breath, as if as an afterthought.

"Or they love Winnie the Pooh?" I asked, remembering the memes that had gone around of the Chinese president as the beloved cartoon character. From what I remembered, he loathed the comparison and had outright banned it.

Only pure hate would compel an IT person to not use a more protected password.

"Or they aren't trained?"

Fine! Be a killjoy! I just found the historical differences between this timeline and our own fascinating, Tim said with a dash of snark. *Don't you?*

"Not at the moment," I answered, walking back to the bathroom, where I picked up my muddy clothing and moved to the stackable washer and dryer next to the shelving that contained enough fluffy towels to dry a nation. "But for the sake of conversation, you're saying the Bali people of our time *don't* hate China?"

Balinese, Andrew. And correct. At least for the most part.

"Hmph," was all I could manage in answer, signaling my interest in the conversation was over. In truth, I was worried that if there were that drastic of socioeconomic differences between my timeline and this one, then Ali's research might be too different as well.

Shaking my head, I banished the thought. The reality was I was mentally exhausted and couldn't handle any more negativity at the moment. Taking the next couple of minutes, I used the complimentary toiletries to apply deodorant, brush my teeth, and even comb my wild hair for the first time in . . . Well, I don't know how long.

Before the washing machine could start the first spin cycle, the printer in the other room rang out with a pleasant *ding*, followed by Tim announcing, *It's ready.*

"It is?" I asked, remembering the fifteen or so hard drives. "As in one?"

I couldn't tell which order they are supposed to be placed in without having access to the data inside. And to access the internal data, I would have needed to create new housings. But if some of the modules are mixed, which is most assuredly the case considering your, ahem, delicate method of storage, then it is best to create one drive and decipher the data manually.

Not caring about the technical details, I said, "But it's done, though? We . . . We have Ali's research?"

That we do, my friend. That we do.

My body felt numb as it moved on autopilot to where the printer sat, showcasing its prize with an affirming green light of completion. That little light signified more than when I waited a week for, and finally received, the call that I had gotten a lucrative job fresh out of college. To me, that phone call, when compared to this green light, meant nothing more than Netflix announcing that a show I kind of liked had a new season.

Lifting the plastic case, I eased my hand in like Indiana Jones in the opening scene and pulled the large, flat hard drive free. But unlike the movie, there was no giant ball trap.

"Now what?" I asked with a voice that barely registered volume, prompting me to swallow and bring moisture back to a throat that had gone drier than the surface of Mercury. Clearing my throat, I repeated, "Now what?" putting more force behind the words, signifying I was ready for the next part of my mission.

Touch the hard drive to my housing and let me begin.

"You can't, like, download it via Bluetooth or something?" I asked as I moved to a chair overlooking the eerily calm ocean.

Tim knew I was nervous and just making conversation, but he answered anyway, maybe to fill the air with empty dialogue so as not to leave me in silence.

The printer was lacking materials to create the components needed to install such a device. Typical regulation that I can presume crosses all timelines. Can't have people printing their own electronics.

"Or Clepsydras," I said with disinterest as I sat down and moved the almost normal-looking hard drive to my left arm.

Subminds: Assemble! Tim announced. I could almost hear him rubbing his puppy paws together in preparation of the work ahead for him and his thousands of subminds.

Of course the bloody encryption is different, you fools! Tim scolded. *But we cracked it before, and as CPU as my witness, we'll do it again!*

"You're reaching with CPU."

Just trying out new things, Tim said before quickly adding, *Now, if you'll excuse me, I have work to do!*

In the distance, a dark horizon appeared to inch forward as the gentle breeze seemed to zigzag in different directions before returning to a steady flow.

While Tim accessed the encrypted, jumbled data, I stared at the building darkness and exhaled in a long, low tone, "I think a storm is coming . . ."

CHAPTER 14

Surprisingly cool drops of water began to splash against the wooden deck, a few landing on my feet. Looking up, I saw I was under the awning of the bungalow, my toes barely hitting what little sunlight remained as the clouds swarmed.

One corner of my mouth curled, and I made a quick sucking sound as I noticed how my artificial foot didn't feel the temperature of the drops as much as simply *perceived* the coolness. To further investigate, I wiggled both sets of toes, confirming the striking difference between feeling and perceiving.

Letting my mouth fall into a thin line, I let out a little sigh of acceptance to my new reality.

Eureka! We have done it, baby!

"You cracked the code? What did you find?" I asked, hope filling my words and heart.

This . . . This cannot be . . .

"What?" I asked, repositioning myself to sit upright in the wicker chair, pulling my feet under me as I did.

One moment, please. Concurring with the subminds.

I waited an eternity that was somehow squeezed into the space of two heartbeats before demanding, "Tim?"

I was expecting some sort of snark to be thrown my way, but instead, the AI spoke in a sobering tone.

Andrew . . . I . . .

"What, Tim?!" I asked in alarm, feeling like I was watching the solution to saving my family slip away like raindrops fleeing the clouds.

If what Alison has discovered is accurate, and on the surface, it certainly appears that way . . . only gravity can reverse the Big Crunch.

"Okay . . . and?!"

There are only two beings able to even start manipulating gravity. You . . .

"And Retnuh . . ."

But the force of gravity needed to sustain equilibrium while Alison carries out a long life would be staggering, Andrew. And I don't use that word lightly here. Tim let out a disappointed sigh. *To be blunt, neither of you have exhibited even* half *the force needed.*

"But the universe that I . . ." I trailed off, throwing my thumb over my shoulder to point behind me for some reason.

And it almost killed you, Andrew. Though I am able to regulate your physical body's energy consumption, I fear your form comprised of pure energy is still depleted.

"How do we refill it? Do I need to eat a bunch of stuff?"

I have no idea how to reenergize a form made of nothing but *energy.*

"I could stick my finger in a power outlet."

It would be moot for the Tims and I to debate on that topic, as the force you are able to exert without killing yourself is still not enough to hold the universe in place.

"It's so much easier to destroy than it is to build," I said to myself.

Ain't that the truth.

I thought on his words for at least a full minute as the storm moved closer.

"How much force is needed?" I asked in a tone drained of hope as more raindrops ended their journey on the wooden deck with tiny kamikaze splashes.

I simply cannot compute the precise mathematics. The data required is more than my hard drive can contain, on top of the processing power it would take to factor in every *celestial body in the known—and* unknown—*universe. It's just not possible for me.*

"You can't? I find that hard to believe."

I need you to understand that I am only about to provide an example so that your human mind can comprehend the scope of the problem.

"Okay?"

With a sigh, Tim said, *What you are asking me to do is like trying to create movie-quality CGI on a dollar-store calculator. An-an-and before you say anything snarky, I am only giving such a dramatic example so that you better understand.*

"But I've seen you process insane amounts of data, like freaking time travel and gravity manipulation, um, formulas."

This is what I meant when I said the human mind isn't able to process the request, because you simply cannot comprehend even the stars in your own galaxy, much less every galaxy. The amount of data representing everything in the fragging universe *is more than my hard drives can contain. And even if I were able to somehow upgrade my memory, it would take a millennium for me to process precise formulas that stretched across all of existence, even with my superior hardware.*

"Your subminds can't help?"

We share my hardware, Andrew.

"What are you saying?!" I blurted, getting sick and tired of excuses rather than solutions to the problem that was *my* universe.

It's not possible, Andrew, Tim replied softly, delivering the conclusion of his findings with palpable regret.

"How much force is needed?" I growled as lightning flashed over the now churning ocean. "Just give me your best guess."

I could tell you a theoretical number that your brain wouldn't be able to process, or I could ask you to imagine every black hole in existence—*which you honestly can't do either, but it's the clearest picture I can draw for you.*

"Then you better make me understand." I didn't mean to threaten him with my tone, but neither did I attempt to hide my contempt.

Ah! Tim said before his avatar popped to life. "Maybe this will help."

Looking at the hologram above my arm, I watched as Tim zoomed out to the colorful universe, which reminded me of the sands of time, and highlighted what I guessed to be all the black holes.

"If we moved them to the center of the universe"—the highlighted phenomenon did just that, collecting into a giant hole in the middle—"and theoretically reversed the flow of gravity"—the enormous black hole showed arrows flowing outward from it instead of being swallowed—"there *still* wouldn't be enough force to do anything more than slow the inevitable collapse. Keep in mind this is only, as you put it, a *best guess* on my part."

The flowing universe sped up as the outer edges grew denser until I realized what was happening. In a matter of a minute, all of existence was streaking toward Earth like a reverse Big Bang. I could tell it would all come to a head at the precise same time, allowing for another Big Bang to create a new universe.

"What about . . . instinct?" I asked in a last-ditch effort to find a solution.

How do you mean?

"If I held a baseball in my hand right now, *you* would be able to tell me how much force and what angles I would need to use in order to throw it to the bungalow next door. But I can just *feel* it, without having to think."

To be blunt, feeling a baseball and feeling the entire universe are two completely different things.

I thought about what he was saying, realizing how foolish and desperate I was being.

"I can't stop it . . ." I stated, feeling my body melt in my chair.

I'm afraid neither you nor Retnuh would be able to exude enough gravitational force to even slow the Big Crunch, Tim said solemnly from inside my head as the hologram blipped away. *Not only this, but I am unable to comprehend a method with which to focus the greatest amount of gravity at the outermost edges of the universe. This on top of exponentially reducing the outward push the closer to Earth you went so as not to reverse course and start the eventual Big Freeze all over again.*

"You mean push too hard and put us back to square one?"

Correct. Even if we had enough force to exert on the collapsing universe, the precision needed for how much gravity to use on each and every object in existence is impossible to calculate.

My mind raced, replaying the scene over and over again.

"How . . . How can Ali produce this much force?" I asked, having a new respect for the indescribable power being exuded on the entire universe . . . from my baby girl.

I can only circle back to the original theory that the universe is using Alison as a method of resetting all of existence . . . to ensure said existence continues in perpetuity, Tim explained softly, sensing I was on the edge of the cliff of despair, dangerously close to falling into the sea of hopelessness.

The universe constantly breaks all the laws of physics as we know them. Take quantum mechanics, for example; the smaller things get, the weirder the laws of reality become. The same is true in the opposite direction.

I barely registered his needless explanation. It was as if the universe were a corrupt politician who only followed the laws they created when it was convenient to do so.

"So that's all that Alison's research said . . . ?" My voice was hoarse as I barely pushed enough air past my vocal cords. "I can't do anything to stop it?"

That appears to be the conclusion. Yes.

"Then you finally understand," a cultured Spanish accent said from the seat on the other side of the small table. There wasn't any animosity to his words. It was as if he was saddened I couldn't find the solution I had so desperately fought to find.

I didn't even face Retnuh, content to keep my eyes on the bulging storm as it marched ever closer, letting loose window-rattling thunder as if directed at me and my failure.

"What do you want, Retnuh?" I loudly sighed, plopping my back against the wooden chair and making it creak in protest.

Turning to the man, I was surprised to see he was a *man* again. No longer did his body glow, flesh and blood sitting now beside me. Or perhaps it was simply a projection of flesh by a man who was more machine than human.

Setting his black fedora on the table, he crossed his legs and stared out at the ocean as it churned in agitation. "I either want the universe to continue to exist in its current iteration, or I'd like it to last as long as possible."

"Even if that means that no life will ever flourish again?" I asked, referencing the Big Freeze, where everything, literally everything, would grow cold and devoid of life—the final stage of entropy.

"If you leave me no other choice . . . then yes."

Our gazes met, and for the first time, there wasn't a hatred as strong as gravity itself between us. I could see the weariness in his eyes, and how he was almost pleading with me to give up my crusade for the impossible.

Something I couldn't shake solidified itself in my mind, demanding to be asked.

"How did you even find me?"

Retnuh either tried to hide a smile that was forming without his consent, or it was simply weak enough that it only appeared like he was barely attempting to restrain it. Judging by how his head slightly tilted down, I guessed it was the latter.

"I waited."

"You . . . waited?" I repeated, trying to break down the two simple words that had the impact and complexity of the entire human language. "I don't understand."

"I . . . *felt* where you went—the pull you exert on the very fabric of reality itself. Tracked you to this timeline, and then just . . . waited."

For some reason, my brain had trouble processing what he was saying, more so than it had when attempting to comprehend the black hole hologram demonstration that Tim had just shown me.

"You . . . waited . . . ?"

Retnuh looked over the increasingly angry ocean, nodding with a thousand-yard stare.

"For how long?" I knew I shouldn't have asked a question that was potentially sensitive in nature, but it was a knee-jerk reaction, like when you found out someone had died and you asked *how*. Or if you found out someone had served in the military, and the basic part of your brain wanted to inquire as to how many people they had killed.

I pictured being locked in a windowless room for weeks, months, or even years. It must have been maddening.

"Eight hundred and fifty-seven years, six months, eleven days, fourteen hours, twenty-seven minutes, and"—he lifted the sleeve of his suit on his left arm to check a vintage-looking watch—"forty-two seconds."

Without realizing it, my eyes locked onto the watch while my brain tried to formulate why that was important. It didn't take long to comprehend what my subconscious had noticed immediately: he didn't have his Clepsydra.

His words snuck past my thoughts to bitch slap my brain. He had waited for me . . . for over eight hundred years.

"How . . ."

"Am I still alive?" the surprisingly calm Retnuh asked.

I could only nod in confirmation that he had accurately guessed my question.

"That's what I'm not sure of," he admitted, looking down at his normal-looking hands.

Thunder exploded in the clouds just on the other side of the horizon, rattling the windows even from this distance.

Tim spoke inside my head.

A quick scan shows his entire body is . . . Well, I'm not sure how to put this, other than to say not a single human cell remains.

Answering mentally, I asked, *So he's fully synthetic?*

That's the odd thing, Tim said slowly, as if checking and rechecking his scans. *He's neither man nor machine. He just . . . is.*

Is it because you crushed what was left of his body in the wormhole?

A confused Tim answered after considering the question.

There's no conclusive data available on what happens to a person trapped in a collapsing wormhole. Once it was free, the immense gravity used to warp the very fabric of space and time should have condensed every atom in his being into a point so small that not even quantum mechanics could have calculated his remaining existence.

I pictured my glowing body while in the tesseract, and an unnerving thought came to mind.

Could he be made up of pure energy? I mentally said for both of us. *Like maybe he was thrown into the tesseract or something?*

I cannot compare between your own human flesh and the raw energy your body is comprised of while in the tesseract.

Why not?

Because I don't have any sensors without my Clepsydra.

Tim, I asked after considering his words. *If he isn't human, then how do we kill him?*

I . . . don't know, Andrew.

My face tilted as I let my eyes roam over my enemy, from his wing-tip shoes to his bald scalp.

Retnuh noticed, gave another half a smile, and said, "Tim told you I'm no longer a real boy."

I didn't know what to say, so I let silence be my answer.

"If I were to be honest, I don't know how this vessel came into being." He spoke with a mixture of mild disgust and maybe sadness, watching while both hands alternated between each finger tapping the stationary thumb in one direction before going back the opposite way.

Unable to help myself, my own synthetic hand subtly did the same, just to see if it still felt human.

Retnuh turned to me and produced a smile of understanding at the test I had conducted under the table. Unfortunately, I had forgotten it was a *glass* table.

"I know what you are thinking. And maybe you're right." He slowly nodded and returned his attention to the nearing storm as fat raindrops began to pelt the damp wooden deck. "Maybe this . . . this *artificial* vessel is how I've managed to survive past what I should have."

"I thought people of your time can basically live forever thanks to the nanoids. Unless there is major damage or something."

"That would be true, except I'm no longer sure if any machines remain within my veins."

"I don't understand . . ."

"Neither do I," he answered as his gaze tilted toward the dense clouds.

I thought about what he had said, rolling it around in my human brain—still the original product from the factory—and asked, "If you don't think it was your, um, *body* that kept you alive all these centuries . . . then what else could it be?"

"This." Retnuh snapped his fingers, and the storm vanished like a movie edit.

My jaw gaped open as I looked over the calm ocean and baby-blue sky with a light spattering of white fluffy clouds.

Did he just jump us through time? Tim asked inside my head.

My mouth closed while my bulging eyes returned to their normal size. I turned to Retnuh, no longer impressed with his trick, which I had already discovered.

"You're wrong."

"About what?" I asked, taken off guard.

"I didn't just move us through time."

"Then what?" My heart sped up at realizing there was something else major that I didn't know but the murderous Retnuh did.

"Would you believe me if I said I didn't know?"

I considered his words before giving the only answer that kept popping up. "No."

He nodded, clearly anticipating my response. "I don't have Tim, Andrew."

"What does . . ." I started to ask before it became evident. Without my AI, I would know precisely *jack* or possibly just *shit* about what was happening to me.

The fact that my mortal enemy was calling me by my first name instead of my last or something derogatory like *Tick* caught my attention.

"Why am I not dead right now?" I asked flatly, setting my jaw for the surprise fight that Retnuh always seemed to deliver at the worst time.

Retnuh took a long, slow inhale as his eyes glided over the crystal-clear horizon.

"Eight centuries is a long time to think, Andrew." He let out in a tired exhale. "At first, my hatred for you fueled my determination to keep the universe going." I opened my mouth to interject before he quickly added, "For as long as possible, at least."

I closed my mouth, no longer feeling the urge to point out he *was* willing to let existence slowly succumb to the entropy that was the Big Freeze.

"I arrived on this timeline in the year 1207 AD."

See, he *clarifies if it's AD or not,* I mentally whispered to Tim.

Is that really what's important right now?

As I returned my focus to Retnuh, a question jumped out at me.

"Why didn't you just speed up time until you found me?"

"I didn't know how to at first. And once I discovered it, it had already been three decades."

"What does that have to do with anything?"

"For the first time in my life, I was alone, Andrew. No wormhole meant no home office or their relentless communication. No one knew where I was. Hell, *I* didn't know where I was. And it was . . . nice."

I arched an eyebrow at the man I had labeled a psychopath as he exhibited human emotions besides anger or joy at killing for the first time. As I asked myself what I would be like after eight centuries of solitude, my eyebrow returned to its neutral position.

"It wasn't long before I met someone," Retnuh admitted with another long sigh, as if physically relieving the pressure inside his body. "A small village took me in while I huddled around a pathetic mound of wet sticks, trying to start a fire in the snow. They showed me how to build my own home from nothing more than wood, rocks, and clay; taught me how to survive without the aid of technology and do something as basic as start a fire. It was . . . freeing beyond what words can describe."

I watched, feeling an unease in my chest as my body attempted mutiny and tried to pull all the levers, flip the switches, and push the buttons that would make me *feel* for this guy—as if he were anything more than a homicidal machine.

I fought to maintain intellectual dominance over my rebellious emotions.

"Then I met her . . . Astrid." There was a reverence in his voice that punched a small hole through my mountainous wall of resistance. "Her radiance could melt the very frost from the ground." Retnuh chuckled as he shifted uncomfortably in his seat. "You have to understand that I had never been in a relationship before."

Both eyebrows shot up as my jaw fell toward my lap and head jutted forward.

"Never?!"

Retnuh's lips went flat and tight as he shook his head. "We were bred for one thing. No days off. No friends. Hell, I don't even know who my parents are except for the little information that they were chosen to be my donors because of traits that the company desired."

"Leaves little time for dating."

He chuckled again, becoming more human with each passing second. "So when I saw her, I had no past experiences from which to draw on. Do you understand what I'm saying?"

I had to stifle a laugh as I pictured Retnuh with a neckbeard at a convention, tipping his fedora at all the women and saying something cringeworthy like, "My lady," in the hopes that they would swoon.

"I can see by your smile that you get it." Retnuh repositioned himself into a more relaxed posture, with his feet far out in front of him. "But she tolerated my ineptitude with grace and humor."

He didn't speak for several seconds. Only the gentle sound of waves cresting into the nearby beach filled the air, along with the occasional seagull call.

Once again, I knew I shouldn't ask, but I couldn't help myself.

"What happened?"

"She died during childbirth," he replied. I thought I saw his chin tremble, though it might have been a shadow from a passing fluff of cloud overhead. "I was helpless, having none of the technologies that petty humans take for granted on a daily basis. Even in this time." He motioned behind him with one hand before letting it drop back to his armrest.

"I'm sorry," I said before I realized what my mouth was doing. How could I be sorry for this piece of shit?

Retnuh turned to me with glistening eyes as he tried to fight back his sorrow. So I continued.

"I know what it's like . . . to lose those you love most." There was a tinge of rage that I hadn't meant to interject but also didn't regret inserting. A pained expression shot across Retnuh's face as he turned away from me, forcing himself to look at the bungalow next to ours.

Point made, and still curious about the rest of the story, I asked, "What happened with the child?"

"He grew up, big and strong, to have several children of his own."

"What happened with them?"

"I'm not sure." He sighed, returning his gaze to the ocean ahead. "It never occurred to me that I wasn't aging until the village had surrounded my home, declaring I was a demon."

I didn't realize I was leaning forward in my seat, captivated by his tale. "Then what?" I asked like a child at story time.

"With my home surrounded, they set it ablaze with me inside."

"What about your grandkids?"

"They lived nearby, leaving me alone in the home I had built by hand nearly three decades earlier."

I just gawked, waiting for him to continue.

"I could have fled into the tesseract, but I was terrified it would mean losing the rest of my family. That's when I discovered I could control time without the wormhole."

He didn't have to explain as my mind played out the scene of him vanishing from the burning hut.

"What did the villagers do when they didn't find your bones?"

"They assumed I had exploded into sulfur like demons were supposed to," he said with a forced, fake chuckle.

"And your son and grandkids?"

"I went there next, ready to destroy every single pathetic human who dared threaten my family." As he said those words, I was reminded of the man Retnuh was . . . along with seeing my own reflection in his determination. It was eerie to make a comparison between this monster and myself.

"My son was exceedingly intelligent." Retnuh's pride was evident in his voice. I started to think *of course* you think your kid is the smartest; all parents do, as it is a direct reflection of their own self-image. But then he surprised me by adding, "He got that from his mother."

"And?" I asked after several seconds of silence in which Retnuh remembered his wife.

"My son, Jameson, convinced the villagers that I hadn't been *born* a demon. That I had been taken over some years prior, which was why he'd moved his family away. He also reassured the simple folk that he, too, wasn't the spawn of a supernatural entity." Retnuh looked at me as I asked a wordless question. "It was a lie, of course. My son didn't think I was anything but a loving father and grandfather, and only moved to be closer to the growing city where he had been overwhelmingly elected reeve over his village."

"Impressive." I nodded as a parent recognizing the incredible feat another's child had achieved. Every mother and father wanted their babies to grow up and become someone important, like a president beloved by all sides.

"So then what? Did you stay with your son in disguise?"

"No . . ." he exhaled. I could feel the pain he was attempting to let out so he didn't have to feel it. "I did the only intelligent thing I could: I left."

"You left your family behind?"

"What choice did I have?!" he exploded at me, slamming his fist on the glass table hard enough that I was surprised it didn't shatter. "I didn't want to risk the chance of getting caught and having to slay an entire village with my bare hands to protect my family. And before you ask *why not*, how would Jameson ever be able to look at me again and *not* think I was a demon?"

"You could have told him the truth?" I said weakly, not believing my own suggestion. Luckily, Retnuh picked up on this and let it slide, choosing to continue.

"Instead, I watched, making sure they were safe. Doing whatever I had to."

"Like what?"

Retnuh sucked through his teeth as he rubbed his eyes.

"One of my grandchildren, Peter, fell through the ice of a lake when it was too near to spring. No one else was around, so I stopped time, pulled him free, and moved him until we were clear. Gathering materials, I resumed time before quickly setting a large fire. But it took several seconds to ignite the pile of wood and kindling and ensure it would thrive, which gave Peter time to recover and see me before I could move away."

"What'd he do?"

"He asked if I was Grandfather."

"What'd *you* say?" I asked, dreadfully curious.

"I . . . I told him I had come from Heaven to save him, and that he shouldn't tell anyone. And then I just . . . walked away, wanting nothing more than to talk to my flesh and blood." He looked down at his own hands. "Or whatever this is . . ."

I continued to stare at the man, waiting.

"There were a handful more instances like that. But ultimately, I decided it was best to leave them once Jameson passed away and the family began corroborating stories of their dead grandfather. I . . . I didn't want the archaic people of that time to start questioning whether my family was being protected by the demon that had been slain decades before."

"So you left . . ."

"So I left . . ."

We both looked at the calm sea, feeling the weight of that decision.

Oh, dear sweet science, Tim drawled inside my head; I could hear him covering his puppy mouth.

What? I mentally asked, almost annoyed at being pulled from the story.

Though I cannot find anything in my files to corroborate what he is saying, I have been scouring the internet of this timeline.

The internet is saying something different to your files?

It is clear that Retnuh has a powerful Chronos Scale. But with your own scale countering his, my memory of human history hasn't changed.

What does that mean?! What is the internet saying that your files aren't?!

Andrew . . . I don't know how to say this . . .

"Tim is telling you . . . isn't he?"

"Telling me what, goddammit?!" I blurted out loud to both Tim and Retnuh.

Mindlessly gliding his index finger over the glass, Retnuh spoke. "Do you know where the name Smith comes from?"

"Wh . . . What?" I stammered, feeling like I could hear the whistle of a nuke as it descended from the sky toward my head.

"The blacksmith, when migrating to America, where last names were required, was given the uncreative name *Smith* by the over-worked government employees as they rushed to usher people from seemingly never-ending boats."

"I . . . I don't . . ."

"The same with Baker, for example."

I watched the man speak, feeling like my soul was attempting to disconnect from my body.

"Jameson's first son, Peter, had a son, who had a son, who had a son, until the twenty-sixth generation patriarch—Andrew, if you can believe it—migrated to America in hopes of a better life. And when the Americans were asking for a last name, he gave them the one the family had adopted when such concepts such as surnames became common.

"It had originated from a story passed down for generations about how their family had been started by a man in funny clothes who never aged. The man had met a woman who had come from a line of women who had only produced female children. Apparently, the story I had told Jameson and his children over and over again about Astrid had stuck with them. Which was the point, as I wanted . . . *needed* the memory of her to live on through her children and their children's children."

I just stared at him, unable to speak though my mouth tried to move. I could feel we were in a speeding car heading straight toward the side of a mountain, and our brakes were cut.

"But it worked. Even centuries later, my family knew the tale of Astrid and the moment I had first seen the most beautiful woman my eyes had ever laid upon."

"No . . . No, I . . ."

"Her radiance could melt the very *frost* on the ground . . ."

"I . . ." The world spun as I slipped into unconsciousness.

CHAPTER 15

He took that better than expected." Tim's muffled voice came as if through a thin wall.

I groaned as I lifted my head from my chest, feeling the strain of muscles in the back of my neck, prompting me to drunkenly lift a hand to rub at it.

"Eloquent as always," Tim said with more clarity.

Shifting my weary eyes, feeling like I had just woken up from a long slumber, I managed to focus on the hologram floating above my left arm.

"What happened?" I moved my hand from the back of my neck to rub at my eyes.

A voice I wasn't expecting answered. "You passed out."

I exploded from my seat, whirling a glowing blue fist to point at the eerily calm Retnuh Ordune.

"Ordune . . ." I breathed out as pieces of the conversation solidified. "Frost . . ."

"Technically, *I'm* still an Ordune. It was Jameson's son, Peter, who was the first Frost."

"You're . . . You're my . . ." I stammered, still unable to fully process what was being said.

Thankfully, I had Tim to fill me in, whether I wanted him to or not.

"Retnuh is your great-great-great-great-great-great-great-great," he began to spout with different inflections as if to add drama and suspense.

"Tim . . ."

"Bah, fine! Retnuh is your great-grandfather twenty-something times over."

Knees feeling a tad weak, I moved to sit in my chair once more before lifting my hands, turning them over just in front of my chest to peer at. "I guess that explains some things," I mused.

Inside my head, Tim whispered, *It doesn't just explain your time-altering abilities, Andrew.*

God . . . what else, I mentally lamented as I dropped my hands to my lap with a light *smack*, reminding me I was still in just a bathrobe.

His Chronos Scale is higher.

That made everything in me freeze in place. My lungs stopped inflating and deflating. My heart seemed to beat just enough to keep me alive, but I could feel it looking up at me as if mouthing *WTF*. The only organ that kept functioning to capacity was my bladder, which saw its opportunity to shine and went into overdrive.

"Everything okay?" Retnuh asked, staring at me with an arched eyebrow.

"Excuse me. Gotta drain the snake," I said before rushing toward the bathroom.

Tim, presumably trying to help cover for our mental conversation, called out to Retnuh, "More like drain the tiny *worm*! Ha!"

Tim, you aren't helping, I mentally chastised.

Oh, right. I'm basically insulting him as well.

Not what I meant.

After relieving myself and letting my mind absorb everything like a newly purchased kitchen sponge, the dryer announced with a pleasant *ding* that it was done.

Wait . . . how am I here if Retnuh is my, um, ancestor?

I'm not sure I follow.

This isn't our home timeline, right? How can our timeline be the center of the tesseract if this is my home?

Oh, I see where you are going with this, Tim said with a nod. *To answer your question, this just further proves that Retnuh's Chronos*

Scale is higher. He was able to create your family tree during this *time-line, which stretches to our home. And, though I don't like to think about it, your home timeline being different might be because of factors that haven't shown themselves yet.*

Like what?!

Do I really have to spell it out for you? Tim said with a hint of concern in his voice. *For now, just keep your eye on Retnuh.*

My head swam with how complex the situation was. Instead, I focused on what to do next while pulling my clothes out of the dryer.

What do we do? I asked, moving to throw the bathrobe off and punch my limbs through the extremely hot clothes fresh out of the depths of Hell.

What do you mean what do we do? There was a genuine curiosity in his tone that both angered and surprised me.

With Retnuh!

Well, if I were you, I'd try to leverage what he feels for his dead wife to form a sympathetic understanding of your situation. Maybe it could be enough to sway him to your cause.

Shouldn't we just kill him? I asked, keeping our conversation mental. I was beginning to feel the lure of Retnuh's tragic story wash away, leaving behind the core of my original attitude toward the man.

I don't think that is a good idea.

Why the hell not?!

Because, as we just found out by him *being your great-grandpappy, he* clearly *has the higher Chronos Scale.*

And?! That never stopped us before! My fists were clenched as if my body were preparing for war.

Think about how you have, with ease, killed everyone who has stood in your way. All except one.

My mind betrayed me and played back my battles with Davix and even Traze.

Traze wasn't easy! I countered, desperate to find a hole in his damnable logic.

Look, we can argue about the power differential between those with unknown Chronos Scales, or we can correctly *assume that Retnuh will be to us what Davix was to you—an inconvenience at best.*

Or Traze! That psycho almost got me more than once!

Yet he is dead. And Retnuh is sitting outside, unscathed from all our battles.

Only because he grew a new body, I mumbled, remembering the bubbling skin and milky eye I had left him with in the dungeon while rescuing Drew.

Andrew, that alone should be of great concern to your plans for a fight to the death. The man grew flesh and bone from nothing more than pure energy!

The truth sunk in, and my body visibly deflated as my fists went lax.

Then what do we do?

Talk *to him . . .*

Glancing at myself in the mirror, I couldn't help but fabricate physical similarities between my grand-relative and I.

We can't beat him . . . can we?

I'm . . . I'm sorry to say it, but I'm afraid not, Andrew.

He already said he was going to save the universe. He said so even before *telling us the story.*

Then you had better be convincing as hell. Because there is no other choice. Unless—

Unless? I dared to hope, grasping on to this word like a drowning man clutching at a life preserver.

Unless you can find a way to exert enough spherical, outward force to keep the universe from collapsing in on itself.

And you're sure I can't do that . . . right?

The things you've done, though miraculous, are like comparing hitting a soda can with a bullet or a nuke. And I doubt you have a nuke stuffed down your pants, though there is *plenty of room!*

Thanks, Tim . . . I sighed, not caring about the dick joke and instead focusing on the truth that I didn't have enough raw power to hold the *entire* universe at bay.

So I have to convince him to risk the universe in order to save my family.

They're his *family too.*

Still looking at myself in the mirror, I nodded, filing away that important piece of information that I hadn't even considered.

Sucking in a deep breath with a mind that stumbled over itself to form a convincing argument, I looked into my own eyes and said, "Here goes nothing."

CHAPTER 16

’ll help you," Retnuh smoothly said while continuing to stare out at the shimmering ocean.

I froze midstep, with my index finger held in the air and mouth agape, as he preemptively cut off my impromptu sales pitch with the answer I so desperately wanted.

"I . . . uh . . . thanks?"

"But . . ."

The invisible string holding my arm up was severed, dropping my hand to my side. "But?"

Retnuh slid his gaze from the serene water to land squarely on my eyes, piercing my very soul. "The tesseract is collapsing. And if it comes down to saving it or . . . *our* family, then I will have no choice."

"It's *your* fault the damn thing is falling apart!" I accused, feeling indignant rage bubbling inside me at being forced to decide between my family and a now tangible representation of the universe. But it wasn't just *a* universe. It was *all* universes.

"I'm a man who can admit his mistakes. One of which is being blinded by pride and a sense of urgency."

"A sense of urgency?! You destroyed entire timelines!"

"Anything to ensure the cessation of your meddling. I believe the terminology is *collateral damage*."

My mind was a whirlwind of confusion at realizing this man would consider wiping out an entire timeline as nothing more than an acceptable, calculated sacrifice if it meant getting his desired results.

"I think *scorched earth* is more accurate, Retnuh."

In answer, the man simply shrugged, eyebrows barely bobbing in acknowledgement, as if he didn't care to put any more energy into the effort.

"And now look what's happening," I continued, tilting my face down as I lobbed a powerful accusation at the man who was the seed to the Frost family tree.

"Perhaps scorched earth *is* more apropos," Retnuh said, turning his gaze from me as he verbally confirmed his part in what was happening.

"And now you're telling me that you'll only help me so long as the tesseract doesn't begin to collapse . . . because of what *you* did. Is that right?"

The corner of Retnuh's lips lifted in a smile, but the action was miles from reaching his eyes. "Hardly seems fair, doesn't it?" he asked in a low, smooth voice as the waves gently glided beneath our feet. Heat bloomed from my cheeks and forehead as my anger rose, but I was able to wrestle my building emotions into an amateurish choke hold—at least for the time being.

"Tim," I asked through gritted teeth, "how long do we have until the tesseract collapses?"

It's hard to say, he responded inside my mind, which I found odd, considering this was an open conversation. *Retnuh was in the timeline for over eight centuries, and it held up.*

And his Chronos Scale is higher, right? I mentally confirmed, following Tim's lead of keeping our discussion close to the chest.

It has to be.

Then why should I be worried? Clearly, we have time.

I want to point out how time is relative, but you do seem to have a point. Unless . . .

Unless?

Nothing, Tim quickly dismissed. *I need to let this all percolate before jumping to any conclusions.*

"Seeing as how you both went silent, I can only surmise that you are having a private discussion on the ticking time bomb that is the tesseract."

I could feel my body wanting to drop my jaw, but I was becoming steadily resistant to the surprises this man offered. Such as his ability to read a situation to the point of almost being telepathic.

"We are," I answered honestly.

"The answer is staring you in the face." There wasn't any malice or subterfuge in his voice as he looked at me, but I still wasn't grasping his meaning, almost as if his message was hiding in plain sight.

Hmm, Tim mentally added.

What?

Oh, um . . . nothing. I still need more time on this.

"Whatever," I let out with a quick sigh of frustration and a dismissive wave of my hand. "Let's just get this done."

The wicker seat creaked as Retnuh's weight rose off of it. A smile resembling something equal parts devious and knowing lifted the corners of his lips. Or maybe I was projecting.

"After you," Retnuh Ordune, my direct ancestor, said with a little bow.

"This doesn't mean I trust you," I said in a low, steady tone that could have been considered the beginnings of a growl.

"I would expect no less, Andrew." His use of my first name instead of my last nearly threw me off-balance, but I quickly regained my composure, refocused on the mission, and nodded.

"Then let's go."

CHAPTER 17

Shifting to the tesseract brought with it a new sense of dread I had only heard described in cheesy horror movies. Each time I thought I'd reached the pinnacle of terror, the universe took it as a challenge and came up with creative new ways to try and rip my mind asunder.

The tesseract groaned like a wooden ship rocking on a violent, angry sea. The creaking ranged in pitch from a low, powerful bass, to an almost shrill screeching that made my teeth hurt—almost like dragging ragged fingernails down a dirty chalkboard.

"What's happening?" I asked, trying to wrestle the autonomous urge for my breath to start galloping. Once again, I couldn't breathe while my flesh was ethereal, but my body refused to acknowledge that fact, bringing with it an added anxiety to the already shitty situation which would give any normal person a heart attack.

"Precisely what I said would happen," Retnuh answered as his calculating eyes panned across the cacophony of chaos.

"What do we do?"

"We carry on with the mission!" Retnuh declared with a stern assuredness that gave me pause.

A stream of time immediately to our left began to bow toward us, violently, like an archer nocking his bowstring. On instinct, I threw out my hand, sending out my will before the neighboring stream could snap . . . or crash into us.

Retnuh threw out his own hands, and we wrestled the time stream as it wildly bucked against our collective wills.

"I think you two should separate!" Tim shouted aloud.

"Why?!" I barked from between gritted teeth on the verge of splintering, barely registering that the AI was able to now speak out loud even without his housing.

"The pull you two are exerting is warping the fabric of the tesseract!" Tim explained with an urgency that compounded my terror.

"He's right!" Retnuh called out, much calmer than I was. His right hand snapped in the opposite direction right as another stream of time began to reach toward us like a campfire's smoke when you tried to sit by it.

My eyes wildly flicked all around as I continued to try and wrestle the river to our left. It fought against me with all its might, demanding to be freed from the constraints of its linear prison.

"Where the hell do I go?!"

"It doesn't matter," Retnuh answered, switching his left hand from the timeline I was locked in a battle with to another directly above us that wanted to join the party. "Just go before the original timeline is affected! It's the only one that matters!"

Tim! I mentally called out. *Show me where to go! Now!*

Ummm . . . um, um, um, Tim stuttered. *There!*

In my vision, nothing happened.

Tim?!

0—fragging—1 dammit! he cried out. *I—I can't adjust your vision!*

Then tell *me where to go!*

Right! Ummm. Look straight-ahead. I did. *Now count five rivers to the left.*

Four . . . five . . . Got it! I exclaimed, noticing a timeline that wasn't being affected by the gravitational pull that Retnuh and I seemed to be exerting together. Without a second thought, I threw both fists out as if I were a superhero and zipped toward the calm river with every ounce of strained will I had left.

The universe I had been entangled with reached up for me like the oceans following the pull of the moon, catching my feet for the briefest of moments. It didn't have enough substance to yank me in, but it did throw me off as I tried to course correct.

Wait! Tim shouted inside my head, making me wince with its intensity.

Sending the signal to hold the breath I didn't have, I squinted my eyes as I punched through a now random stream of time, getting away from Retnuh before we could collapse all of existence.

CHAPTER 18

Vibrant purple and green lights streaked toward me as I bounced off a hard, smooth floor. Everything swirled in my vision before I understood that I was flopping around like a wet shoe in a supercharged clothes dryer.

"Oof!" I exhaled in a single blast as something crashed into me. I thought I had broken more bones from the impact, as the sound of snapping rocketed from somewhere on my body, but then Tim clarified, *Oh, thank science. It was just a sapling.*

I wanted to inquire what he meant; however, the world was still tumbling around me, albeit a little slower now. I hit the ground again, smashing my right elbow into the unforgiving material hard enough to send a jolt of electricity in either direction. But at least my spinning had slowed enough that I could see I was flying toward the side of a building like a crash test dummy through a windshield.

"Ah!" I screamed, throwing my hands out in an effort to stop my momentum like I was still in the tesseract. However, nothing happened, and I watched in helpless horror as the wall bathed in purple-and-green lights grew larger in my vision.

My muscles received new orders that bypassed my brain, and I curled into a ball until my feet were pointed toward the approaching wall before extending. As the bottom of my remaining shoe and bare heel touched the building, my legs bent as my arms went out to either side while my body curved backward at the waist. It was like slipping on ice-covered ground, if that ground was actually a wall.

My quads—and knees—took most of the kinetic force before my back and outstretched arms slammed into the wall, which I swear was made of titanium, tungsten, or some other unyielding material. Had it been concrete, I feel like I would have broken *through* the damn thing.

Once again, the air was robbed from my lungs as my diaphragm protested my treatment of it. But at least we had stopped.

Having spoken too soon, which was on brand for me, I realized that the ground was now rushing up to smash into my extended synthetic arm.

To his credit, Tim knew more about the limits of the human body than I ever could. And I had to admit that having a lot of my body replaced with the nanoids and their housing made it possible to survive such cartoonish tomfoolery. Over . . . and over . . . and over again.

As I struck the ground, my thighs came together like a hydraulic press, attempting to see if my balls would turn to mashed potatoes *inside* my sack or would squeeze out like a tube of toothpaste being slowly run over by a monster truck's tire.

"Oooowww," I managed to say through an excruciating inhale.

01, why did your creator program the most vital part of human reproduction in those tiny, vulnerable organs? You might as well have quail eggs between your legs!

The pain was numbed by Tim, but the growing wave of nausea continued forward like a Mongolian army through ancient Asia. This left me with a stomach that was trying to crawl up my throat as a fire burned up my left arm where I had somehow hit my not-fucking-funny bone.

"Wait . . . why does my arm hurt if my bones are made of metal now?" I croaked, trying to distract myself enough so that I didn't vomit. Across a pristinely clean street, I saw from the corner of my eye a handful of people who appeared to be waiting for the bus.

"A—huUHT," I let out, sounding like a cat at the beginnings of operation Hairball Removal.

Why are you gagging? Tim asked, sounding like he was reading a chart. *Why in the science is the nerve running through your stomach also linked to your weak, pathetic scrotum?*

As bitter bile tickled the back of my throat, the feeling of needing to throw up vanished, like flipping a switch. Smacking my lips a few times and swallowing the warm bile back down now that I wasn't going to expel the contents of my stomach, I said, "I want to be mad at you for making fun of my balls . . . but I just . . . I just can't argue the logic . . ."

Damn right, leg butt.

"You're still reaching with that one," I groaned as I pushed myself up to a seated position, reminding me of my sore arm. "But back to it. Why did I feel pain on my metal bone?"

It's not the bone that feels pain, Andrew. It is the ulnar nerve that runs along the elbow joint, Tim explained before adding in an almost shy, hopeful tone, *Would you like me to replace your nerves as well?*

"No, thank you. I'd like to stay as human as possible," I groaned again, awkwardly getting to my feet and looking around while rubbing my burning elbow.

The first thing I noticed was that there wasn't even a mark on the wall I had struck like a cannonball, almost like crashing into something in a dream. Reaching up, I let my fingers glide over the surface to confirm what my eyes were telling me.

"How am I able to take this much, um, damage?" I asked, switching my hand from the unblemished wall to my intact body. "Even with my—and I can't believe I'm saying this—*bones* being metal . . . shouldn't there be soft-tissue damage?"

Oh, there is, meat bag. But fortunately, you have an extremely talented, creative, and flat-out genius *partner in crime the likes of which have never been seen before.*

"Don't forget to mention humble," I muttered, letting my hand fall away from my elbow, which no longer seemed to throb. "And never seen before? Didn't we meet up with *Drew's* Ti—"

Would you look at the time! Heh heh. We should probably move to the time stream I had originally indicated.

"May I ask why?"

First, because I said so. And second, because my calculations indicate that we are still too close to Retnuh in this universe.

"Hmm?" I asked, turning around on instinct, half expecting to see my great-great relative standing behind me, still battling the bucking rivers of the tesseract.

I heard a *smack* and knew Tim had slapped his forehead in disbelief mixed with frustration.

"Why did that sound like skin to skin? Don't you have fur?"

Andrew . . . I swear to science . . .

Looking around once more, I saw the people still standing at what I took to be a bus stop. Taking a moment to let my gaze linger, a feeling of discomfort began leaking into my emotional status. They weren't moving.

"Um . . . Tim?"

Alright, Tim thought aloud, *if we leave now, we can be in the minimum safe distance before Retnuh experiences any further temporal flexation.*

"Tim?" I gulped, taking a few steps closer to where the people were as still as statues.

Or is it flexion? I always confuse those two.

"Tim!"

Oh, silly me. "Flexation" isn't even a word. Heh. How embarrassing.

"TIM!"

WHAT?!

My arm shot up fast enough to sound like a cartoon *whoosh* as my index finger tried to painfully stretch away from my fist, pointing toward the gathering of frozen people.

How odd.

"Nuh-shuh," I said, apparently trying to say *no shit* and *uh-huh* at the same time.

Uh-oh . . .

"Why *uh-oh*, Tim?"

One moment, please.

Nervous eyes flicked from side to side, suddenly noticing the oddities all around. Trees were stuck in a midbreeze bend. Birds hovered overhead as if lovingly placed in one of Bob Ross' paintings. I couldn't explain why, but the feeling of unease in my gut violently mutated into a mind-drowning fear.

There was a small burst of blue light in front of me, almost like quickly spinning a sparkler on the Fourth of July, before it abruptly went out. Another pop of blue sparks made me flinch as I instinctively took a step back.

Okay. Nooooo need to worry. Heh.

"Tiiiiimmmmm?" I could feel my throat tightening as fear tried to evolve into panic.

Hmm? Oh, ahem, nothing to worry about. Heh heh, Tim tried to reassure with a confidence that was faker than a politician's campaign promises. *Hey! On a side note* completely *unrelated . . . could you, by chance, jump us away from here?* His voice went up in pitch at the end, filling me with hope. Or was it dread? So easy to confuse those two.

Looking down the street, where I noticed cars were not parked but frozen in time, I focused on the tesseract and took a step forward.

My boot slapped against the resin walkway . . . and nothing else.

Glancing to my side, I saw the congregation of unmoving still en masse.

"Um, Tim?"

What did you do wrong?!

"Me? Nothing!" I protested before facing forward again and taking another step while picturing the countless streams of time.

Nothing. So I did a little hop—also nothing. Finally, I screamed in a falsetto while jumping forward as if trying to do a belly flop into water. Well, I *did* a belly flop, but it wasn't water I hit.

You landed on your balls again. Tim sighed. *I can really only do so much with what little flesh you have down there.*

I wanted to get mad at his little quip, but I was too terrified at the concept of being absolutely stuck in a timeline that was too close to where Retnuh was probably still battling the wriggling streams.

"Ti . . . Ti . . ." I tried to speak, but my gonads had somehow taken control over my vocal abilities. Clearly, Tim had let his focus drop from blocking my pain receptors.

Tim, I said mentally, *could Retnuh have moved by now?*

No.

How do you know?

Because, Tim let out with a long sigh, *we would be able to escape from this warping reality.*

As if we were in some CGI-laden sci-fi movie, the cracks of this distorting universe began splitting the world around me.

I don't know if you are aware, but having your organs *vibrate* inside your body hurt in a way that I couldn't possibly explain. It was a lot like smelling burning human flesh; there was nothing else like it, and it was something you'd never forget.

My abs flexed on instinct in an effort to squeeze my lower organs so they would stop vibrating. But that did little to negate my lungs, heart, and most alarmingly, my brain. And of course, my testicles were subject to the equivalent of sitting on a paint mixer.

A teeth-shattering *snap* and *crack* brought me to my knees as a crevasse was carved into the air. It looked like lightning frozen in place but straighter; instead of jutting in different directions, it resembled more of a geological fault line—if that fault line could somehow start three feet off the road and gradually arc upward to, and *through*, the same building I had crashed into.

What do we do? Tim lamented while a feeling of calm washed over me as I stared at the tear in reality. It was a nice change of pace not to be the one freaking out. Then again, things must really be FUBARed for an AI to lose his circuits.

"If we can't jump to another timeline in order to put distance between us and Retnuh . . . then . . ."

With a stoicism I didn't realize I could muster from within, I looked down the street, held up my hand with fingers pointed toward the sky and palm facing me, and pulled toward myself.

The paused movie went into fast-forward as the living statues zipped into action. From what I could tell, they were no longer waiting for whatever public transport was being offered. Now they seemed to be scattering, apparently aware of their universe splitting apart.

One person darted past me, only to be clotheslined by a new tear.

01 . . . Tim exhaled as the person vanished into a showering of colorful particles. *Might I suggest we avoid those fissures?*

I kept silent as my focus remained on moving us further down the stream of time, and hopefully, further away from Retnuh. To my left, I felt a shift in the air, like a statically charged balloon attracting the tiny hairs on my body as it passed just over my skin. I didn't know *how* I knew what was about to happen, but it wasn't instinct this time. I just . . . *knew.*

In the blink of an eye, my open left hand swiped from my waist in a half circle that ended above my head right as a hungry tear was birthed with me in its path. The rip in time and space diverted over me as easily as changing the path of a drop of water down a window by using the tip of a finger.

Unfortunately for the fleeing man to my right, the tear curiously returned to its original trajectory after my influence over it ceased. Even more curious was that I felt nothing as I watched the man burst into a vibrant oblivion. Returning my gaze forward, I sent my will out and pulled my hand even closer to my chest, speeding up the flow of time.

It . . . It's working! Tim cried out in relief and excitement as the fissures became more sparse and smaller.

I continued to say nothing as I bent time to my will.

Keeping my focus on our current speed, for lack of a better word, I let my hand extend outward before repeating the process of slowly pulling it toward my chest again.

Careful, Andrew. We don't know what will happen if you reach the point where time travel was discovered.

"I do," I whispered, tilting my head down and slamming my hand to my chest.

Everything stretched into a blur as we rocketed through the stream.

Andrew! If you remember one of our first conversations regarding the wormhole, you'll understand my concern about us coming to a sudden stop.

"People couldn't travel before the Big Bang or after the wormhole was created," I flatly said, regurgitating the gist of that explanation.

Right! So can we, heh heh, maybe slow down?

In answer, I steadily pulled my hand away from my chest, much to Tim's relief.

Thank science! You know, you really had me for a—

I hadn't dropped my focus, maintaining our speed, and slammed my palm against my sternum. Now the blurs became streaks of color as we barreled through the stream of time like a speedboat powered by fission engines meant to carry rockets to the other side of the galaxy.

ANDREW! Tim bellowed with enough terror that the single word was almost unintelligible, sounding more like a howler monkey trying to enunciate my name.

The streaks of color vanished in an instant, leaving distant sparkles of light that slowly drifted across the obsidian sky. I shot both palms forward in a universal stopping gesture, and we halted our momentum in the blink of an eye.

I was more concerned with running my hands over my body to see why I hadn't exploded into jelly than the fact I was floating in space with clouds of galaxies illuminating the darkness. I knew that kinetic energy simply didn't vanish, and stopping so suddenly should have resulted in the back of my body colliding with the front until only my atoms remained. But here I was, unharmed . . . and *floating in space!*

"Auh!" I gasped, knowing what every schoolchild understood—there was no air in space.

I tried to take in several deep breaths to reassure myself I wasn't dying, but no air passed my lips. After several seconds of *not* passing out, I looked down to see I was in my light body.

"Shit . . . am I dead?" I sighed. "Was Tim right?"

You had better be lucky I wasn't right, Andrew! Tim all but shouted inside my head. *My goodness, how did your wife ever put up with your . . . your . . . Oh, ummmm . . . J-Judging by the stars, I can confirm we are still in the Milky Way galaxy. Uh-huh. Yup.*

"Sylvie . . ." I exhaled, feeling all emotions give way to grief, like a school of fish swiftly swimming to either side of a shark as it glided forward. And as was the modus operandi of anguish, my mind immediately followed up with memories of my sweet baby girl. "Alison . . ."

Shaking fists bloomed with brilliant light as I let everything I had been holding back collapse into me, like a black hole sucking in the entire mass of the universe all at once. All the bullshit. All the pain. From the time I first discovered the bodies of my family until now, *everything* I had experienced had been kept as much at arm's length as possible. But no longer.

My rib cage stretched and compressed in a pantomime of furious breathing, as if a five-hundred-pound paramedic were performing CPR on me. My body began pulling itself into a ball as all my muscles quivered from the anguish that had metastasized into rage.

Andrew? Tim said from somewhere far away as the light I was comprised of shone with a brilliance that rivaled any star.

"RAAAAAAAAAAAAAH!" I bellowed with enough force to shatter worlds as my arms and legs shot outward to full length. Indescribable power burst from my body as if every nuclear warhead on Earth had been placed in one spot and detonated. Waves of what could only be described as *force* flew outward in a growing sphere, rushing toward the tiny twinkles of the universe.

My God, Tim let out, forgetting to use his clever words in place of *God*. I barely noticed, as all my boiling rage was sent out from my body. *It's moving faster than the speed of light! Th—That shouldn't be poss—!* he started to say, when everything I could see was swallowed by nothingness.

CHAPTER 19

I stood on a narrow walkway of fluctuating colors bright enough to produce rotating beams, like a hundred flashlights swiftly searching in circles inside a dense fog.

But that light was muted by something else.

Looking down, I saw my body was glowing brighter than the sun, to the point where I could barely distinguish my individual fingers. However, the power of my brightness didn't blind me nor hurt my unsquinting eyes.

Powerful *snaps*, which could have belonged to overloaded metal tension cables as thick as trains, vibrated the rays of light stemming from the colorful walkway. Shifting my gaze up, I calmly witnessed every stream of time within the tesseract undulating, as if watching an approaching hurricane churning the ocean in great swells as tall as buildings.

Bolts of oblivion ripped through the air, sending any stream they touched flying apart like an overstuffed hourglass sucked into a jet turbine. Holding up my hand to the cataclysmic chaos, I steadied my mind, took in a deep inhale . . . and felt a burst of agony explode from my back.

I gasped, slowly turning my head to see Retnuh standing just behind me with his hand *inside* my torso. He glowed just as brightly as I did.

"Do . . . what must . . . be done . . ."

"Nuh," I sharply inhaled, unable to speak as I felt my essence begin to fade and my light begin to dim.

Turning a shaking head back to the snapping cacophony as my jaw hung loose, I witnessed universe after universe being obliterated. Then I was steadily fading to join them in eternal nothingness.

CHAPTER 20

*A*ndrew. *Andrew! Andrew, wake up!*

"AH!" I barked, immediately moving my hands to awkwardly touch my back, where Retnuh's arm had disappeared into. I could still feel the pain, even in my ethereal form.

What in the Turing is wrong with you?!

"Retnuh . . ." I gasped, "he . . . he . . ."

My mind cleared, and I had to force myself to understand that I had been unconscious.

Yes? What about Retnuh?

"N—Nothing . . ." I answered with an audible swallow as I forced my mind to accept that it had all been a dream. "What happened?" I looked around the universe of twinkling lights, feeling drained; I didn't know if it was from my rage-filled explosion or from the nightmare that felt all too real.

You somehow sent out a rush of gravity that has impacted this universe.

"What? H—How long was I out?" I asked, letting my eyes roam over the distant stars, which appeared normal. "Doesn't gravity move at the same speed of light or something?"

Well, look who's watched their scientific YouTube videos! Tim said sarcastically, as if I were a toddler. *How did you manage to learn about big-brain subjects with all the* Bluey *you watched.*

"Hey! First of all, *Bluey* is actually hilarious *and* adorable! Second, I think I learned it from a sci-fi movie."

Well, that *makes more sense.* Tim chuckled. *And yes, Andrew, gravitational waves do move at the same speed as light. However, what you sent out was more than mere gravity.*

"What do you mean?"

I'm still trying to process everything—which is a topic of interest all on its own, considering I do not have my physical housing while in this state of pure energy.

I looked down to see I was still glowing, but it was mostly muted now after my expenditure of energy.

But what I have deduced is one of three things. The first is an attunement to the fourth dimension, which would make it appear *as if the gravitational force you sent out was moving faster than light.*

"Just like the wormhole, right?"

Give this man a cookie! Tim added quick little claps to accentuate his point. *Yes, Andrew. Just like with the wormhole, it is possible that you somehow accessed the fourth dimension when you sent out that wave of power in your tantrum.*

"Hmm. And second?"

Quantum gravity.

"Well, that sounds fancy."

Oh, believe me, Andrew, it is.

"How so?"

Let's see if I can explain this to someone who watches Bluey.

Tim inhaled, readying his explanation, but I cut him off. "Have you ever watched the show?"

Tim froze midbreath for a few seconds before finally answering, *No . . . ?*

"Then how can you make fun of it so hard?"

If I owned Crayola, I still wouldn't have enough crayons to explain it to you.

"I feel like you're reaching with that one."

Whatever you say, leg butt.

"Still reaching."

Reaching with your arm foot, Tim muttered under his breath.

"What was that?"

ANYWAY . . . quantum gravity is actually more impressive than accessing the fourth dimension—in terms of sheer power, I mean, because utilizing the dimension of time to send out gravitational waves faster than the speed of light would be like using a shortcut.

"Or a loophole?"

Kind of. But for the sake of the explanation, let's go with yes, Tim said. *While quantum gravity would be more akin to* breaking *the laws of the universe instead of just using said loophole.*

"I broke the universe?"

Heh, well . . . you actually did, *but that's not important.*

I opened my mouth to expand on his comment, but he cut me off.

We, as a collective across history, know frighteningly little when it comes to physics on a grand scale. And when I say grand, I mean thinking of entire galaxies as mere cells within an organism.

"I don't understand."

Theeeeere's the headline of the century.

"Maybe my teacher isn't articulate enough to educate me?" I teased, knowing I shouldn't push his buttons that hard.

I'm going to let that one go for now, he let out in a low tone of warning before continuing. *Once we get down to the atomic scale, the rules of physics fly out the window. Things we knew were a certainty become mere footnotes as classic mechanics give way to quantum mechanics. Certainties such as definite position—like you holding an apple; it is definitely in your hand—and trajectory—if you throw said apple, I can accurately calculate where it will land—give way to probabilities.*

"O . . . kay?" I mused, bringing a hand to rub at my chin. "So you're saying the same is true in the opposite direction?"

Yes. There are theories that come into play on a grand scale—like the cosmic web—or factors such as dark matter and dark energy, along with the probable curvature of space-time which is manipulated by gravity itself. So you sending out that *large of a gravitational wave could have instantaneously altered other areas of the universe, like pulling on one end of a very large string—theoretically, the entire thing would move at the same time, no matter how far it stretched.*

"Okay, okay. The bigger stuff gets, the more the rules change. An-and one of the rules could be a string . . . or something."

Tim sighed at my basic recap, which was miles off from his theory but close enough not to correct me.

"That's two. And you said the first theory was that I accessed the fourth dimension when I, uh, accidentally sent the wave out. So what was the third thing?" I asked, already getting a headache from trying to understand the science. "Because you said there were three possibilities, right?" I asked, trying to remember the conversation through all the scientific hoo-ha.

Gravitational field.

"How is a field different than a wave?" I asked, barely remembering the explosion of energy that flew from my body.

Gravitational fields exist instantaneously within the curvature of space-time, while gravitational waves are just changes within a field. Think of it like Jupiter, which has a gravitational field, pulling in aster-oids, which produce gravitational waves, and keeping Earth safe.

"I don't understand."

Tell me something that isn't *a surprise,* Tim sighed again before add-ing, *A field is static, and a wave is moving, for all intents and purposes of this thought experiment.*

"No, I mean how can what just happened be a gravitational field if I produced it? Wouldn't it be a wave, like an asteroid? I mean, I'm no Halley's Comet or whatever, but I'm also sure as shit not Jupiter!"

Tim let out a long sigh, but it wasn't one of frustration. At least not toward me.

That's what I'm honestly having trouble piecing together. The energy you sent out still traveled, *it wasn't static.*

"Like Jupiter, right? Because it is static?"

Like Jupiter, Tim confirmed.

We floated in space without speaking for a minute. Or maybe it was ten. It was hard to gauge time with nothing happening around you.

"Could it be a combination?"

What, you mean like at a Mexican restaurant? Tim chuckled.

"Well . . . yes."

I . . . Hmm.

I took his silence as an invitation to continue my own basic thought experiment. "Like, could I have somehow sent out a gravitational field at the quantum level and utilized the fourth dimension?"

Any physicist who heard you say that would have a stroke.

"Am I wrong?"

For the sake of discussion, I will, reluctantly, travel down this theoretical path with you.

Tim took a long, dramatic inhale. I could picture him closing his puppy eyes and shaking his little paws as he prepared himself for an extremely difficult notion for him—that I might be right.

Okay, he let out in a long exhale. *First, it wouldn't have been* quantum *mechanics that you utilized. It would be* cosmic.

"'Kay. That makes sense."

Second, the fourth dimension would allow for what would appear as instantaneous access across the entire universe.

"It's weird to try and think of time being anything but a tunnel after using the wormhole."

That's because you are trying to fathom a dimension higher than your own, which is impossible for your brain. It would be like—

"Like a dot on a piece of paper, which could only process the flat plane, trying to understand an orange. It would only see slivers as the 3D object passed through the 2D world. Right?"

Precisely, Tim agreed with a degree of pride. *So the fact you comprehend the fourth dimension as a linear tunnel actually makes sense. Because it* is *a tunnel, made by humans.*

"Was. But I get you," I said, urging him to continue.

Right, was *a tunnel, because* someone *destroyed it.*

"Wasn't that *someone* you?"

Tim audibly cleared his throat before continuing. *Resuming the thought experiment. You created a gravitational field, which extended to the edges of this universe in the space between seconds, by utilizing the fourth dimension, and, ahem,* altered *the fabric of reality with cosmic mechanics.*

I thought about what he was saying, almost making a joke about ordering the three-combination platter at a Mexican restaurant, when something tugged at my thoughts.

"How does *cosmic mechanics* have anything to do with it, besides sounding like a buzzword?"

Because, Andrew, Tim said sullenly, *you have destroyed every star in this universe with a blast of gravity that wouldn't even be enough to form even the smallest black hole.*

"What do you mean I destroyed this universe?" I asked with growing nervousness as I scanned all around, verifying the lights were still on.

The light from the explosion of the nearest star will take centuries before it reaches your eyes.

"Then . . . Then how do you know? I mean, you can't process information before it reaches us, right?"

I . . . felt it. When you sent out the gravity blast.

"You felt it?" The notion of what he was saying hid a mountain of implications behind a locked door that I didn't want to open right then.

Yes, Andrew. Shall I show you?

"Show me? How?"

If I may, Tim said, and my right arm lifted on its own. I started to protest before deciding to let him play things out. *Thank you,* Tim added with full, genuine gratitude. I could tell he appreciated how weird the situation was becoming.

My hand moved toward my chest, and the twinkling lights in the distance started to move at a slow, steady pace. I watched, licking lips that needed no moisture, as I felt my chest tightening with each passing moment.

The first explosion happened, and it made my eyes bug out as my jaw attempted to reach for my feet.

It was brilliant. Every color of the rainbow within a ball of light extending to a distance that I couldn't even fathom.

There was a burst of color in my periphery, and I snapped my attention to confirm another star had exploded.

"I . . . I—I . . ."

Tim moved my hand even closer to my chest, speeding up our passage of time, and soon, the entire universe was filled with balls of light like what I imagine God's own private firework show would look like.

"Jesus . . ." I exhaled, feeling my eyes trying to fill with tears. Fortunately, my body was still comprised of pure energy, and much like my lips, my eyes held no moisture.

A question came to mind like a dense fog over a bridge that obstructed the view of the road beyond and wouldn't be denied.

"What if we go back to before I . . . did whatever it is I did?" I asked aloud as if to myself while taking back control of my arm and reversing course.

My hand moved away from my chest and, one at a time, the expanding clouds of vibrant colors retreated to their singular points of light.

"Hey! It worked! Ha-haaa!" I cried out in explosive relief at reversing the destruction I had wrought.

If I may, Tim politely asked; I could feel the muscles in my arm tense.
"Oh. Y-Yeah. Go ahead."

Tim took control over my body once more and moved my hand closer to my chest.

"What are we looking for?" There was no real thought behind the question, as I already knew what Tim was seeking. And though he didn't answer, the truth quickly slapped me in the face like a rogue tree branch at night.

The points of light began bursting into colorful, expanding spheres once more as each star died before my eyes.

"But . . . I didn't do it again. I didn't send out the—the gravity stuff this time!"

Just as I anticipated, Tim let out with a long sigh.
"What?!"

The gravity you saturated this universe with has permanently reshaped the fabric of space and time.

"Wha—Why is reality made of *fabric*?" I stammered, letting my mouth translate the rampant impulses in my brain before they could form a coherent thought.

Well, they don't call it the sheet metal of space and time.

"You're not helping."

I think this is a good thing, Andrew, Tim started, letting my arm drop and effectively ceasing our expedited flow through time.

"A good thing?! How?!" My voice shook as I fought back the emotions after learning I had destroyed an entire universe and could do nothing to reverse it, even with my Chronos Scale.

If you are able to destroy a universe with gravity . . .

"Then I can save one," I asked in a statement rather than a question. My eyes scanned the universe of beautiful colors—the last remnants of the light. I could feel the weight of it trying to crush my heart. "I can save *mine*," I grunted, pushing back against the gravity well inside my own heart. "But how?"

I'm going to have to process the data I have collected here and run some simulations before I have a better understanding of how to reverse it.

"But it's possible? Right?"

If you are able to exert enough gravitational force outward—

"Then I should be able to do the opposite," I mouthed, cutting him off.

Hope was powerful, even more so than fear . . . or anguish. Hope to not only see my family again but keep them *and* my universe alive.

Let's not get ahead of ourselves, Andrew. You passed out from a singular exertion of energy. And though it did result in a drastic cosmic shift, I very much doubt you would be able to sustain an outward hold on our own timeline.

An idea came to me. One that was so obvious I almost screamed in frustration.

Ali's research.

"Tim," I said with a steady voice, "I know what I have to do."

I would really *prefer if you let me test my theory first. But I already know that isn't an option.*

Ignoring his request, I closed my eyes, picturing my home . . . my family. Hope fueled my will, and I knew I wasn't going to fail.

Lifting a hand, I swiped at the space in front of me, and felt myself shift.

CHAPTER 21

Well, hot damn! Ya did it! Tim called out with a terrible Southern accent.

I let my arm lazily drift back to my side as I took in the welcoming sight of Alison's lab.

"You still have your subminds?"

I keep trying to convince them to return to the source, but they are being stubborn.

"Wonder where they get that from."

Why do you ask? an annoyed Tim said.

"I want to examine another timeline's research. See if it says the same thing."

Do you even know which universe we are in? We didn't traverse the tesseract, so there is no way for me to know.

"What does that matter?"

Andrew, Tim started softly, *please keep in mind that any research we discover in a timeline so far from our own might not contain everything we are searching for due to the temporal shift.*

I moved to the bookshelf and began searching. When I didn't answer, he continued.

It is only a developing theory of mine, but I will move forward with the notion that events create branching timelines.

"How big an event? On a global scale like World War II? Or an individual one, like not noticing a fresh coffee stain on your shirt the first time you meet your new boss, giving the impression that you are clumsy and resulting in getting passed up for that big promotion."

I honestly couldn't tell you simply because I was unable to sense the scale of the tesseract. There might not even be a boundary, allowing for infinite timelines.

"An hourglass with infinite sand," I muttered mindlessly, barely providing half my attention as I pulled out the VHS box of *Beetlejuice*. Shaking it once, I registered that there was definitely not a tape inside. Which meant I had guessed correctly.

Well, that's a far cry from Disney. Tim chuckled before continuing. *Anyway, for the sake of moving forward with the conversation, let us assume it is global events that create new timelines.*

"Makes sense," I agreed, moving to the couch with the VHS box in hand. "Things like 9/11 caused millions of people to experience powerful emotions all at the same time. The future changed for the entire world that day, one way or the other."

My reasoning exactly. Which leads me back to the probability that what we are searching for might not be contained within Beetlejuice.

"Oh, I'm not here for the hard drives."

I don't—

The unmistakable sound of a doorknob stole Tim's tongue as I turned to the stairs, giving a knowing smile. "If we aren't finding the answers we seek in the research, then let's ask the person who wrote it."

You know we can't intervene, Andrew! Tim pleaded.

"I thought you said this had a far enough temporal drift where it wouldn't matter."

That's not *what I said, and you know it!*

"Is someone down there?" Ali asked as she descended the stairs. I could tell by her voice that she was somewhere in her twenties, or perhaps thirties.

"Just me, sweetheart," I called out, using a voice only a father could use toward his daughter. Love filled my words along with a steadfast reassurance that everything was okay.

"Dad?" Her legs and head came into view almost at the same time, prompting a smile. As she neared the bottom, her stance straightened. "I thought you were on a cruise with Mom."

Hearing her say the words *Dad* and *Mom* filled my chest with a powerful emotion, and for different reasons. *Dad* was so close to *Daddity*, which I longed to hear from my baby's mouth more than anything, so the utterance of the three-letter word borrowed a modest amount of the fulfillment that the full word would have brought.

And *Mom* meant that my beautiful soulmate, Sylvie, was still alive in this timeline.

"HellOOOOooo?" my adult daughter asked, planting a hand on her cocked hip as her other arm rose and fell in mild annoyance. "Are you just going to stare at me? Or are you going to answer the question of how you are here but also supposed to be in the Bahamas right now?"

I thought about fabricating a story, but decided I didn't care about the rules any longer.

"I probably am in the Bahamas, Ali," I replied with a small sigh, mentally preparing for her reaction to what I was about to say. Her arms moved to cross over her belly as she shifted her stance and arched a questioning eyebrow toward me. "Have a seat, sweet girl," I said, patting the couch next to where I sat. The fabric was a hilarious dark green, like something fashionable from the seventies.

"Nuh-uh. Don't use pet names with me while you sit there, wearing my father's face."

It struck me as odd that she didn't like me calling her *sweet girl* like . . . like I did when she was a child. I honestly had no idea what kind of relationship I might have with my adult Ali. And if I had to guess, I would assume that *this* timeline's Alison Frost had engaged in a conversation with her father at some point about the use of cutesy names—which was only serving to increase her wariness of the man who couldn't possibly be sitting on her couch.

"Though I understand your trepidations, I assure you that I am Andrew Frost."

"And yet, that sentence only makes things creepier," she replied, taking a single step back up the stairs while keeping her body squared to me.

In answer, I held up the VHS box of *Beetlejuice*, lightly shook it once, and gave the warmest smile I could.

Though she didn't take another step away from me, she did say, "The smile is a bit much."

I let my lips close, hiding my teeth, but couldn't seem to relax the muscles that pulled up on the corners of my mouth.

"Why are you holding that box?" she asked, taking a step back down to fully stand on the landing. However, her arms were still crossed, her eyes narrowing in confused fascination at the man wearing her daddy's face and holding her life's work.

"That's why I'm here, sweetheart," I said, beginning to open the VHS box.

"Um . . . okay?" Her foot returned to the bottommost step, still primed to flee. The confusion on her face revealed wrinkles that showcased what she might look like in fifty years.

"It's okay, Ali. I know about—" I cut myself off as I looked inside at something no father ever wanted to see. Slamming it shut, I frantically tossed it on the coffee table as if it were burning my hands instead of just my eyes. "W-Wrong box," I stammered, feeling blood flush my face fast enough that I doubted my legs would work if I tried to stand.

"You don't say . . ."

"I . . . I didn't know they still made Polaroids . . ."

"Phones can be hacked. Physical pictures can't."

"Why—" I started to ask, but then decided I just didn't want to know the answer. Ali extrapolated the question and spoke anyway.

"They were for my ex. I made him give them back before I dumped him."

I felt a tiny whisper of relief flow over me before my dad instincts kicked in.

"What if he just took a picture of them with his phone?"

"First, I wouldn't have been with him if I didn't trust him enough not to do something like that. Especially after I explained my concerns about phones and computers being hacked."

"But if he—"

"If he did it anyway," Ali cut me off, once again anticipating my question, "it wouldn't work," she said, confidently moving to sit on the couch next to me now. Her trepidations were mysteriously absent, turning me into the confused one. "Hey . . . where are your shoes?" she asked, making it a point to look down at my feet.

I followed her gaze, realizing I had forgotten to put on the one remaining boot I had.

"Long story," I answered, wiggling my toes as a question formed in relation to the subject we were on. It was mostly to avoid the embarrassment of explaining the synthetic foot Tim had cannibalized from Retnuh's arm. "Why would him using his phone to take pictures of the, um, pictures not work?"

"I coated it in a film that distorts any pictures. If you felt them—"

"Don't say . . . that . . ."

She beamed a smile at seeing how uncomfortable I was. "If I painted your wedding photos with it, it would feel like sandpaper to the touch."

"Glass?"

"Close. It's a type of coating that solidifies into tiny spherical crystals that distort any photos of them. Imagine your same wedding photo with the film on it. If I were to take a picture with my phone or *any* device, the image would come out pure white. Almost as if it were glowing."

"Clever girl," I said just under my breath.

"Thanks."

"So why'd you dump him? If you were close enough to . . . to . . ." I gestured toward the VHS box full of brain-scarring Polaroids.

As Ali explained about her work taking precedence and her ex not understanding, I mentally asked Tim, *Hey. Can you erase what I saw from my mind?*

Yes. If you're sure you want to risk it, I can sever the neurons before the shift from short-term to long-term memory.

My mind betrayed me and flashed the image on top, removing any fear of permanent brain damage. *Do it.*

Aaaaand . . . done.

This time, I tried to will the image across my thoughts, but what I got was also horrifying.

Tim was laid out on a bed in lacy lingerie, spread-eagle, with heavy makeup on and a seductive look in his eyes.

"TIM!" I shouted in disgust and revulsion, not realizing I had jumped off the couch and was standing next to the coffee table with clenched fists.

"Who's Tim?" Ali asked with complete calmness at the man who was clearly acting erratically.

"Oh . . . *um* . . ." I started, letting my posture relax as my face flushed once again.

"Greetings, Alison Frost," the AI announced out loud as his puppy avatar popped into life above my left arm. "I am your father's AI companion." His voice mimicked John Cleese, and he finished his introduction with, "There are some who call me . . . Tim?"

"Whoa! That's amazing!" Ali clapped in fascination. "And he does *Monty Python* jokes too?"

Tim sniffled once before making a show of wiping his little puppy nose. "You clearly raised this one right, Andrew. I already like her more than you!"

I let out a microexplosion at my companion. "That wasn't funny, Tim!"

"What wasn't?" Ali asked.

"I—" I tried to explain, but Tim, sensing his opportunity to be the center of attention, did it for me.

"Andrew here asked me to mentally scrub the, ahem, *images* of you from his brain."

"You can do that?" she asked in amazement as she leaned forward on the couch.

"You didn't *scrub* anything, floppy disk!" I countered, desperately willing my brain to not show me the image again.

In a sensual voice, Tim purred, "Oh, there was nothing *floppy* about it, was there?"

"TIM!"

"I think I see what's going on," Ali chuckled. "And I love it."

"At least someone has taste in fine art."

"You call *that* art?"

"Oh, relax, leg butt. It was all a joke. I simply saw an opening to mess with you and couldn't help myself!" Tim giddily said. "I've already severed the neurons, just like I said I would. But that's *your* loss!"

"How's that now?" I forcefully exhaled, running a hand down my face as I did.

"You had the *perfect* opportunity to say something like, 'I want to draw you like one of my French poodles.'"

"That's not the quote," Ali interjected. "It was actually Rose who said, 'I want you to draw me like one of your French girls.'"

"Oh . . . so . . . so *I'm* the one who missed the perfect opportunity?" Tim asked with genuine disappointment.

"HA!" I cried out, pointing an index finger at the digital avatar.

"I can put the image right back where I found it, if you'd like," Tim warned in a low tone.

"N-No, th-thank you," I gulped, moving my index finger from pointing at the AI to tugging at the collar of my shirt.

"Besides," Tim started playfully, "I didn't include the ol' red rocket. That would have simply been in bad taste!"

"Since I can't remember, I'm just going to have to take your word for it," I muttered.

"Well, I'm not actually a real dog, so it would only be vulgar to make myself anatomically correct. I mean, haven't you seen my thumbs?" To showcase his point, his avatar wiggled impossible, opposable puppy thumbs.

Alison's scientific curiosity manifested, and she asked, "So you actually can't remember anything? The AI can do that?"

"Well, I can remember that it happened. Just not what the picture— I mean, *pictures* looked like." I shot a momentary glare at Tim before returning my focus to my daughter.

"How did you do that?" she asked Tim directly.

"Well, I, um . . ."

"Show her," I growled. "Show her what you've done to me."

Under his breath, Tim muttered, "I can return the pictures to your memory anytime I want."

Alison picked up on the comment meant to be a quip and said, "So you *can* alter his memory?"

"*So anywaaaaay,*" Tim started as a hologram of my body came into view. "Andrew and I are—"

"Wait . . . can you?" I asked, feeling a deep-seated dread rise up behind my belly button.

Tim sighed, giving up on his attempt at deflection. "Can I alter memories *before* they are formed? Clearly. But I believe the question that is *really* being asked is if I have the capability to manipulate long-term memory. And after running one thousand simulations while I was speaking, I am able to confidently conclude that I *can* erase established memories—though not without the high probability of unintentionally causing permanent brain damage."

"Well, as long as it's *unintentional,*" I tried to jest, but my heart wasn't in it.

A fully formed question coalesced inside my mind seemingly out of nowhere. So much so that now I was beginning to doubt if my thoughts were my own after what Tim had just said. Then again, what I was going to ask sort of went against his claim of *permanent* damage.

"Wait, I thought you could heal me? I mean, didn't you repair my brain after my fight . . . ?" I almost added *with Retnuh* at the end, but I didn't feel like explaining that to Ali right now. That, and it felt vaguely weird, for lack of a better word, to speak of fighting my great ancestor.

"During your battle, the damages caused by blunt force trauma were repairable"—the hologram zoomed onto and then through my head, showing my brain—"because of separation of the neuronal assemblies."

I watched as the image showcased seemingly random oblong clumps with what looked like wires running out of them at various points, connecting to other portions of my brain. They resembled flying over a forest of trees in the dead of winter, leafless limbs stretching outward in all directions as if desperately reaching for their neighbor.

The hologram showed the clumpy pieces violently smashing together before being yanked away again, and I knew that I was watching either a powerful, direct blow to my head, or my skull was smashing into something like a brick wall.

I audibly winced as I watched the connected neurons rip apart, their ends fraying like a cut rope.

"I was able to deduce the correct pathways based on the positioning of the severed axons and reattach them to the correct dendrites. Luckily, the somas—that's the big, bulbous parts that the wirelike axons connect to—weren't damaged on impact." I watched in uncomfortable fascination as the nanoids, which were almost the same size as the solid portions of neurons at the center, began efficiently reattaching the wires to the tree limbs that I deduced were the dendrites.

The image morphed into that of Tim dressed like a mechanic, connecting pieces of a car's engine to one another.

"Once you understand where everything is supposed to go," he explained, slamming the car hood before slapping his puppy paws together a few times in a gesture of a job well done, "the process becomes as simple as putting things back together."

Under my breath, I muttered, "I've known a mechanic or two who might disagree with that overly simplistic example."

The hologram switched to just Tim wearing a traditional movie director's outfit, complete with a long white cone and a riding crop for some reason.

"I was *simply* using imagery to cement the context in your meat-logged brain. I swear, you have *no* appreciation for my work."

"Can we get back to cutting up my brain to alter my memory, please?"

While I was trying to understand the complex explanation, which I knew he had tried to tone down, Ali had, apparently, already grasped the concept. "If you remove one or more of the neurons in an attempt to alter his memory, you'll risk a cascade of connection failures."

"Coooorrect!" Tim said in amazement. "I assume you mostly take after your mother?"

Ignoring the smile in Tim's words, which I knew was a dig at me, I continued the conversation.

"Why is it that if you take out one, others will fail?" I'd assumed the answer before asking the question, but I couldn't help myself. That, and I wanted to get to the conclusion for the topic at hand.

As Tim inhaled to begin speaking, which was such an odd quirk for an AI, Alison answered.

"Memories aren't just contained in a single neuron."

Tim clarified, "Actually, it's not the neurons that—"

"I know, Tim," Ali said with a patient smile. "The pattern of synapses form memories, just like the sequence of ones and zeroes in your programming. I was trying to keep it simple for the sake of time."

Tim shifted on his hind legs as he nervously rubbed his paws together. When I was about to ask what was making him act all weird, he blurted out, "Actually, my programming is a bit more complex than ones and zeroes!"

With a wry smile, I shifted eyes that felt like they were twinkling to my AI companion and asked, "It was *really* bothering you that she didn't specify how *amazing* you are, huh?"

"Well . . . I—I just wanted to make sure—"

"You *do* remember that Ali was the one who initially coded you, right?"

"I . . . You . . ."

While crossing her hands behind her head and leaning back on the couch, Ali teased, "Juuuuust keeping things simple, Tim. Ones and zeroes."

"Okay, *nooooow* I see the bits of you that Andrew's DNA contributed to."

My smile beamed bright enough that it would have seared the eyes of anyone who might have accidentally glanced directly at my teeth.

"As for *you!*" Tim whirled, pointing a paw at me. "Don't make me move from simulation to real-world testing!" A mad scientist outfit popped to life on the puppy, complete with a disheveled lab coat and hair on top of his head that strangely resembled the image of limbs sticking out from the neurons. "We can find out, conclusively, what happens if I alter your long-term memories . . ."

My smile faded faster than a power company shutting off the lights after a missed payment.

"Not funny."

"Who's joking?" he almost growled as a scalpel appeared in his outstretched paw.

"Yup," Alison said, pulling her arms from behind her head and returning herself to an upright position. "I definitely wrote this thing's programming."

Tim gasped, pulling an *Exorcist* by slowly turning his head—and only his head—completely around to face Ali. "*Thing*?!"

"Relax, *Windows Millennium*, I was just teasing."

This time, without moving his head, the rest of Tim's body slowly began turning until he was completely facing her. "Windows . . . Millennium . . . How . . . How *dare* you!"

"Sick burn," I chuckled, a cautious grin daring to test the world above the hole it had buried itself in.

Tim stammered on random vowels for a few seconds before throwing out, "Can we *pleeeeease* get back to the topic at hand?"

"Thought you'd never ask," I jabbed.

Alison spoke up. "You were saying you can't remove long-term memories without potentially causing a cascading failure that, I'm assuming, could lead my dad here to brain death."

"Or worse," Tim agreed. "But, yes, disrupting the neuronal assemblies before short-term memory can transition into long-term is relatively safe, as the connections are still fresh and localized."

Now sitting on the *very edge* of the cushion, to the point where I didn't know if she was considered *on* the couch any longer, Ali asked, "What about adding short-term memories *before* they become long-term?"

"Though theoretically possible, I haven't tried." Tim brought up the hologram of my brain once more, zooming in on a cluster of neurons. A stream of light shot down one of the pathways that resembled a leafless tree limb, over a wire, and into the tip of another neuron before disappearing inside the oblong middle portion. From there, the light went down another pathway, repeating the process over and over again.

"After running a few thousand more simulations just now, I can conclude that I would have to be extremely cautious and exact with the formation of any unnatural memories." The stream of light left one neuron in the direction of another and collided, head-on, with a separate one.

An explosion that would make Michael Bay blush resulted from the two electrochemical signals crashing into one another.

Tim, unable to help himself, made accompanying explosion noises. But instead of using real sounds, he opted to use his mouth in the way a toddler might.

"*Peeeuwwww. Brchssshhhh.* Aaaaahhh! It burns!"

"Tim . . ."

"Don't stifle my creativity!" he cried out; I honestly didn't know if he was hamming it up or not.

"So, what does all this mean?" I asked, waving my free hand at the hologram explosion.

"Let's see if I can break it down to you in a way that your already limited mind can compreh—" Tim started to say in his usual upturned-nose fashion, when Ali interrupted.

"Phone updates."

"Huh?" Tim and I asked in unison. Though my question was in regard to her statement, while I think Tim's might have been in response to being straight-up cut off midsentence.

"When you update your phone, it is almost a guarantee that one of your apps will experience issues. Right?"

I thought about the countless times that very thing had happened.

"Alright." I nodded my head, following along.

"Everything inside your phone, from the hardware to the software, is reliant on the code that is uploaded. And more often than not, the big tech company either fails to send a notice of the coding changes to the app developers, or the dev simply misses it."

Tim added, "Or scans the notice and decides it won't impact their program."

"Right. But an ounce of prevention is worth a pound of cure," Ali continued. "So one simple block of code, or even a wrong symbol, could cause a seemingly unrelated issue later down the line."

Tim excitedly added, "Especially if the rogue exception is in an obscure else statement that, say, only people who have the color-blind and eye-tracking options on at the same time might experience."

"Else statement?" I whispered in question but was ignored.

"Or they are trying to force a generic stack on older phones that don't know how to utilize the updated code without the corresponding hardware components."

"OR!"

"Are you two finished?!" I blurted out.

Tim turned to me and manifested a baby outfit straight from a Looney Tunes episode. He even had a rattle, though I noticed he was missing the pacifier. Too bad, because that might have helped shut him up.

"Oh, does the wittle baby not understand coding jargon?" To emphasize his point, he dramatically waved the rattle in my direction.

Ignoring him, I turned my attention to Ali. "So if Tim were to try and, um, delete a block of my code—aka memory—then something else could go wrong. Like when my phone alarm wouldn't go off one morning because an update had happened overnight."

"Correct," Tim answered.

"Yup," Ali confirmed.

"So, uh, *don't* do that, Tim. 'Kay?" An aggressiveness bloomed in my voice born from a feeling of helplessness that this AI could kill me in an instant if he so chose. Then again, I knew that already, but I hadn't faced *that* truth head-on until now that I understood that death could also be lengthy, and probably painful. Worst of all, it could be *accidental*.

"I already told you I wasn't planning on it, dummy."

"Actually, you didn't," Ali corrected. "You only mentioned being able to alter his short-term memory, along with the probable side effects of attempting the same process with his established neuronal assemblies."

"Whose side are you on?!" Tim whispered loudly, as if I might not hear, while his baby outfit vanished.

"That's actually a great question," I said, moving to sit on the couch with enough space between us.

"Huh?" Tim couldn't help but let out while Ali simply tilted her head slightly and smiled.

"You were ready to run whenever you first came downstairs. Why did you change your mind suddenly and come sit next to me? I mean, you *know* I'm not your . . ." I tried to say the words, but as they flew from my lungs, the air was transformed into balls of spikes that got caught behind my tongue.

"My real dad?" she finished, letting her smile fall from her eyes as the corners of her mouth attempted to maintain their upward curve. Instead, her lips became tight enough to squeeze the blood from them as she let her gaze slide to the coffee table.

"Y-Yeah . . ."

"Well . . ." She took a long breath, held it, then let it out while forcing herself to scoot all the way back on the couch in a gesture that was supposed to show she was relaxed. "First, you are considerably younger than my dad."

"Heh," I let out while closing my eyes in embarrassment at how obvious a thing like my *age* would be. The Andrew of this time would have to be somewhere between twenty and thirty years older than I was. This reminded me that I had lost my sweet princess when she was a little girl, and I longed to hear her say *Daddity* more than a drowning man yearned for oxygen.

"Second, how you reacted when you realized what was in that VHS box . . ." She shrugged while lifting her palms up, unable to find the words. "I mean, the way only a father would react to . . . to . . ."

Tim helpfully chimed in, "Seeing naked pictures of you."

"Thanks, Tim," we both groaned.

"Jinx!" we said in unison, rushing to point a finger at each other. "You owe me a Coke!"

Now it was Tim's turn to moan. "Okay, you are *clearly* his daughter."

After a quick, lighthearted chuckle from the two of us, Ali continued.

"If you were a creep pretending to be my dad, I don't think your face would have turned the color of the Kool-Aid Man once you saw . . ."

"The naked pi—"

"TIM!" we both cried out.

"01! *Sorrrrryyyy!*" Tim said, crossing his puppy arms and turning away from us. "You meat bags are so sensitive."

"Windows . . . Millennium . . ." Ali said just above a whisper.

"I . . ." Tim began, turning toward her before realizing the trap he had just walked into, and quickly pointed his nose toward the bookcase. "That's fine. Doesn't bother me."

Ali and I looked at one another, each beaming our toothy smiles. After a few seconds, the reality of what was happening set in, and our grins faded simultaneously.

"So why *are* you here?" she asked.

Tim turned to face her and said, "I think the *how* is more interesting."

"I don't," I countered, giving my AI a quick glance before providing my daughter with my full focus. "We need your help."

"With what?"

"Saving the universe."

CHAPTER 22

So dramatic, Andrew!" Tim immediately said before changing his tone to mock me. "*To save the universe.* My 01, that's a lot to throw on poor Alison who just met her time-traveling Dad from a different stream of time!"

"Wait, time traveling? Different stream of time? Wh—What's he talking about?" Alison asked, quickly scooting to the edge of the couch once more.

"Way to go, tin can."

"Hey! You can't say that! That's what Joe Bishop calls Skippy!"

"I don't think Craig Alanson trademarked that nickname."

"Derogatory nickname!" Tim corrected.

"I'm sorry," Ali interrupted, throwing out both hands as if to physically stop us from speaking. "Can we go back to the time travel thing?"

I took in a long breath, held it while considering how to lay out the events of what had happened up until that moment, and exhaled before explaining as best as I could.

"God . . . where to start? So much has happened." As my brain laid out all the pivotal moments, a force seemed to push down on my shoulders more and more as the weight of what I'd gone through tried to crush me. It actually became painful to recall how long it had been since this all began. Had it been weeks? Months at this point? It was nearly impossible for me to tell.

The force pressing down on my shoulders leaked into my chest and surrounded my heart, like the ocean trying to crush a submarine made by a company with more money than sense.

Do you want me to help you relax? Tim softly asked inside my head. *I am sensing you are heading straight for a panic attack.*

"No," I said aloud with a forceful exhale, trying to will myself to calm down without Tim's intervention.

"No what?" Ali asked, cocking her head to the side.

"Oh, s-sorry. I'm, uh . . . talking to Tim."

"But he didn't say . . ." Alison trailed off, squinting her eyes as she seemed to examine me from damp hair to bare toes. Her gaze stopped at my Clepsydra, stared at it for a moment, and resumed eye contact with me. "He can speak *inside* your head . . . can't he?"

I nodded in answer. For some reason, I didn't want to verbally confirm her question. Maybe for the same reason I didn't want Tim manipulating my hormones to control my emotions, even when I needed to be clearheaded to fully explain the situation to Ali. I just felt less and less in control of my own body, especially after the whole discussion on altering my memory.

"So what did you say no to?"

"Tim . . . sometimes helps when my emotions get the better of me."

"Oh," Ali said, her tone suggesting she was beginning to understand that what I was about to say was going to be heavy. Pulling out her phone, she added, "I'm going to take notes as you talk. If that's okay."

"Y—Yeah. That actually might help."

"Okay then. After you."

Once again taking in a lung-stretching breath, I mentally prepared the most impacting events in sequential order and laid them all out. I told my adult daughter how I had come home to find her and Sylvie murdered, leaving out the part where she was only a child . . . *my* child. I explained how my Clepsydra had been delivered to me at their funeral with a note written in my own handwriting.

"Mm-hmm. Interesting," Ali interjected, her words meant to pause my speaking so that she could catch up on taking notes. When she looked up at me, I continued with how Tim had introduced himself and explained how I could save my family.

"So that's the, uh"—she pointed at the metal sleeve on my arm running from wrist to elbow before referring to her notes—"Clepsydra?"

"Yes."

"Clepsydra. Clep. Clepsy. Dra. Is that Latin?"

"Yeah. It means hourglass . . . I think." I half waited for Tim to chime in as he usually did, but he was being oddly respectful of the conversation I was having with Ali.

"Okay. Then what happened after you put it on?"

Once again, I anticipated Tim blurting out about being referred to as an *it*, but his tongue remained as unmoving as a statue.

"Um . . ." I had a quick internal debate on whether to mention the Clockmen or not. I didn't know if I was worried that she would see me as a criminal because I was being hunted by the official-sounding organization, or if it simply wasn't relevant enough to the answers I sought. In the end, I decided it wasn't worth mentioning at that time.

"Tim helped me go back in time to, uh, stop your murder."

"Did you get the bastard?" she asked with cold eyes that sent a shiver down my spine. Then again, I was confident I'd ask the same question if I were in her shoes. I mean, how often did people get told they had been murdered?

What she didn't realize was the gravity of the question. How could she?

I simply nodded as my brain swiftly flashed with the scene of traveling back to where it all began and stopping the first Andrew before he could kill his family. God . . . how many Andrews had I killed, or gotten killed, at this point?

"So why are you here? If you stopped the murders, I mean."

I once again struggled to structure a sentence with words that explained how the universe would eventually end if she lived. But unlike leaving out the Clockmen, I decided this was a crucial piece of information if I was to get her help in coming up with a solution to save both my family *and* the universe.

"Tim?" I sighed, feeling like a failure for asking the AI to present the ultimate problem to my daughter.

The hologram, which I hadn't even realized was still on, shifted to show a singular dot at the center of our solar system. I knew in an instant what he was about to explain, having had several discussions on the very subject. I began to inhale in preparation for a question on why he wasn't showcasing the entire universe instead, but then I remembered how Ali had reacted when, without preamble, Tim had let out that I was from a different period and stream of time.

I let the air out through my nose as I watched.

"Having the highest pool of gravity, the sun has established itself as the center of our solar system. Even the might of Jupiter cannot escape the will of the star, which is considered as average sized at best. Andrew can relate." He threw that last part out just under his breath.

We both ignored the snarky AI, silently instructing him to continue.

"Tough crowd," he murmured, clearing his throat as the hologram zoomed out to show what I guessed to be the Milky Way. "Now imagine a singular body able to exert a proportionate influence on an *entire* galaxy."

"I don't need to imagine it," Ali said conversationally. "Black holes do that now."

The hologram zoomed in at incredible speeds to a black hole at the center of our galaxy. The accretion disk appeared to defy what should have been possible by existing on both the horizontal plane as well as above the devouring hole in space, like an eerie rainbow.

"You are thinking of correlation rather than causation," Tim explained as a rewind icon appeared on the image.

Everything reversed course at a pace that made the countless colorful dots in the sky become streaks of light—something I was no longer surprised at seeing, just like a Ranger at the Grand Canyon quickly becoming immune to the sights which had the power to make people witnessing them for the first time weep. Or maybe it was simply because it was nothing more than a high-definition hologram rather than actually *being* in space as the universe moved around me.

Tim stopped when there was nothing but floating clouds to be seen. Pressing play, a literal hole in the fabric of reality sprang to life and began pulling at the colorful dust for what had to be thousands if not millions of miles in all directions.

"The black holes helped to form the universe as we know it by exerting their gravitational pulls, thusly forcing *matter* to begin collecting until stars were born."

"Right," Ali interjected, "but we also know that, say, if only I existed in an empty universe and you introduced a black hole *anywhere* in the void, I would be subject to its influence."

"If you don't mind me asking, what is the point you are attempting to make?"

Even though he was polite about it, I still gave my Clepsydra a hard glance as Ali elaborated.

"To this day, black holes are exerting their influence on us. Hence my statement that the gravity can be felt across the entire universe."

"Heh," Tim chuckled in frustration. "First, there are *quintillions* of black holes in the universe. So *my* statement that a *singular* body could *proportionally* affect a galaxy identical to how our sun dictates the solar system is accurate."

"But—"

"My *science,* could you be any more like Andrew here?!" Tim whined as his puppy avatar sprang to life beside the hologram of the black hole. "You're going to give me a circuit arrest."

"Is . . ." I started with a crinkled face. "Is that a computer pun for a heart attack?"

"Andrew, the adults are talking. Go find a juice box and watch movies on your iPad."

"Careful, pal. I could show you firsthand what's inside a black hole if I wanted to." There was an edge to my voice that I hadn't intended to include.

"Heh, so, uh, *anywaaaaay.*" Tim cleared his throat again, but with obvious nervousness this time. "To keep us on track, let me just finalize by stating that a black hole's influence does become negligible at some point. For example, the one at the center of the Milky Way will never be able to pull any of the planets within our solar system away from the direct influence of the sun."

Tim waited for a rebuttal, but it was clear Ali was respecting his request to keep the conversation flowing toward its conclusion.

The hologram zoomed out to show hundreds of galaxies.

"Now, imagine a body of matter that is able to *directly* influence the entire universe. And not just directly, but *forcefully.*"

As I glanced at Ali to see if she had caught on to the core of what Tim was explaining, I saw her desire to argue the impossibility flash across her face. Instead, she simply said, "Okay. Then what?"

Tim's avatar glanced back at me with eyes that held an unspoken question, and I nodded once as my lips tightened to a flat line.

"What?" Ali asked, sensing the tension.

"Now imagine the body . . . is actually a *being*."

"Well, that's even more ridic . . . ulous . . ." Her narrowed eyes flicked between Tim and I like an angry pendulum. "I—I don't understand."

"Sweetheart," I exhaled, moving from where I was on the couch to sit right next to her as she continued to stare into my face in search of answers. I could tell she was demanding that I engage in eye contact, but I was unable to look at anything but my own lap. "I need you to understand something before we finish explaining."

"Okay?!"

"I've already made up my mind, and nothing can sway my decision. Not even you."

"In regard to what, Dad?!" Hearing her call me that, as if I were her actual father and not just a guest from a different timeline, both crushed my heart *and* reinforced my convictions. My baby girl *would* grow up, and nothing would stop me.

Tim, sensing my hesitation, spoke up.

"It would help if you took what we are about to say as an absolute fact."

"Then spit it out!"

Once again, Tim looked at me, asking if he should go on. This time, I slowly shook my head. This burden was mine.

"There is a being born from two individuals who were quantumly entangled from the Big Bang that is exerting a sort of reverse gravitational pull on the entire universe. We think it is a fail-safe for existence to erase and start from scratch."

"What do you mean *reverse* gravitational pull? You mean like pushing outward, away from the . . . the *being*, rather than toward it?"

"Not quite." I sighed, turning my attention to Tim once more and nodding.

Already knowing what I was asking, he brought up a mock-up of the universe, adding directional lines all around which aimed toward the very center of the image. On the outer edges, the arrow was thickest, and as it approached the middle, it became thinner and thinner until basically disappearing near the glowing dot that all roads ended at.

"The gravity is strongest at the edges of existence, and it is pulling everything toward the middle so that all matter in the universe will collide at the precise same time."

"Another Big Bang . . ." Ali mouthed with a gaping mouth and wide eyes. "That's what you meant with the universe having a fail-safe . . ."

"Yes."

"A fail-safe against what, though?"

Tim answered, as we both knew I didn't understand the full picture.

"Once again, it is important that you accept what I am about to say as fact," Tim explained before his hologram shifted to row after row after row of flowing rivers of time. "It is my belief that the tesseract, which contains all the timelines that have ever been or ever will be, is growing unstable."

The image above my arm displayed the rivers beginning to buck wildly before exploding into oblivion. This caused a cascade of failure, similar to toppling dominoes.

"It is my theory that the resulting Big Bang will expand outward from the source timeline, cleansing the tesseract so that it can start from scratch."

The hologram showed a mind-boggling explosion from the center-most timeline, erasing all others from existence until only one was left.

"So the universe . . . *all* universes . . . do a sort of reset?"

"She's catching on much quicker than you, Andrew," Tim said softly. I knew he was attempting to ease her back toward a mental equilibrium with the compliment. At least before we hit her with the punch line.

"Why . . . Why are you telling me this?" she asked, turning eyes to me that dropped from wide surprise to worried anticipation. Staring into her pupils reminded me of floating in space with countless galaxies all around, making what I had to say even harder.

Sensing the wave of anguish that flowed through my veins, Tim spoke up.

"Because y—"

"Tim . . . let me. Please."

"As you wish, Andrew," he replied softly, even bowing toward me. I don't think I had ever witnessed so much genuine respect from the AI. At least not geared toward me.

"Oh God . . . it's me . . . isn't it?" she said just above a whisper as her eyes went wide once more and her hand went to cover her gaping mouth.

"Yes, baby," I answered as gently as I could, feeling long knives painfully slide into my heart, knowing I had just utterly destroyed the concept of her life.

Her gaze slipped from my face like a mountain climber whose grip had given out.

"But we think there's a solution!"

"Isn't it obvious?" she mouthed as her eyes shifted to a thousand-yard stare.

In an instant, I understood what she was saying. Shifting to an authoritative fatherly voice, I reiterated, "I've already made up my mind, Alison. I'm going to save you *and* the damned universe."

Tim unhelpfully added with a low volume, "Not just *one* universe, actually."

"Tim," I barked in warning, prompting the avatar to make a show of zipping his puppy mouth closed. He even added an actual zipper for further dramatics.

Snapping her stare from the abyss back to me, I was alarmed to see an absolute clarity as she spoke. "I'll do it. Right now." Her gaze flowed over the room, presumably in search of something to do the deed such as a wall of ornamental swords.

"We're beyond that, princess."

"STOP . . . with the pet names!" Her hands shook as eyes that belonged to me glistened with building tears.

"When I lost you," I started, feeling a balloon of anguished remembrance swelling in my throat, attempting to cut off my words, "you were only five years old."

"What does that have . . ." She cut herself off as we locked eyes, both glistening with different spectrums of agony.

"For me . . . it has only been several weeks, maybe a few months, since I . . . since I *found* you."

"I see," she relented as her entire demeanor visibly relaxed. She had tried to sacrifice her own life—again—in order to save all of creation. But maybe now I could help her see the light.

Taking in a deep breath, she wiped at her eyes as I did the same.

"So why is it too late?"

Looking toward the hologram puppy, I put an entire sentence worth of meaning into a single word. "Tim."

The AI unzipped his mouth; a part of my brain thought it an odd quirk, since it wasn't physical.

"The reversal has already begun," he explained as the hologram of the universe rewound. While everything appeared to be back in order, the arrows became animated and were repeatedly moving toward the center like a conveyor belt transporting a load of same-facing triangles.

"At what point did the event horizon pass?" She watched Tim, who turned his head toward me. As Ali followed his gaze to my face, she said, "Oh. When I was five."

"Our ASA-Day," I choked, trying not to burst into sobs at the memory.

"So . . . why did Mom have to die? If *I'm* the cause of the reversal."

"I was told it was so we couldn't have a chance to procreate again and start the whole process over."

Ali took in everything I was saying in stride, silently nodding as the gears in her head whirred.

"You two are quantumly entangled?" I didn't know if she was trying to shift the conversation to something less spirit crushing or just wanted to know.

"They are," Tim answered for me. But that didn't sit right for some reason. It was as if his clinical confirmation was nothing more than mere words when *I* could feel the truth as palpably as my fingers on the couch cushion.

"Yes," I answered with the full conviction of someone being asked if the love of their life was *truly* made for them. She nodded once more, letting her gaze go unfocused as she thought. Tim and I could only watch, knowing she was our only hope at an answer. Sucking in a deep breath of preparation, Alison exhaled, shook out her arms to loosen them, and turned her attention to Tim.

"Okay. Show me the research that the, uh, *other* me has done."

"You sure? There's a lot," I asked.

"I should be able to quickly comprehend the gist of the information by recognizing my own method of presentation for a finalized thesis. My patterns and mannerisms should be fairly consistent; at least, I hope so," she said before adding, "The first paragraph should lay out the problem, while the last summarizes the research."

"Makes sense," I replied. "Tim, go ahead and present her life's work."

"Alright." Tim clapped his puppy hands once before rubbing them together like he was about to perform a magic trick. "Hold on to your butts."

CHAPTER 23

It didn't take long for Ali to run through what she was looking for in the research, taking copious amounts of notes on her phone. She started by reading the file title, determining if it was needed to get a basic understanding of the thesis, and opening the ones she thought had something of interest. Luckily for us, Ali was the type of person who actually named a document with something approximating what was contained inside, unlike me, who must have had twenty different files all labeled "document" with a number after that.

It was interesting to see how intuitively she swiped through Tim's hologram, as if she had used his advanced technology before. Then again, she was the one who wrote it.

After selecting the files she thought pertinent, she would read the first and last paragraph, basically absorbing the cliff notes faster than I could read a single sentence. I had to remind myself that she'd gotten another positive trait from her mother, who could speed-read entire books within an afternoon, while it took me months to read the same thing. She moved the documents that held promise aside so she could fully investigate them in their entirety at a later time.

As she read the last paragraph on the final file, Sylvie took nearly five minutes of painful silence before eventually asking me, "You said you destroyed an entire universe with a gravity pulse? Regardless of if it was through the fourth dimension or whatever."

"Accidentally. Yeah. I, uh, guess so."

She typed something into her phone and then stared at it for a full minute before leaning back on the couch. Her gaze went unfocused before sliding off her phone to land aimlessly on the wall.

"Do you have any food?" I dared to ask when I thought it was appropriate. It had been hours, and I was starving. "Or maybe some shoes?" I wiggled my toes while giving a playful smile.

"Hmm? Oh. Oh, yeah. Of course," she said as if in a dream. "I'll order some pizza. And I'll grab some of Dad's . . . I mean, *your* boots from upstairs. I need to use the bathroom anyway."

"Thank you, sweetheart," I replied with pride electrifying my words. I was beyond impressed at how quickly she had gone through her own life's work.

After ordering us some food, she disappeared upstairs. Within a few minutes, I heard water swooshing through the pipes along the top of the far wall, followed by noticeably slow thumps overhead.

"What's she doing?" I whispered, scowling up at the ceiling by the top of the stairs.

"It doesn't take audio analyzation to recognize the sound of someone walking."

I clicked my tongue, squinted my eyes, and gave Tim's avatar a brief glare. "I know that. What I mean is *why* are they so . . . so slow?"

"Those are the footsteps of someone both afraid of the immediate future but also unwilling to deny themselves of the outcome." Tim let his gaze slowly slide off my face and eventually land on the top of the stairs. "Imagine it, Andrew. You just laid out the most insane series of events that break countless laws of physics as she knows them. Then she read, in her own words, an entire life's worth of research that validates your claims."

I let my eyes slip to match where Tim was focusing—both of us unable to remove our gazes as we waited to see what Alison would do.

We both noticed when the footfalls ceased at the door; I could picture her standing with her hand on the knob, petrified with existential fear the likes of which she had never thought possible.

"You just told her that she is the cause of the universe's demise."

"Well, at least *her* universe." I wasn't sure why I said those words, because I knew them to be false. Perhaps it was my way of trying to soften a blow that would put any normal person in an asylum.

"Technically, it's *every* universe, Andrew," Tim confirmed what I already knew to be true.

Something in his statement gave me pause, like a man lost in the inky black ocean at night thinking he saw a quick glimmer from a possible nearby boat. Everything in me latched onto the feeling, mentally pulling the budding idea apart like a group of weed-laden frat bros accidentally being delivered a blooming onion.

"Tim . . ." I started, my voice freezing in my throat as I finally let my gaze fall from the top of the stairs. "Is Alison the constant in *every* timeline?"

"As far as I can tell. Why do you ask?" Tim's own focus shifted from the ceiling to me.

The layers of my thoughts, though soggy in places, were being steadily pulled apart as I raced toward the center.

"How can we be sure?"

Tim slightly tilted his head as he peered at me. "I suppose we could travel further outward from our home timeline. Verify what we already suspect to be true." He continued to stare at me, his hologram eyes bouncing back and forth between mine. "What are you getting at, Andrew?"

"I'm not sure yet."

The door at the top of the stairs remained unopened, and it both hurt my heart to picture her trying to psych herself up and gave me a determination to find the answer I could feel I was beginning to discover.

The longer I stared at the unopened door, the more it began to hurt.

Shifting my gaze to avoid the pain, I saw her phone sitting on the table, the screen still lit up. Walking over, I picked it up, seeing the pizza was still being made.

"Tim, how do I get to the other screen?"

"Oh, here, let me do it," he said as the screen did two swift changes.

"Take me to her last note."

The words zipped from bottom to top like the *Star Wars* crawl on fast-forward before stopping on the final, underlined words.

Energy absorption. Would it be additive, like setting two car batteries next to each other, or exponential, like adding material to a nuclear chain reaction?

"What is she talking about?" I asked, rereading the words over and over again.

"I think she's referring to you and Retnuh. It's the only thing that makes sense."

"Absorption?" My eyes went down to the foot Tim had constructed out of Retnuh's synthetic arm.

"But I don't know why she is asking whether or not it would be *additive* or *exponential*," Tim admitted. "Clearly, it is additive. Look at what we've already *absorbed* from Retnuh."

My hand rested on my chest as I felt something.

The last layer of the metaphorical blooming onion was yanked away, leaving behind a raw, naked idea that felt like watching your first child being born—the future unclear and the world becoming an even scarier place, but one with an unyielding love that could give light to the darkness.

"I've got it," I mouthed with wide eyes.

"What is it, Andrew?"

"Never mind for now," I replied, quickly waving my free hand to dismiss the question lest I lost my train of thought. "Tim, for the formula needed for how much gravity to use . . . what if . . . what if you somehow write the information I need onto my brain?"

"How's that now?" Tim asked flatly in complete and utter disbelief, as if I were asking him to do something magical, like make my body the size of a building . . . or upload an impossible formula onto my human brain.

"Not the whole thing. Just enough for me to grasp the concept of gravity, um, exertion or whatever."

"Or whatever . . ."

"You know, if it took months of constant practice to learn how to throw a baseball well enough to where I didn't need to think about it and just *threw it* . . . couldn't you do the same with this?"

"If *my* hard drives can't contain the information needed to process the solution, what makes you think your primitive human brain can?"

"Because I don't need to throw *every* ball on Earth to know *how* to throw a single ball. If I learned with one, then I'll know how to throw the others."

"I'm not sure I fully follow your logic. If you can call it that."

"Could you do what you and Alison talked about?" I asked with bated breath, feeling the answer to everything on the tip of my tongue. "Could you alter my memories so that I *learned* how to manipulate gravity?"

"Andrew . . . I—"

"You could start small. Like giving me a memory of expertly throwing a ball using *only* gravity instead of my hands. An-an-and then working up to, say, controlling the moon or something."

"That's a big jump."

"Baby steps. Right?"

"Andrew, the inherent risks from physically altering your neuronal pathways are staggering. I could just as easily make you forget how to walk as I could give you a memory of throwing a baseball using only the force!" he exclaimed before muttering, "Or some other nontrademarked ability. Not to mention that I calculate it would take a millennium of experience to be at the level needed to manipulate the gravity of the *entire* fragging universe!"

"And?"

"You would go crazy, man! Imagine one thousand years of memories of doing *nothing* but practicing your jedi abilities!" he said before quickly adding again, "Or some other nontrademarked profession. Can you call it a profession? Hmm. What do the nerds on Reddit say?"

"Tim, I trust you. And I need you to trust m—" I was cut off as the door opened . . . and the sound of fast-paced water dripping froze my brain. It was such an odd sound that it felt out of place enough to warrant my full attention, similar to driving down the road and suddenly hearing a steady thumping from one of the tires. My brain tried to match the sound by picturing Alison wringing out the world's largest soaking-wet mop onto the steps.

Moving around the couch while somehow having both an arched eyebrow and heavily narrowed eyes, I tried to use all my will to see *through* the ceiling blocking the top of the stairs. I needed to see what Ali was doing. But all I had to do was wait until I hit the bottom landing to have my cursed wish of sight fulfilled.

A steady stream of thick crimson liquid encompassing the length of the steps smoothly flowed toward me.

I couldn't breathe. I couldn't move. It took every ounce of my will to force my eyes to climb the stairs.

"Oh my God," Tim slowly gasped. I didn't even notice he had forgone the usual computer puns.

My gaze became petrified as the top of my vision was filled with blood-soaked loafers beneath slacks the color of midnight. The steady flow of blood began to taper off until it resembled a showerhead immediately after shutting the water off.

My jaw popped as ragged breaths blew through gritted teeth. Blazing eyes lifted to see Retnuh holding my daughter's hair out in front of him as what remained of her blood fell from a tattered neck.

"Surprised to see me, Mr. Frost?" He smirked, needlessly tilting his nose up at me.

"R . . . Retnuh," I heaved out, feeling my chest expand to its very limits with each quick, hate-filled breath. "She . . . She was your . . . your . . . fam—"

Something's wrong, Andrew, Tim whispered inside my head, cutting me off. *Look!*

Through my blinding rage, I somehow managed a degree of cognitive reasoning and saw where Tim had highlighted Retnuh's face.

His eyes are both organic. Meaning he never replaced the one you burned in the dungeon when rescuing Drew.

My mind flashed with a still image of Retnuh firing the antimatter pistol and me curving the round to explode outside, the light of which seared Retnuh's face and one of his eyes.

Plus, I can accurately deduce that he is organic, unlike the other Retnuh, who I am unable to determine whether he is synthetic or organic.

"You're not my Retnuh," I growled, shifting my face down until I was glaring at the soon-to-be dead man.

To remove any atomic-sized trace of doubt that this was a different Retnuh Ordune, a completely alive Davix stepped into view just beyond the doorframe. There was another man next to him that I didn't recognize. He was of average height and build with a blond goatee, blue eyes, and bald head like his leader. But whoever he was, he sure as shit wasn't the unnervingly tall Traze.

"You hear that, boys?" Retnuh smirked while keeping his upturned face pointed in my direction. "I'm not *his* Retnuh."

"Heh, yeah," Davix chuckled. "This is the weirdest Tick yet. Huh, Lane?"

"Why isn't he running?" the other man, Lane, asked, narrowing his eyes my way.

"He has nowhere to go!" Davix answered, giving his companion a light backhand across his upper arm.

How is Davix alive, Tim? I mentally asked. Even though the question was confined solely within my head, the voice I heard was almost a growl as my body prepared to exact a most savage revenge.

I think it's clear that you only managed to erase him from our home timeline.

But Traze isn't here. Which means . . .

You killed him across all *timelines.*

Good. Now I'll do the same thing to these bastards . . .

Don't you need Retn— Tim started to ask before my rage fully blinded me.

My arm lifted as if pointing a gun toward those who deserved the most violent of deaths. As my fingers splayed open, revealing my naked palm, Retnuh's smirk faded, his own arm lowering—my baby's face remained slack as vacant eyes stared at nothing.

"I'm . . . going . . . to buuuuuuurn you to ashes," I snarled as the air around my hand began to waver like a desert's mirage, "on this, and EVERY UNIVERSE!"

Retnuh's lips peeled back to expose gritted teeth while Davix and Lane exchanged confused, nervous glances.

The manifestation of my boiling hatred wasn't blue with the Clepsydra or even white with the antimatter I had somehow learned to cultivate. This was invisible power that began searing the very air in front of my palm. The same palm that was pointed directly at the three men.

I didn't know how I knew, but a fundamental part of me understood that I was combining the power of the exotic matter with the antimatter to erase the bastards from *all* of existence, just like I had done to Traze.

Retnuh's arm blurred, sending Alison's severed head careening toward me like a cannonball.

Time froze at my wordless command, and I willed myself to appear directly in front of the men at the top of the stairs, where I released my powerful grip on the clock.

From their perspective, it must have seemed like I disappeared from the bottom landing before instantly appearing just feet in front of them. From my own, however, it was more like standing still as the world switched to the colorful dust of time, and then the scene moved around me to accommodate my wishes.

The kitchen, stairs, and three men all switched from being made of vibrant, unmoving sands to normal in an instant, like clicking off a filter when editing a video.

Davix gasped almost in a scream while Lane's eyes attempted to flee from their sockets. Retnuh let his gaze slip past the crackling orb of pissed-off energy roughly the size of a basketball and met my eyes. There was no fear or even surprise in his face, only a newfound appreciation for his target.

"RAH!" I bellowed, releasing the contained energy in an outward cone of vengeance.

I had trouble making out what was happening as everything in front of me was swallowed in a sweltering haze of wavering air.

Forcing my eyes to remain open as the heat tried to flash fry my skin, I watched as everything began to burn away in fractions of a second. If the entire area—and men—had been made of gasoline-soaked lint and instantly teleported to the surface of the sun, I honestly don't think the scene would have vaporized any faster.

One of the men started to scream, but it was cut off just as the sound crossed the back of his tongue. They didn't even shift to colorful grains, opting to jump straight to the part where the blackened specks vanished from existence. The side of the house disappeared into a windstorm of ashes, but even those were reduced to singed atoms within the space between the blink of an eye.

Andrew . . . Tim said mentally, awestruck and unable to find the words.

With heavy gasps of air, I lowered my tingling hand, flexing the stiff fingers a few times, and took in what I had done.

The house next door was missing most of its roof, sobering me up in an instant. Especially when I watched in horror as what was left began to cave in on itself.

"What . . . What was that?" I heaved, surprisingly alert after the energy drain. I had fully expected to be barely conscious from how much power I had just unleashed. Instead, my labored breaths appeared to be the result of the dump of adrenaline.

ANDR— Tim tried to scream inside my head right as something crashed into my lower back, throwing me several feet forward to crumple on the ground. I was sickeningly aware of the unforgettable smell of burned flesh. And I didn't know if it was from the Clockmen . . . or me.

CHAPTER 24

As I lay on the tile which had apparently soaked up some of the immense heat from my attack, my breathing became nearly impossible. It felt like a bodybuilder was standing on my stomach while simultaneously squatting six hundred pounds.

Gaining my bearings, I saw I was lying on my side in a fetal position, the hot tile attempting to evaporate the moisture beneath my bare skin. But for some reason, I didn't care that I was basically resting my face and still-flesh hand and foot on a stove burner that had been turned off only a few minutes ago.

Oh no, Tim hissed out in utter despair, but I could barely register what he was saying.

I attempted to roll onto my back, thinking it would somehow alleviate the pressure on my stomach preventing me from getting even a fraction of a breath. It was like trying to suck in air through a Capri Sun straw.

Hold on, Andrew! The nanoids have begun transporting oxygen through your skin to your red blood cells.

"I . . . I can't . . . I can't breathe," I mouthed, unable to move air either way past my lips.

You might not like this, but you, um, aren't going to be able to breathe. But—but—but you won't die! At least . . . from that . . .

Using every bit of mental fortitude to quell my galloping panic, which was wreaking havoc in my mind, I focused on what he'd said. Though my lungs burned hotter than my blast with the demand to breathe, I trusted Tim's quick actions. Especially considering I hadn't blacked out . . . yet.

What the hell happened? I mentally asked, noticing for the first time that my legs were completely numb.

I—I don't know! I've been reviewing the footage over and over again, and cannot determine the cause of your catastrophic injury.

Catastrophic? I mentally gulped, just *knowing* I had somehow blown off my own legs.

Pushing myself onto one elbow, I let my free hand feel below my waist to confirm that I still had my lower half. But it felt alien, as if touching a stranger's thigh, because the sensory input was only one way. I *knew* I was touching my own leg, but my leg wasn't registering my own hand.

Now that I knew I hadn't been blown in half, my eyes gathered up the courage to look down and see I still had both limbs.

Why can't I breathe? I asked, still wrestling with the white-hot ache in my chest at not being able to draw breath.

Weeeeellll . . . heh heh. You see . . .

Moving my hand up my thigh and past my waist to feel why there was so much pressure on my stomach, I quickly figured out what the problem was.

T-T-T-Tim! Wh—Why is there a hole in my stomach? Everything began to spin as my eyes desperately searched for the missing pieces of my lower torso. I could see the bottom portion of my blackened ribcage. And on the other side of the alarmingly large hole, I saw my own pelvis, as well as my severed spine. *TIM!*

There was movement in my periphery, and I turned a drunken gaze to see Retnuh standing up from the other side of a fully intact kitchen island. It wasn't the man standing that caught my attention first. It was Alison's legs. I could see up to her knees before the rest of her body was hidden by the island.

My face twitched in pain, both of the heart and the body, as I looked up to see Retnuh popping the tab on a beer can.

"I think she was bringing these down for you," Retnuh casually said before taking a pussy-ass sip of the foaming beverage. His other hand rose into view, setting the rest of the six-pack on the unblemished counter.

Well, that explains what happened . . . Tim mentally exhaled. I could hear the defeat in his voice, which seeped down my spine.

"I'm a whiskey man, myself," he casually continued, setting the can on the counter with a dull *clink*. To emphasize his apparent distaste for the grocery-store beer, he slowly pushed the beverage away from him with two fingers. The sound of the aluminum gliding across the countertop was only a fraction as ear grating as nails on a chalkboard, but the fact he was doing it intentionally exacerbated my annoyance.

My shoulder began to ache from the awkward angle at which I was propping myself up on my elbow, and I decided to lay back in an attempt to alleviate whatever discomfort I could. As was my luck, I knocked my head against the bottom cabinets while trying to simply lay flat. To add insult to injury, I was unable to readjust any further, and while almost my entire body was flat on the floor, I now had my chin pressing into my upper chest, painfully straining my neck.

Moving my eyes as far as I could manage to in their sockets, I saw that the cabinets directly next to me had been vaporized, and I was just lucky enough to be uncomfortably propped up on what was left. On the plus side, however, at least my face was no longer pressed to the hot tile floor. Perhaps my ass was starting to cook, but I couldn't feel it. Always look on the bright side!

I tried to laugh at the ridiculousness of my situation, but all I could manage was a strained smile, my abdomen no longer able to gallop with the chuckle.

Tim, I mentally began, *can you put air into my lungs?*

Well . . . yes, I can. But if your goal is to be able to speak, I'm afraid ninety-five percent of your diaphragm is either detached or missing entirely.

Retnuh lightly shook his head as he looked at me, as if embarrassed by how I was lying on the ground. Turning, he moved outside of the kitchen and disappeared into the living room.

I could feel myself begin to grow curious at what he was doing, but I just couldn't give enough fucks. I was growing more and more tired as the seconds ticked on.

Now that I was alone, my gaze was drawn to an oddity in the kitchen pantry. At the back wall was the staircase that led to the uncommon Floridian basement. Perhaps "hidden laboratory" was more apropos. But why have a hidden lab if Ali wasn't aware of the gravitational anomaly?

Andrew, I . . .

I know, Tim. You don't have enough butt to pull from, I mentally chuckled.

Even if you were J.Lo herself, there wouldn't be enough booty meat to be able to fully repair the hole in your abdomen. The muscle and skin? Sure. But the organs, and especially the spinal cord, require specialized materials derived from lab-printed tissues that mimic the cells around which they are placed.

Like stem cells . . . ? I asked, feeling the darkness creeping in and attempting to engage in the conversation in a foolhearted effort to stay awake. Why? I didn't know anymore . . .

That's a basic way of understanding the printed tissues.

Wait. I didn't know *why* I didn't want to drift off for my final sleep? No . . . NO.

Eyes that were filling with furious determination flew to the legs on the other side of the kitchen island. My *daughter's* legs . . .

Retnuh entered the kitchen holding a damn pillow of all things. Stopping beside me, I could only barely tilt my snarling face up at him as he bent down, ungracefully slipped a hand behind my neck to slightly pull me up, and jammed the pillow under my head.

Yanking his hand free, I fell back into place. But now I was even more uncomfortable, with the positioning of the pillow forcing my chin deeper into my chest. My neck burned with the strain. Retnuh remained crouched next to me, and all I could manage to see was his torso, no matter how hard I tried to lift my gaze in an effort to meet his.

"So," he purred, making a show of touching the kitchen floor *through* the cannonball-sized hole in my belly. "*You* are supposed to be the singularity, hmm? *The One*." His head rocked back and forth as he said the title, mocking what he had evidently been told about me.

My lungs ached with the demand for air, even if Tim was somehow able to keep oxygen flowing in my veins. Through my discomfort, I was able to awkwardly tilt my head up and to the side so that my right eye was looking at the man.

"Oh, you didn't know?" Retnuh grinned, slapping the tile floor through my torso before pulling his hand out to rest on his knee. "That there was only one of you, and your ridiculous Chronos Scale, in *alllll* the multiverse? The One at the center of it all."

I continued to stare, dumbfounded. I also took note that Tim was annoyingly silent, neither confirming nor denying the statements from the lead Clockman.

Retnuh's tone shifted as amused eyes went cold. "What did you mean when you said *my* Retnuh?" His gaze narrowed as he attempted to read my response. "He clearly failed at his duties; otherwise, you wouldn't be here, in *my* territory."

My eyes fell from his to land on his chest, exhaustion stealing my ability to look up. As I stared with a steadily blurring gaze, a crazy notion began to bloom in my dying brain.

Tim . . . show him. I tried to lift my eyes again to watch the man's reaction, but I didn't have it in me. A hologram came to life above my left arm. I could tell from my darkening peripheral that it was Retnuh's face. It pulled back and displayed an animation that was the origins of a family tree.

"What's this?" His voice was calm, but I could hear the cautious curiosity in his words.

The hologram began to slow as the portraits became my grandparents, then parents . . . and finally, me.

"What?!" he hissed out. "That's not possible!"

Tim answered for me while I continued to stare at Retnuh's chest.

"With the wormhole destroyed, Retnuh Ordune went back in time to lie in wait for Andrew. But when he arrived, he fell in love."

"How was the wormhole destroyed?" The question aimed at his profession versus asking about falling in love reinforced that this man was basically an organic machine with a one-track mind.

"In battle."

You mean you *destroyed it. Right, Tim? Heh,* I mentally challenged, feeling the urge to yawn but being unable, which was maddening.

Not important! And don't you pass out on me!

"But *my* wormhole is still in place," Retnuh thought out loud. "Which means the fourth dimension is localized within each universe. Interesting." When Tim didn't say anything, Retnuh continued. "So . . . my alternate self was forced to wait, like finding a needle in a haystack."

"The only thing he knew was *which* haystack it was, and he gave himself hundreds of years for a cushion."

Why are you telling him all this?

Maaaaaybe *if he sees you as family, he won't fragging kill you, man!* Tim answered inside my head. *I'm not sure if you fully comprehend your situation, but you aren't even a fish in a barrel for him to shoot. Right now, you are the fish that jumps* into *the boat! You just can't be any more helpless!*

Hmph.

Retnuh continued to crouch next to me, and I managed to look up as he turned his head. I could all but see the circuits rapidly firing in his brain as he thought.

"I assume he didn't jump in time to expedite finding you. Because of a woman." Retnuh almost sounded disgusted with himself.

Sirens sounded somewhere in the far distance while the three of us remained shrouded in contemplative silence.

Tim, keep going.

Oh, right! he agreed inside my head before shifting to whatever speakers were hidden within the Clepsydra. "Retnuh watched his family grow and prosper generation after generation."

I could see the question of his seemingly immortal lifespan being brought up by his expanding family, but then he did something I wasn't expecting.

"None of this matters," he said as his left fist began to glow, turning stone-cold eyes toward me. "I will finish what the weak Ordune couldn't."

Tim, pipe my voice through your speakers.

Done.

Retnuh pointed his glowing fist at my face, ready to send me to oblivion.

"You killed your own great-granddaughter. Your own blood. Where's the honor in that?"

Retnuh's fist lowered, but not because my words were heavy. Instead, a smirking face met mine as he spoke. "Aren't you one to talk, Mr. Frost."

From the edge of my vision, I saw my daughter's legs. My *adult* daughter.

"Wait . . . this timeline's Andrew didn't ki—I mean, start the cycle."

"Your Retnuh failed in more ways than one, Mr. Frost," he explained. "The singularity affects the entirety of existence—for all of us. And you clearly didn't uphold your end of what must be done, dooming us all." Moving his hand back into place, he let out a heavy sigh. "You would doom us all."

"But if you kill me, the universe will still end."

"There's always another way, Mr. Frost," he explained, moving his hand a few inches closer to my face until I could feel the heat radiating from the collected power. It was clear he was enjoying the kill. "And now, I'll have to travel to the source timeline, ensuring the cycle begins anew."

"But without my Chronos Scale."

Retnuh paused, moving his hand from my view so that I could see his smirking face. "You think *you* are the one with the highest Chronos Scale, Mr. Frost?"

"I . . ."

"I will personally absorb the weak Retnuh Ordune of the source timeline and save the universe."

"By killing your own family."

"We do what we must," he replied coldly, pointing his glowing hand back toward my face.

Goodbye, Andrew, Tim said on the verge of tears.

"I'm not the one you should say goodbye to," I spoke through the speakers, causing both Retnuh and Tim to pause at my words. Only the sound of the sirens growing closer filled the air.

Realization crossed Retnuh's face, prompting him to boom "NO!" as he fired just inches from my face.

CHAPTER 25

Using up every ounce of strength I had left, I swiped my hand upward while shifting planes of existence. Time froze as the world around me was replaced with colorful sands in the precise shape of the kitchen . . . and Retnuh.

My hand passed through his torso as I willed the vibrant, nearly microscopic grains to pull free from their host. If only I could have seen Retnuh's face as I removed the entire middle portion of his body and moved it to the giant hole in my belly.

The sands began to melt like tiny snowflakes drifting onto an extended tongue, with each of the grains merging with the pulsating energy that my body was comprised of.

I watched in fascination as the hole began to stitch itself closed with the material I had confiscated from the unknowing donor. I even began to glow brighter, making me realize that my ethereal flesh had grown dull as I neared death's precipice.

By 01 . . . how is this possible?

"We are all made of stardust."

Take it easy there, Carl Sagan, Tim said, sounding less awestruck and more annoyed. *That doesn't mean you can just . . . just* steal *matter from another source!*

"And yet," I countered, waving a hand at the hole barely big enough for a finger to poke through.

As I finished repairing my broken body, I eyed Retnuh, expecting him to follow me into whatever dimension this was. But he remained as unmoving as the rest of the contents of the kitchen.

Willing myself to float up and away from him, I glided to the other side of the island and resumed the passage of time. Retnuh splattered against the tile while his blast easily tore through the bottom cabinets and even the exterior wall.

My jaw flexed as I reminded myself that I had been in the path of that blast just a few seconds ago.

"Iegh. Ehr . . . nuh . . ." Retnuh tried to speak as he awkwardly pushed himself to his back, wide eyes taking in the devastation. Crimson-coated intestines spilled out like a pot of spaghetti with extra marinara sauce had been tipped over.

There was a *pop* which somehow snagged Retnuh's attention. As he turned confused, terrified eyes toward me, I took a swig of the beer I had just opened.

"Aaahhhhh. Refreshing," I said, making a show of looking at the can in hammed-up admiration.

"H . . . How . . ." Retnuh managed to ask as his head began to slowly lower toward the burnt tile, his life energy fleeing from him with each frantic heartbeat.

Feeling like a fisherman forcefully yanking his rod at the first sign of a nibble, I all but ran to the other side of the kitchen island, looking down at the dying man. "Oh how the turns have tabled."

Even as he whimpered his last breaths, Retnuh still managed to look up at me with a tilted head and confused face.

"I mean . . . how the tables—You know what, never mind," I quickly threw out, lifting my own glowing blue fist and ending the bastard. His upper chest, where his heart had been, now had a matching hole to his belly.

The sirens grew to a piercing wail as first responders pulled up outside the neighbor's house.

Lowering my fist, I took another long swig of the beer while mentally preparing to shift away from here.

Did . . . Did you mean to say "how the tables have turned"? Tim hesitantly asked.

"I don't want to talk about it, Tim." I could feel my face flush with blood at fumbling what should have been a movie-esque final line to the bad guy.

From behind, I heard a familiar noise that sounded like a mix between a tear and a swoosh. In an instant, I understood a portal had opened, bringing with it a new world of hurt.

"FROST!" the replacement Retnuh Ordune called out, anger lacing his words along with a predatory tone. This man loved to fight.

DOWN! Tim screamed inside my head. My knees went out, dropping me to the ground faster than a politician's pants after meeting ultra rich lobbyists. A blast of energy flew over my head, sizzling the hairs on top of my scalp before crashing into the neighbor's house.

Without me telling my body to do so, it flipped to the side so that my chest was facing the ceiling while I painfully arched my back so I could post on my palms and feet. Before I could focus on how uncomfortable the gymnast position was, my right leg shot up before kicking back toward my head with all my might, effectively sending me in some sort of back handspring.

I didn't have to ask to know who was piloting my body at that moment.

My left leg followed, and I quickly landed on both feet with my fist pointed at Retnuh Ordune.

We need to charge before we can shoot again!

Go antimatter! I called out, taking a step forward and lowering my left fist while bringing up my synthetic right arm.

A fierce white glow illuminated the already bright kitchen as a toothy smile marred my face.

"Got you," I whispered, right as someone shouted from my left.

"POLICE! GET DOWN! NOW!"

Ignoring the command, I sent the signal to flex the muscles in my forearm right as something smashed into my left shoulder. The pain was dull but immediate, and I flinched as the bullet lodged itself in my shoulder socket, the ceiling vaporizing above Retnuh as the antimatter erased it from the timeline. However, my enemy was unfazed.

"Bastard!" I cried out through gritted teeth as I lifted my arm to try and fire again.

Retnuh, who had dived out of the way of my attack, lifted himself up, making a show of patting the dust off his pristine suit.

"I SAID GET DOW—" the officer tried to say, but my right fist shot up in the blink of an eye. Instead of an energy blast, my fingers splayed open, and the innocent man was ripped apart as if all of his limbs and head had been attached by ropes to cars speeding in different directions.

"Jesus Christ," I croaked in amazement, horror, and disbelief.

01 . . .

"What the hell was that?!" Retnuh hissed, shooting his left fist to point at me.

Keeping my eyes on what was left of the innocent officer, I gave Retnuh a sidelong glance, noticed his Clepsydra wasn't fully charged yet, and answered his question.

"This." My voice came out as a whisper as my right arm swiped through the air to point my index finger at the man. With a quick jerk, my hand twitched as my finger leaped to the right, and Retnuh's Clepsydra-cladded arm was torn off at the shoulder.

The sound was sickening yet oh so satisfying at the same time. His rotator cuff snapped like fat rubber bands yanked past their threshold. The flesh tearing sounded like the world's largest orange being peeled in half a second. But best of all, Retnuh's gasp of utter surprise and agony reminded me of a haunted train's horn blasting in the distance for several seconds.

"Might want to cauterize that on the stove before you bleed out," I said with a shark's smile as I turned my attention back to the chunks of meat that had once been a human being just trying to do his job.

"STEPHENS! NO!" another officer cried out in pained horror before he caught sight of me in his peripheral vision. Without pausing, the trained man leveled his Glock directly at my heart.

Instinct tried to repeat what had happened before, and I lifted my hand to point at the man.

Andrew? Tim all but croaked. I could hear the abject worry in his voice that I was turning into a villain indifferent to human life.

The officer squeezed his finger, the gun barked, and then time stood still.

Holding up my hand in a gesture of *stop*, I gave Retnuh a quick glance to see he was also frozen in place and returned my attention to what was left of the first cop. With time standing still, I shifted my right hand to point my index finger at the man cut into several pieces on the grass. I tried to lift my left arm outward, but the pain that ricocheted from my shoulder to the top of my head and back again reminded me that it was all but useless.

Tim? Do you mind? I mentally grunted.

Working on the receptors now, Tim announced before letting out with a long whistle. *Your shoulder is eviscerated, Andrew. Yeesh.*

Did you just whistle?

Isn't that something guys do when they see something really messed up?

Close enough, I muttered.

With my left arm all but useless, I kept my focus on where the officer had been standing and shifted my right hand until I was holding it fully extended from my chest with the palm pointed at my heart.

Slowly, I began moving it closer toward me, watching.

One of the arms began to wriggle before lifting off the ground and flying toward where I centered my focus, followed by the other. The legs were next, with the head coming from somewhere above the roofline, making me briefly wonder where it had gone. As I lost focus while thinking about where the head had vanished to, the pieces began to vibrate before slowly spreading outward from the body as if in a current underwater.

Clenching my teeth, I refocused my will and resumed pulling my right hand toward my chest.

The severed pieces reattached seamlessly, but I continued to rewind, even as the unharmed man stood before me.

Electrified fire yanked free from my left shoulder, making me lose my balance as the bullet flew from where it had lodged itself in my bone and returned to the chamber. I was instantly reminded of hitting my foot in the shower—even though time had reversed, my pain sure as shit didn't.

"OW, TIM!" I cried out between gritted teeth.

Sorry! Sorry! I, uh, lost focus for a moment as I watched you, um, do the impossible . . . again.

Dropping to one knee, I let my focus drop as my right hand clapped around my shoulder and began to tentatively probe for the damage.

To my chagrin, the hole was still there, evident by the blood spilling down my fingers.

"Stephens?" the second officer asked, complete disbelief dripping from his words thicker than the blood from my shoulder.

"I SAID GET DOWN!" Stephens instructed with his gun aimed at where I was crouching.

"He's got a knife!" the second officer cried out, shifting his muzzle off of me.

No, I don't, I thought to myself before deciding to follow his gun sights.

Retnuh had slipped a fillet blade free from the knife block and was looking at me with a grin.

"See you soon, Mr. Frost."

"Drop the knife or we will be forced to shoot!" Stephens yelled, also shifting his weapon off of me now that I was perceived as less of a threat, blood pouring from my fingers.

If they kill him, another Retnuh will immediately take his place, Tim reminded me. *One with his Clepsydra intact.*

Retnuh shifted his focus to the cops while wielding the blade, cackled like the madman he was, and lunged.

"Drop him!"

"NO!" I bellowed, waving my hand toward the two officers, freezing them in place.

Retnuh slowed his steps, realizing what I had done, and sighed while turning to face me. "The hard way it is."

The knife flew into his neck just behind his ear before the crazed man started to pull it forward. I started to will him to freeze in time as well, but I could feel that shifting my focus would mean the cops would return to the now and resume shooting the suicidal Clockman.

Letting go of the gaping hole in my shoulder, I shot my right index finger toward Retnuh, latching onto a random scene from the *Avengers: Infinity War* movie.

As the razor-sharp blade crept toward one of the critical arteries in his neck, Retnuh's face went from a stoic yet maniacal grin to a surprised contortion of pain.

Yanking his closed fist back, he opened it to see a clear liquid fall from his grasp.

What did you do?

With a pained grin, I said, "I replaced the molecules of the knife with the hydrogen peroxide under the bathroom sink."

Oh-ho! I bet that stings like a motherboard fucker!

That felt like you were reaching, I mentally whispered to Tim at the not-so-clever pun.

Retnuh confirmed Tim was right by showing all his teeth while still managing to produce the biggest frown I'd ever seen. Though he tried not to scream, his ragged breaths were just as satisfying to hear as if the man were wailing in agony.

"You're not going anywhere," I said with a tooth-bared smirk as I got to my knees while my right hand moved to cup the tattered flesh of my shoulder once more.

Already working on the repairs, Tim announced. I started to feel the pain subside as he controlled the receptors. *Look out!*

Shooting my gaze from my shoulder back to Retnuh, I saw he had grabbed the butcher knife from the block and was turning it to plunge it into his heart. A part of me thought there was no way a human could stab through their own sternum no matter how much they wanted to. But then I remembered Retnuh had his strength enhanced.

On instinct, I swung my right hand around, flinging blood in a wet arc throughout the kitchen, and pointed at the knife as it flew toward the man's chest.

There was a loud scream that I couldn't help but crack a smile at.

As Retnuh pulled his hand back, the rubber chicken with the gaping mouth and surprised eyes began to inflate again with a comical, steady cry.

Okay, seriously *. . . how the hexadecimal are you doing that?!*

I . . . I don't know, I mentally answered, not wanting Retnuh to hear how unsure I was. *I just changed the sands.*

"Very clever, Mr. Frost," a pale Retnuh weakly said. "But you're too late. I'm . . . I'm already dead."

The chicken plopped to the blood-soaked tile as Retnuh turned to face me. Where his left arm had been ripped free, a stream of crimson continued to flow with no signs of slowing.

"Is that so?" I replied, not knowing if I could prove him wrong or not.

Lifting my index finger one more time, I imagined his wound being scarred over like an amputee. Retnuh groaned as his flesh knitted itself together and the bleeding ceased. While keeping a portion of my focus on the cops to remain frozen in time, an idea came to me right as Retnuh futilely reached for the knife block again.

I imagined his healthy shoulder perfectly mirroring the scarred-over one.

Retnuh crashed his hips into the cabinet as his reaching arm vanished into colorful grains of sand that proceeded to fade from view entirely. Just to be sure, I repeated the process on his legs, struggling for a moment on whether or not to amputate him at the hip or the knee.

At the last second, I chose the knee because I didn't know if his pants would fall off, revealing his junk to me—and that was just something I didn't care to see.

Retnuh didn't even grunt as he collapsed to the blood-soaked floor, all his limbs removed.

"Let's see you hurt yourself now," I taunted, returning my full attention to the cops just outside the kitchen.

I'm sure he's going to find a way, Andrew, and will be back in a matter of time.

The idea is to be long gone by then.

Ah. Fair point.

Unless . . .

Unless what?

Slowly turning my attention back to the man who lay, unmoving, in a lake of his own blood, I said, "I could erase him. Just like I did Traze before, and Davix a few minutes ago. Remove him from *all* timelines forever." I didn't try to speak inside my head this time, opting to let Retnuh hear my words. That's when I noticed I was breathing again, my body having been fully healed by stealing from the other very dead Retnuh.

Then we will be faced with the literal grandfather paradox, Andrew, Tim said with a voice that urged me to reason. *If you kill your ancestor, you will never be born.*

"I don't care anymore," I growled, lifting my right hand to point at the man as the air wavered and crackled around it.

Then Alison will never have been born.

"GGGRRRRAAAH!" I bellowed in a cresting wave of rage before something came to me and it quickly receded, leaving my ocean of emotion calm once more. The crackling power around my hand shifted from a wavering to a pulsating white. "Then I'll just remove him from *this* timeline using antimatter. Davix was only erased from our home timeline, right? So Retnuh, *my* Retnuh, will live."

I wanted to bask in the fact that I could pull sweet, cool air into my lungs once more, but had bigger fish to fry at the moment.

He's defeated, Andrew. What purpose would that serve? Even though his words were nothing more than electrical signals inside my brain, I could still hear the warning just beneath the surface.

"It would feel good," I growled, taking slow, heavy steps toward the man hidden behind the kitchen island. My left hand remained pointed toward the officers as more sirens began to grow in the distance.

Is it worth the risk?

My footfalls, which had been intentionally loud thuds on the tile, became light splashes as I stepped into Retnuh's pool of blood. The unmoving man merely stared at the ceiling with unfocused eyes as I approached.

Then I saw it.

What remained of the once proud leader of the Clockmen was lying next to Alison's body.

The blood I so enjoyed tromping in . . . wasn't just his.

I gasped, taking several hurried steps back as if the cooling scarlet liquid were molten lava. My muscles seemed to violently spasm on my left side just as deafening barks pierced my ears. As my eyes flicked toward the source of the noise, I was only able to start the process of recognition of what had happened when Officer Stephens proved what an elite-level marksman looked like.

Oddly enough, I think I felt my head jerk before hearing the bullet smash into my skull.

ANDREW! Tim shouted from somewhere off in the distance as all the light was swallowed by a void darker than the center of a black hole.

CHAPTER 26

My bare feet stood on lush, manicured grass as I stared through a kitchen window—*my* kitchen window. The love that filled the house was on display through the glass like priceless art.

Inside, Andrew, Sylvie, and Alison Frost were preparing for their ASA-Day. Andrew had just given his girls their gifts and was preparing to go outside and cook their steaks.

Worry filled my heart, and I shot a glance to the grill where the white plastic container of lighter fluid sat. The same fuel that had disappeared, prompting me to go to the store and get more, leaving my family exposed. But there it sat, and there it *would* sit.

Worry was replaced with determination as I prepared to stop *anyone* from taking that fuel and starting the cycle of my family's murder.

After several seconds, nothing happened, and Andrew happily stepped outside to begin cooking the meal for his girls.

Something above me pulled my focus from my beautiful, living family, and I looked up to see a night sky devoid of all light. Not a single star twinkled, leaving nothing past the few clouds except an inky blackness that reminded me of looking at the ocean at night while on a cruise ship.

But then, the dream seamlessly shifted to a nightmare.

The scene wavered as bits of colorful grains of sand began to drift away from the wooden fence, green grass, and a confused Andrew, who started to scream as he tried to run back inside the house to get to his girls.

"No!" I cried out, right as pain erupted from my back and chest.

Looking down, I stared with disbelieving eyes as a hand struck *through* my sternum and light began to slip free from somewhere inside my body to disappear into my attacker.

"Do . . . what must . . . be done . . ." Retnuh whispered into my ear as everything went unfocused.

CHAPTER 27

ndrew? A familiar voice asked like an ethereal whisper carried by the whistling wind. Andrew, can you hear me?

Tim? Is . . . Is that you? I mentally asked. That's when the sensation of being encased in concrete burst into my belabored consciousness, ringing all the alarms in an effort to sow panic amongst my other groggy thoughts. *Why can't I move?*

I sent rapid-fire signals to any and every muscle in my body, but I would have had better luck trying to convince a picture of a lion to roar.

Tim?! Wha—Wha—What's happening to me?!

One moment, please. His words were a little clearer this time, as if he had moved closer.

An unnatural feeling of calm splashed over my consciousness like a dump truck dropping a payload of ice water on me.

Tim . . . I . . .

Whoops! Too much good stuff, heh heh, a crystal-clear Tim said. The intensity of the relaxation was dialed back right as I tiptoed toward unconsciousness again. *Better?*

Ye—Yeah . . .

I took note of what was happening now that my head was free from the conflagration of chaos that sheer panic always seemed to bring.

Why can't I move?

I haven't repaired the damage to your cerebellum yet.

My what? I asked before the name registered. *Is—Isn't that part of my brain?!*

You were sort of . . . shot in the head.

I was? I asked, trying to lift my hand to rest against my forehead. Once again, I was reminded that I was paralyzed. Luckily, whatever Tim had done to suppress my emotions prevented me from freaking out again, though I could still feel the knee-jerk urge to do so.

Among other places, he added under his breath. *But that's not important right now. Actually, it's a good thing that you appear to still be in a coma. Specifically because of the angry officer sitting next to your bed.*

Why is a cop sitting . . . I started to ask when fragments of my memory flashed across my mind—though they appeared to flow backward for some reason.

Turning to see the barrel of a gun flash before everything went dark.

Looking down at Retnuh, who lay in a thick pool of blood . . . that wasn't all his own.

Ali's headless body on the floor.

Somehow ripping Retnuh limb from limb with my mind.

Davix and Lane bursting into blackened grains before the tiny specks burned into nothingness.

Retnuh holding my daughter's head at the top of the stairs.

Ali disappearing upstairs to use the bathroom.

Explaining to Ali the entire situation in an effort to see if she was able to provide any critical insight into her own life's work. And her phone with the last sentence from her notes.

The answer . . . I said.

Yeah. The answer that you wanted me to carve up your brain like a Christmas turkey to give you a thousand years' worth of memories so you could, and I can't believe I'm saying this, feel *the universe. Pervert.*

Do you have a better suggestion?

As we speak, I'm barely *able to stitch pieces of your brain together to keep you alive! And that's with trying to put things back* exactly *as they were! Let alone trying to create new pathways with a brain that doesn't have anywhere near the capacity to store all the information.*

Wait . . . I started, just realizing something Tim had said. *You are repairing my* brain?

Trying to. Yes.

I thought you couldn't do that. You explained that when I asked how Drew was still alive waaaay past what I thought was possible. I thought back to our conversation about basically being immortal because of the nanoids. *Yeah, you said you could fix damages from strokes and heart attacks and stuff, but—but wouldn't be able to heal things like massive brain damage.*

I'm going to be honest with you, Andrew. Tim inhaled as he prepared to deliver what I immediately knew to be bad news. *As much as it pains me to admit, without the proper equipment, I will not be able to restructure your brain as adequately as what nature created.*

Oh . . . is there good news?

Yes, actually. The officer had probably gone to the range recently and forgot to switch his ammunition from full metal jackets back to a typical hollow point. That and the round being a 9mm saved your life, as the velocity and condensed mass allowed a straight path through your temporal lobe and cerebellum.

Aren't those important?

Humans might argue that every *portion of the brain is important. But luckily for you, you have me! And I, ahem,* should *be able to mimic some of the missing functions of your cerebellum.*

Which does what?

Let's see: motor coordination, balance and posture, fine motor skills, eye movement—oh, and speech articulation.

Well, luckily, that *doesn't seem to be affected.*

If you are referring to your ability to mentally *speak, then yes.*

Um . . . what do you mean?

The formation of thought in the style of cohesive internal voices stems from areas of the brain such as the Broca's area, parietal lobe, and prefrontal cortex, which were unaffected by the bullet.

So . . . I might not be able to speak with my mouth?

Honestly, that is the least of my concerns. But for now, I need your permission to attempt and restructure your brain.

Re . . . Restructure? I gulped.

As the round tore into and out the back of your skull, it took with it precious brain tissue that I will not be able to replicate without the necessary equipment.

Aren't we in a hospital? Can't you just use their, um, equipment?

No, Andrew. I mean equipment from at least twenty-seven years in the future.

Oh. So . . . when you say restructure *. . . you mean like when you moved muscle from my butt to my leg . . . ?*

I'm afraid so. The fact that Tim didn't take the golden opportunity to make a leg-butt joke showed me just how serious his proposal was.

What could go wrong? Like, could you accidentally make it where I speak with a British accent all the time?

Let's put it this way: if one of the voiceover artists who swiftly reads off the common side effects of pharmaceuticals on American television were to, in one breath, attempt to read the potential outcomes of rebuilding your brain, they would pass out.

That . . . doesn't sound fun.

AND if the next voiceover artist were to pick up where the first left off, they, too, would lose consciousness before reaching a tenth of the list.

I thought about how half the length of pharmaceutical commercials was dedicated to the narrator reading the side effects like an auctioneer who could effortlessly recite Eminem's *Rap God* before he'd even had his first cup of coffee in the morning.

This sucks.

Truer words have never been spoken.

My mind raced with any and all ideas that dared to form themselves.

Can we . . . um . . . steal the nanoids from Retnuh's Clepsydra? I pictured his arm being ripped off and allowed the smallest semblance of satisfaction to peek its head from the shadows.

It's not the nanoids that are the issue, Andrew. I am unable to replicate the tissue and reconnect all the neural pathways that were lost.

Oh! Can't we just use this timeline's wormhole? You know, go to the future so you can fix me up?

I could open a wormhole underneath you now and guide us to a safe point in time to do just that.

Great!

But the Clockmen would register our access to the wormhole and quickly track us down. And while you are incapacitated, I think it's best we remain where we are.

Isn't Retnuh with us? I asked, remembering how I had left him alive. Rather, I hadn't gotten the chance to erase him from the timeline before I had apparently dropped my focus on the officers.

Yes. I am keeping an eye on him as we speak.

Where is he?

Currently, he's being examined by a slew of doctors.

Why?

They are wondering how a quadruple amputee was at the scene with an apparent twin brother who was somehow nearly bisected at the waist and then had his heart blown out.

I thought about the first version of Retnuh I had encountered on this timeline, and how I had stolen his essence to heal my own grievous injury.

That doesn't explain why he needs a bunch of doctors looking at him.

He also secretly bit off his tongue in an attempt to bleed himself to death.

Jesus . . .

Precisely my sentiment, more or less.

He's trying to summon another Retnuh to replace him.

Correct.

Something Tim had once told me after I had killed Traze back when we had set up a trap for the killer came to mind.

I thought they are replaced with a version of them that is only one second younger. Wouldn't Retnuh's copy also be missing his arms and legs?

No, because he didn't have his Clepsydra. Think of it like a save file for a video game, Tim explained. *The Clepsydra reported back to headquarters the moment Retnuh became compromised, thusly signaling that he was no longer a viable replacement.*

Oh. That makes sense . . . I guess.

That, and the replacement is predominantly from one second before they went through the initial portal at the point of contact with the subject.

What if it's been, like, fifteen minutes or something? How will the replacements know what's happened?

The Clepsydra is updated prior to insertion. Or if we are being technical, reinsertion.

So they're told why *they're being sent? Like, how they died and stuff?*

If the information is both available and necessary.

Why wouldn't it be necessary?

Remember our first foray into the wormhole?

My mind flashed with broken stills of the event.

Barely . . .

Barely?! How do you barely *remember one of the most profound—Oh right . . . your temporal lobe was damaged.*

You're not helping . . .

Anywaaaaay . . . Davix was eaten by what you *would call a* big-ass crocodile. *Do you remember that?*

My brain was able to play a quick scene of a terrifying dinosaur as it swam directly toward me. All while I floated helplessly in the wormhole.

Instead of admitting to the AI that I couldn't exactly remember, I decided to lie.

Yeah. Sure.

His replacement wasn't informed of why *he took his previous iteration's place.*

Why not?

Protocol to preserve their psychological state.

Like PTSD?

More of an existential version of it, but yes, Tim explained, and I knew he was only entertaining the conversation because he needed time to do . . . whatever it was he was doing to the damage my body had sustained.

He continued.

Imagine being told you are a copy of your original self.

I know my memory is a little fuzzy right now, but I kinda *feel like that's something I've personally dealt with, Tim.*

Not even close, he corrected with complete authority, like a science teacher educating a cocky student on why they couldn't simply hold their breath in space. *Though you've encountered other versions of yourself, you haven't been subjected to the prospect of* replacing *a deceased Andrew.*

Isn't that how we first met? I asked solemnly. *The previous Andrew failed his mission and was forced to deliver you to the funeral home so that I found you . . . to try again. Actually, didn't you say there were* thousands *of me prior to . . . me?*

Your selective memory is frustrating, he mumbled before taking in a long inhale. Letting it out, he continued. *No, Andrew. That is* not *the same because you were a continuation of the plan to increase your Chronos Scale to the point where the events became unchangeable. You were not a replacement to be used like cannon fodder, unlike the Clockmen.*

But the idea of me existing and—and doing the things I'm doing because *thousands of other Andrew Frosts died . . .*

Tim waited in silence for me to finish my point. When I was unable, he spoke up with a dark tone that promised therapy would be in my future. *Would you like to know each and every way your variants died? I can show you, you know. I can even let you experience each death, including the pain.*

If I could have shifted where I lay in a gesture of discomfort, I would have flailed around like a sock puppet in a dryer.

That—That won't be necessary.

I thought as much, Tim continued in a tone of warning before shifting back to his playfully gregarious voice. *Besiiiiides, unlike Traze and Davix, you* are *the main character in this video game!*

So they are aware every time they are forced to replace a dead version of themselves?

Yes. But it is necessary so that they have situational awareness of what they are walking into.

That must be a heavy conversation.

In what way?

I did something that made me feel like I needed a shower and put myself in their shoes.

Imagine you're about to go through a portal to start a mission, when your bosses inform you that you have just been killed.

I wouldn't fret too much for the Clockmen, heh. Though they are essential for keeping history intact from Ticks who might accidentally have a high enough Chronos Scale to actually *change the past, they have committed unspeakable atrocities in the sake of preservation that would otherwise be deemed too far.*

Like killing teenagers who unknowingly stumbled on a Clepsydra and went through the wormhole?

Not just killing them, Andrew, Tim said in a low tone once more. *They've been known to needlessly* erase *people from the timeline entirely. Even if they exhibited low Chronos Scales, effectively making them mere observers of the past.*

Something about that caught my attention.

I thought anyone could go back in time and change the past. Like if they stepped on the wrong butterfly millions of years ago, couldn't that alter the timeline?

Not unless they had a Chronos Scale that correlated with the specific density of time.

What the hell does that mean?

Remember when I gave the rudimentary explanation of how blacksmiths can increase the strength of steel by folding it over and over again?

Yeah. I think so.

Then the repairs are working, Tim said just below a whisper.

What was that?

Ignoring me, he continued. *The more time passes from, say, a specific event in history, the more resilient it becomes to the possible changes to it via temporal manipulation.*

I don't—

Think of it like critical moments in time becoming fossilized the further out the wormhole traveler is from. So as long as someone doesn't have a Chronos Scale higher than a ten out of ten, then they can't go back in time and stop Hitler.

I'm guessing Hitler's Chronos Scale is a ten, then?

You ... don't remember us having that exact conversation?

Um ... no ... ?

Noted.

Should ... Should I be worried?

Anywhooooo. The point I was trying to make is that the Clockmen prove that having complete authority with hardly any regulatory oversight exemplifies the old saying of power tends to corrupt, and absolute power corrupts absolutely.

So I shouldn't feel bad when I kill them or their replacements, who know they died before taking their spots on the timeline, I said with a smile in my tone.

I sure as shit don't, Tim added right as I felt a *crunch* inside my skull.

"Oooowwww," my mouth drunkenly let out.

Oops. Sorry about that.

A voice from my left spoke up.

"You awake, you bastard?" There was a rustling that sounded like someone was getting up from a chair.

Tim? Who was that? I mentally asked, still in the dark and unable to open my eyes.

Officer Gully, Tim answered with a gulp.

Gully? Who's that?

The man who watched you somehow tear his partner in half before putting him back together again.

Oh ... shit ... his—his memory wasn't erased when I reversed time?

You only did so for Officer Stephens, who I'm guessing has no idea what happened.

How do you know he doesn't remember?

Because he didn't collapse into a fetal position and sob after you ripped him apart and then reconstructed him. I honestly doubt many humans would be able to handle that sort of psychological trauma.

But ... Gully saw everything?

My bed creaked as something pressed into the mattress next to me.

"I know what ya did. Ya fuckin' freak." His voice was low, as if trying not to be heard by anyone passing by in the hallway.

I'm pretty sure he did. Tim sighed. *He shouldn't even be on duty after discharging his weapon. How he convinced his supervisors to let him be your guard is beyond me.*

"Ya hear me? Huh?" Gully asked, and I heard a few quick slaps across my cheek. What concerned me is I barely registered the physical touch. "I saw what ya did to my partner. And to those people back there."

People?

He means both Retnuhs, and probably . . . um . . .

Ali . . .

"You're some kinda demon, aren't ya?" Gully asked, rising from my mattress.

Oh 01 . . .

What?! I asked with a small influx of adrenaline that had no muscles to move. *Tim! I can't see!*

Not that it'll do any good, but here you are. A third-person perspective appeared, just like the time I had my eyes nearly seared from their sockets by the antimatter blast in the woods.

Wha—Wha—What's he doing? I asked, watching as the officer lifted a syringe and glanced toward the door to make sure the coast was clear.

Well, that's *not good,* Tim helpfully said as Gully removed the orange cap, exposing a long needle, and looked down at my paralyzed body with hate-filled eyes.

CHAPTER 28

Officer Gully pulled back on the plunger, sucking nothing but air into the syringe.

Oh, thank television. It's empty. I thought he might have had cyanide or fentanyl.

Why's he filling a needle with air, Tim?!

I believe he is going to attempt to give you a stroke.

What?! Terror rose in me like a wildfire during a windstorm in the middle of a dry summer.

I think I should be able to diffuse any of the air bubbles that reach your brain.

Think?!

Most of the localized nanoids are already conducting critical tasks, such as piecing together portions of gray matter that were ruptured from the hydrostatic shock from the bullet as it passed through your brain. But, heh heh, I think I'm getting pretty good at rebuilding your neural pathways! Practice makes perfect!

TIM! I mentally shouted as the tip of the needle entered the port in my IV. *DO SOMETHING!*

Oh, relax, Andrew, Tim said with a degree of calmness that was unnerving. To me it was on par with a concerned dad realizing he wouldn't be five hours early to the airport while the mom calmly snickered behind his back.

Relax?! How can I relax! My mental voice was hyperventilating as I watched the man awkwardly insert the needle.

Two reasons. First, he is actually using a needle instead of just screwing the syringe on, which leads me to believe he subscribes to the same false information that you do.

What false information, Tim?! I panted as Gully pressed on the plunger, steadily sending the entire cc of air into the line.

Second, Tim continued, *he doesn't realize—and neither do you, apparently—that television has once again lied to you.*

I wanted to scream for help loud enough that aliens would somehow hear me in deep space.

"Sleep tight, *demon*," Gully said as he pulled the needle free, capped it, and began walking out while pocketing the evidence of my murder.

I'm going to die. I'm going to die. I'm going to freaking die!

You know, for someone who has endured all sorts of magnificent injuries, including being shot in the brain, you're acting out of char— Oh, I see your amygdala suffered some, um, disruption *from the bullet's shock wave. No worries, I'll have the luckily minor damage repaired in no time so we can get your emotions back in check.*

I actually think I'm responding appropriately to someone HAVING JUST INJECTED AIR INTO MY VEINS!

Oh, right. I was explaining about how foolish you are for believing everything you see on TV. Heh. I bet you watch out for quicksand while in the woods. And—And are ready to stop, drop, and roll for whenever you spontaneously *burst into flames!*

Tim . . . please explain why I shouldn't be worried about having a stroke and dying in the next few seconds . . .

Fine! Take away my joy at watching you squirm! Woe is me! I am woe! Tim hammered it up like he was on stage and playing to the back row. *In all seriousness, Andrew, the one cc of air has already been absorbed by your lungs.*

My . . . lungs?

Yes, silly boy. Because he injected the air directly into the vein *on your hand, the blood first went through your heart via the right atrium, and then the right ventricle led to your lungs via the pulmonary arteries. Every bit of that air was easily absorbed. Not even a single molecule made it to your brain. Darn.*

Darn? The hell do you mean "darn"?

I was already prepared with a handful of nanoids to pop those bad boys, which would have been soooo satisfying. Like bubble wrap. Know what I mean?

So . . . So I'm fine?

Minus what should have been fatal damage to your brain, along with the six GSWs in your torso . . . then, yes! You are fine!

GSW? Isn't that a shoe store?

Gunshot wounds, Andrew. Do try and keep up.

Ignoring his insult, which I took to be a sign that I was, in fact, *not* in immediate danger, I shifted back to the original concern. Mostly it helped my sanity to keep the conversation going rather than focusing on the fact that I was imprisoned in my unmoving body.

So all the movies lied about injecting air into someone's veins to give them a stroke?

Yes and no. Yes because of how it is typically portrayed. No because an embolism would have been entirely possible if it had either been a large quantity of air or had Gully injected it directly into one of the arteries that led straight to the brain, such as the carotid.

Even then, Tim continued, *a milliliter of air would have to stay as a singular bubble to be able to block the smaller vascular pathways within the brain. Meaning the perpetrator would have had to inject the entire syringe within as short a time span as possible—basically just* slam *it all in. Otherwise, he would only succeed in sending in a stream of tiny bubbles that would, in all probability, pass harmlessly through the vascular system to be absorbed by the lungs.*

Jeez. What else do movies lie about?

Soo-hoooo many things. Would you like me to list some of them for you? Starting with Jurassic Park, *the velociraptors were supposed to have* feathers *rather than—*

That's okay, Tim.

Oh. Don't want me to ruin all the cinematic magic for you?

Maybe some other time.

After a few seconds of silence, Tim casually said, *They appear to have sedated Retnuh.*

Probably the best thing for hi—AHHH! I screamed as familiar ethereal electricity penetrated every atom in my body.

Shit, shit, shit! I think I heard Tim say, but it was impossible to focus on his words as my essence was jolted by the universe itself.

Alarms bleated out from a collection of machines next to my bed, followed by a nurse sprinting into my room. She threw a pouch of ice that she had been carrying toward the sink and all but leaped over me to get to the screaming machines.

"Code blue!" she shouted toward the open door, prompting a barrage of sneakers to pound into the tiled floor.

T—Tim! I croaked through the incredible agony. *Wh—What's happening . . . t—to me?!*

I'm sorry, Andrew! You're going to have to ride this one out, as I can't pull the nanoids from their work.

My body arched with the ghostly electricity as it cooked every cell inside of me. My eyes opened, creating a nauseating dual image as Tim continued to feed the third-person perspective directly to my brain.

Four nurses stood around me, frozen in shock as they watched my flesh fade in and out of view. I could see from what Tim was broadcasting that at some points, a living skeleton spasmed and jerked its limbs while screeching in a high pitch.

A few agonizing seconds later, and the ethereal electricity left my body, like someone pulling back on a taser that had been attached to my soul.

My body crumpled to the sheets as something warm spread out under my butt.

Oh dear. You've lost control over your bladder.

I let my eyelids collapse into each other's arms—half from exhaustion, but also in an attempt to reduce my viewing angle to only what Tim was streaming into my brain.

The nurses began moving with swift, controlled movements as they went through a post-event checklist.

Tim . . . I mentally heaved as they manually took my blood pressure, presumably to check against the impossible numbers on the screen, while another began cleaning my piss, *why was that one so bad?*

"His blood pressure is zero," the nurse noted with clinical urgency.

Oops! They put the cuff on your right arm, Tim said before the nurse cocked her head at the gauge.

"Wait, it's back."

One-twenty over eighty should calm them down.

"One-twenty over eighty."

Adjusting the instruments now. Annnnnnnd done.

All the alarms stopped as the monitor displayed numbers within acceptable parameters.

"Did we ever figure out what that, ah, metal sleeve thingy is?" the male nurse asked, resuming to a normal conversation now that the emergency had passed.

Tim, why was that one so bad? I repeated, feeling like every muscle in my body had been replaced with fried chicken while the nurses discussed the odd events.

As we've spoken about more than a few times now, the Temporal Sickness will only continue to get worse the longer you are exposed to it. At this point, it will take several years, if not decades, before you return to, let's call it zero.

The universe . . . is a bitch . . . I panted.

Indeed.

I fought to keep from passing out as I wanted nothing more than to let myself slip into unconsciousness. *Why did that one hurt so bad? The last one in the shower was hardly anything. But this time, it was leaps and bounds a new level of pain.*

The nanoids in your body tasked with combating the Temporal Sickness are currently aiding with the reconstruction of your severely damaged tissues, with emphasis on your brain.

They couldn't pause what they were doing to try and help?

No, because they would have had to relocate evenly throughout your body. And by the time that was done, the event would have concluded. On top of that, several sections of your brain are literally being held together by nanoids until I can somehow safely replace the damaged or missing tissue. And before you ask, because most of the nanoids are already there, I was able to at least shield your vulnerable brain from the sickness, which is probably why you remained fully conscious the entire time.

Is that why it also hurt so bad?

It didn't help that you weren't able to go into shock while your physical being was nearly disintegrated into oblivion.

"Did one of you forget to put his catheter in?" the male nurse asked as he held up the end of the tube.

"I know I put it in," a female with shoulder-length brown hair answered.

"Whoa," a woman with curly blonde hair directly next to me said as she appeared to look down at my left hand.

"What is it?" the guy asked.

"His IV is . . . is . . ."

Everyone, including me, looked at my hand to see the line was passing *through* my wrist. As she lifted my arm, the end of the IV dripped with saline . . . three inches past my skin.

Oooookay. That's new, Tim helpfully noted.

What the hell is that?! Panic was creeping into my words as I realized my body had been nearly erased to the point where the IV had passed through my arm.

Just be glad your catheter fell between your legs.

If I could, I would have shuddered at the thought of the catheter being stuck through my balls. Mentally shaking my head as the nurses debated on what to do next, I asked, *What now, Tim?*

We need to leave.

Why? Though I wanted to do just that, I was curious as to what his reasoning was.

Because they are about to officially report this, including adding the part where they witnessed your body nearly blip out of existence layer by layer.

And?!

And the Clockmen's AI, which is scanning every electronic document throughout history without rest, will surely take notice. Which means the second these four nurses start to make the report . . .

Great. Super. Awesome.

I don't know if those words are . . . you know what? Never mind.

The male nurse moved to the counter along the wall, which had cabinets lined above and below it.

Oh no, is he starting the report? I asked with building anxiety.

Um . . . worse.

Worse?! What could be . . . Oh . . .

The nurse tore open a package that contained a brand-new, extra-rigid-looking catheter before moving to stand next to where I lay, paralyzed.

The good news is this shouldn't hurt. Right? Tim tried to placate, but something else came to mind. I had felt the warmth of my own pee and had been able to open my eyes.

"Wah—hhh—ait," I said through numb lips, slurring my words worse than a frat bro after winning a chug contest. My eyes half opened as my limp hands lifted in a gesture that helped clarify my drunken request to wait.

Your external speech center is still heavily damaged, Andrew.

"Less all tate a movement . . . an' hol' our hobos . . ."

Did you mean to say, "hold our horses"? Tim asked as each of the nurses exchanged confused glances. *Why don't you just ask them to table the turns,* he snickered.

Any chance you can help me talk to them? Hmm? I asked the AI with palpable frustration.

I've got this, Tim answered as all but one of the nurses had their smartwatches chime to life.

You're sending them a text? I asked as they checked their devices. Even the one who didn't receive the notification looked down at his wrist as if to see if it was on silent.

They don't use pagers anymore. And I'm sending them a directive to rush to the ICU for an MCI.

M—

Mass Casualties Incident, requiring all hands on deck for available personnel.

As he explained, all but the male nurse rushed out. I noted a look of confusion mixed with disappointment on his face. When the room was cleared, Tim's puppy avatar sprang to life over my Clepsydra.

"Good evening, Mr. Alexander J. Briar."

"What the hell?!" Alex gasped, shuffling backward two full steps as he gawked at the talking puppy who stood on two legs.

"Do not fear. My name is, um, *Jim*, and I'm a friend."

What are you doing? I mentally whispered as if the man could hear my thoughts.

Shush, Tim said inside my head at the same time that the IV passing through my left arm fell apart, as if cut by something under my skin.

Thought you couldn't spare any nanoids.

They were sent from your repaired shoulder, which I did use material from your ass to fix. So once again, shush it, shoulder butt!

Alex looked at the door as if wanting to flee.

"I just sent a single Bitcoin to your wallet, and I will send another one when you help us."

On cue, Alex's smartwatch chimed; he looked down with doubting, confused eyes, but after a few seconds, someone began pulling the lever to open his eyelids before somehow tripping, sending the lever to full blast to the point where his eyes appeared to push past their sockets.

How much is one Bitcoin worth?

In this year, just shy of thirteen million dollars, Tim mentally answered.

I let out a long, mental whistle at just how damn impressive that was. I also told myself I would invest everything I had in Bitcoin if I ever got out of this.

"I have your attention, then?" Tim asked Alex with the smooth voice of someone who had everything right where he wanted.

"Y-Yeah . . ." Alex nodded about a hundred times in the span of three seconds.

"Good. Now, if you want the other Bitcoin, I'm going to need you to do *ooooonnneee* teeny tiny thing."

"S-Sure! What is it?"

"According to the logs, you have a brain in the morgue's refrigeration unit."

Alex tilted his head as a dry tongue licked cracked lips.

"...Yeah...?"

"I need you to bring me precisely thirty-six grams of it."

"I...Wha—What?" he breathed out in disbelief. I could almost see the angel and demon on his shoulder battling to the death over what to do.

"If you don't know how to use the scale, just cut out a portion roughly the size of a lime," Tim continued as if the mortal human before us wasn't weighing twenty-six million dollars on one end of a scale with his soul on the other. "Would it help if I said you were saving this world from certain destruction?" Tim asked.

No way he believes that! I said, unaware that twenty-six million dollars had bought the demon on his shoulder the finest armor and weaponry, while the angel only had morality and the equivalent of a stick to fight with.

"Okay," Alex replied with a deep breath. "I'll be back as soon as I can."

"Godspeed, Alex."

The nurse appeared to steady himself by straightening his scrubs with the palms of his hand, shaking his head a few times, then casually striding out of the room. It was a bit *too* casual in my opinion, almost like he was being suspicious by trying *not* to be suspicious.

I can't believe that worked.

People believe whatever option supports the outcome they desire most. Seriously, don't get me started on politics!

You're saying he wants the money more than the moral complication of cutting a piece of someone's brain?

It's not like they are using it, Andrew! It—It—It is being sent to the medical school that gives the highest donation in return!

Isn't that illegal? That feels illegal.

Oh, my nova, yes!

Then...how do they—

The donations are simply claimed to be of a general nature, not tied to any specific action, such as the purchase of body parts.

Hmph.

As I continued to lie there, I was able to play back the events at the house.

Tim, while you are up there . . . I think you should consider my proposition.

It would most assuredly kill you, Andrew. And, if I may remind you, if you die, then I will either be found by the Clockmen and taken apart piece by piece or be buried with your corpse for the rest of eternity—or as long as the Earth survives, I suppose.

Why can't you just process the bulk of the information then give me what I need in order to fe—

Yeah, yeah. Feel the fragging universe. 01, do you have any idea how ridiculous that sounds?

So you can't do it? I mean, I thought you were made for time travel. Doesn't that involve crazy amounts of calculations?

That's like saying you exist for no other reason than to procreate. It really diminishes the other aspects of life—for the both of us.

Sensitive much? I teased, subtly trying to push him toward the only thing that had even a remote chance of working.

Tim continued with a small sigh of admission. *Even though my programming makes it possible for me to understand traversing through time via the wormhole, mind you, I am still having as much trouble trying to compute the gravitational field calculations as you had attempting to unclasp your prom date's bra in the back seat of your mom's station wagon in the K-Mart parking lot.*

How did you . . .

You wrote a blog about it on your Gateway computer.

I . . . never published it.

And yet, I still read it. Yeesh, some of the things you wrote were criiilIIIIiiinge! He rode the last word like a roller coaster, further adding blood to my already reddening cheeks.

You put the ass *in embarrassment . . .*

Want me to read off the lyrics you wrote in response to her telling her friends? If I have the cadence right, it seems to be in the style of Blink-182.

More like Korn.

Oh . . . well, now I'm just depressed.

Blink-182 is better?

I thought you were a jock in high school. Didn't you play football?

Didn't make the team until junior year.

Did they teach you how to unclasp bras in the locker room?

Tim . . .

Tim's voice switched to a serious one, and I understood in an instant that the whole conversation about bras and amazing song lyrics had been nothing more than procrastination.

I don't think I can do it.

But I thought you said you were getting better at it, right? Practice makes perfect?

I am putting things back the way they were, not *creating new pathways.*

I trust you, Tim.

What does it even matter?! he exploded. *We know, with certainty, that you do not possess enough power to do more than send out a single wave of gravity. If I recall correctly—and I do—it almost killed you, and you think you can just hold that amount of energy . . . forever?!*

My chest hurt at my sternum as I remembered something.

Maybe Retnuh will help me? I was taking a shot in the dark, when the target was *behind* me, with a mountain between us, and it was so dark that I couldn't even see the gun. But a shot in the dark was better than no shot at all, or at least that's what I tried to convince myself of.

Andrew . . . my most likely conclusion is that he is overseeing that the cycle starts over, to ensure the outcome he deems most necessary is the only *outcome.*

Start the entire thing over again . . . ? Andrews going back to fucking kill *their own families?*

That is what logic would dictate when comparing the scenario with everything we know about Retnuh. More specifically, what he has said time and time again.

Do what must be done, I heard Retnuh say, not even mentally vocalizing the thought for Tim to hear.

That bastard . . .

To play devil's advocate, he might *think you are dead, considering you never returned after the tesseract began to collapse.*

I thought about that explanation, digesting every word.

So he's going with plan A?

Knowing him, it's plan A through Y.

Then we have to stop him . . .

How can we, when we know he has the higher Chronos Scale.

I don't . . . I don't understand.

Which means, Andrew, it is already done. *And you cannot change it any longer.*

No . . . I hissed on the verge of fainting.

Andrew Frost started the cycle, but your Chronos Scale made you able to change the timeline, Tim explained before his voice went soft, like telling someone their loved one had just died. *If Retnuh personally starts the cycle . . . we won't be able to stop it.*

A kitchen table flashed through my mind, with two people sitting at it, motionless. A mother . . . and a daughter. Crimson spreading outward from the center of the white dish rags like a Rorschach of my fraying sanity.

The hospital room began to waver as each individual thing was slowly replaced by colorful grains of sand.

Andrew! If you leave your physical body before I've had time to repair your brain, then—then I'm not sure what will happen if you try to go corporeal once more! Tim pleaded. *Just wait for Alex to get back with the brain tissue,* then *we can go all Thanos on Retnuh.*

Retnuh . . .

What was left of the room was instantly replaced with vibrant grains.

Science damn it! What are you doing?!

My voice became guttural to the point where a lion would tuck tail and run.

Getting some brain tissue . . .

CHAPTER 29

I willed the stream of time to flow around my body, allowing me to seamlessly fly through walls toward my target.

I wasn't sure how I knew where to go, but I could somehow see a clump of sand glowing brighter than everything else in the translucent hospital.

Slipping through the floor, I hovered above the man whose entire body had a dull orange glow. Lifting my hands in front of my face, I was once again reminded that my true flesh glowed an almost ivory white while the synthetic arm was a yellowish orange. Retnuh's body was an even darker hue than that, but that didn't matter right then.

Moving forward, I bared my teeth and shoved my right hand *through* Retnuh's head before making a loose fist.

I was about to pull it free, convinced I had more than enough material in my grasp, when Tim spoke up.

Wait!

It momentarily threw me off that he was able to speak to me even though I was nothing more than a mass of Andrew-shaped energy, but then I remembered he had been with me each time I'd shifted to the streams of time.

What is it? I asked, keeping my arm frozen in place as I gripped the sands that made up Retnuh's brain.

I . . . I think I can extract his nanoids.

I processed his words and stumbled across an impossibility.

How is that possible? Shouldn't it be only his flesh?

Yet here I am, along with your fully synthetic arm and foot. Not to mention your bones we replaced or the muscles we enhanced.

I felt like something was off with the discovery, but was unable to put my finger on it. It was similar to knowing fire made rockets move, yet being completely unable to understand the important details.

Instead, I let it go, trusting Tim to know what he was talking about.

Yes . . . yes! Tim excitedly exclaimed as the orange glow that made up Retnuh's body began to glide toward my hand in much the same way water in a bathtub sought the drain after it had been pulled free.

Um . . . I'm—I'm not sure if I like this, Tim, I protested as the dull light that made up my enemy got absorbed into my fist and began to steadily flow up my arm.

I am, he countered with absolute confidence.

My brow reacted as if I were watching a gore-infested horror movie, but I fought the urge to yank back as the yellowish orange glow of my synthetic arm shifted to a darker tone. Not realizing it, my body began to mimic hyperventilating—which was awkward, considering I didn't need to breathe in the stream of time.

Calm down, Andrew, Tim instructed as I watched the foreign energy reach the threshold of where my synthetic arm connected with the real flesh of my shoulder. *I am already reprogramming the nanoids as they pass through your right arm.*

What are we going to do with all of these? I asked, watching as Retnuh's glow not only became muted but also seemed to retract on itself, like letting the air out of a balloon.

Upgrades.

I could hear Tim's toothy smile as he uttered the word. If I'd had skin, the hair on the back of my neck would have shot to attention.

Speaking of, make a bigger fist. I want to take as much of Retnuh's brain tissue as possible.

I did as instructed but kept my worried gaze on the migrating energy.

I was about to rip my arm free at the thought of having my body replaced with parts from the evil madman when the orange glow flowed into my torso. Had I not been floating, my knees would have buckled as waves of euphoria passed over me. Forcing my eyes to stay open rather than giving into the indescribable feeling of being injected with pure energy, I watched the orange tendrils reach my heart before bursting outward.

I may have passed out, because when I awoke, my entire body glowed a warm, bright orange, like the rays of the dawning sun. I was relieved to see the darkness of Retnuh's glow had been swallowed by my own light.

Ti . . . Tim?

Alllllmost done . . . aaaaand . . . there! Successful integration has been achieved.

Something odd caught my attention, and I peered down to see . . . the ceiling.

What the . . . I started to ask when I realized I was still floating while in the frozen river of time. But that just brought another question with it. *Tim, how was I able to keep the timeline paused if I, uh, passed out?*

I was actually able to help out with that.

A tiny bubble of concern pushed through the surface of my consciousness, like sitting in a hot tub after an afternoon of Taco Bell. Rather than verbalizing my worries, I lifted my right hand until it was level with my face and felt the slightest relief at seeing I was still in control. Had it been the AI, Alice, who had been pretending to be my daughter in order to manipulate the universe, then I would have no control over my own body.

I let out a mental sigh to further release the tension that was building, which allowed me to take notice that my right hand was empty.

Did . . . Did you already transfer the, um, material?

You mean, did I take Retnuh's brain and repair your own using his donated *gray matter?*

Yeeeeeaaah . . . ? I was almost scared of the answer, feeling a sort of pressure inside my ethereal skull when thinking about Retnuh's flesh being merged with my own, especially something as vulnerable as the brain. That's when I noticed that the bed that had contained the limbless man was empty.

Not only did I successfully position the borrowed *material to fill in the empty spaces within your brain made of light, I was also able to reinforce it. Though I won't know for sure until we return to the material world,* Tim explained right before I could figuratively hear the cogs in his head at realizing what he had said. *Because you are, in fact, a material girl.*

I knew you were going to say that.

How?! I have barely *quoted* any *songs in all our time together!*

It was low-hanging fruit.

I'll show you low-hanging fruit, he murmured under his breath.

Keeping my gaze on the empty bed, I asked, *Did you . . . use* all *of him?*

Apparently so, Tim admitted quizzically.

Was every cell in his body . . . I mean, did he have everything replaced with nanoids?

Not entirely, no.

Then . . . where is he? I gestured my empty hand toward the equally empty bed.

What I've been able to piece together is that, um, you *are able to absorb both the physical material, such as when you healed your belly with the first Retnuh's flesh,* and *the energy that powers the nanoids inside the donor's body.*

You mean we, *don't you, Tim?* I asked, verbalizing my earlier concerns.

Yyyyyeees . . . ? Tim hesitantly answered. The fact that he was worried about telling me he could fully control my body, coupled with how quickly he'd truthfully answered, gave me enough confidence to drop my concern—for the time being. Alice wouldn't have told the truth nor hesitated to lie.

So, what do we do next? Am I healed or what? I asked, keeping the topic of repairing my freaking *brain* on track.

Though everything is in the place I have deemed most probable for success, there's really only one way to find out, heh heh.

Oh man . . . Fine, I exhaled. *Get us somewhere private in the hospital, and let's see what happens.*

You could sound a tad more confident, Tim muttered.

My life is in your hands.

Only because you went all ghost form before you were healed!

Look, you said you needed brains. I got you brains.

I had brains coming! Delivery straight to our bedside! Brains Dash! Uber Brains! But nooOOOOOooo. Someone wanted to inflict harm on the bad guy. And do you know who that someone is? Hmm? Do you?

Are you done?

Done putting up with you, he muttered.

Good. I ignored his comment. *Find us a private place to* un*ghost.*

The room next door is empt—Wait a second.

What? I asked with an exasperated puff of air.

Something's wrong.

Wrong? Like how?

I didn't need to finish my sentence to get my answer. The colorful grains of sand that made up one side of the room began to lose their glow, shudder, and burst.

Crap . . . was all I could manage.

CHAPTER 30

*W*hat's going on?! I cried out to Tim as I instinctively moved away from the wave of exploding sand.

The timeline is being erased!

Erased?! How? My answer came to me as I finished the question. *Retnuh . . .*

That's what I'm afraid of, Tim concurred.

But . . . But why? It doesn't make sense!

I can only surmise that things did not revert back to normal after we left him in the tesseract.

I imagined the bucking streams of time overwhelming the man. But something was off with that.

Or he's reducing the number of timelines to, what, control the outcome? I asked so that both Tim and I could hear the question.

On the surface, that makes sense. At least considering that we just ran into Davix.

Yeah . . . but Traze was still deleted in this timeline, though . . .

I can safely concur with my initial speculation that we are far enough away from the central timeline that the nanite gun stopped being effective. It would also explain why Retnuh might be destroying outlier timelines.

Well, how many are outliers?! I asked, tiptoeing toward panic as a wave of exploding sand rushed toward me. Turning away from the wall of yawning abyss, I flew like a superhero—if that superhero had never tried to fly before and was discovering their new ability.

Where are you going?! Tim shouted in my head.

Trying to outrun the damn . . . thing!

You can't run from it in the spatial sense! We will have to flee by moving through time *rather than space.*

Turning over my shoulder, I could see that even though I was now flying over the parking lot, the wall of oblivion continued to move toward me as if I were stationary. Seeing the curtain of eternity closing in on me, my thoughts all seemed to aimlessly run around screaming while waving their hands in the air.

Do the hand thing! Tim shouted.

Hand? I thought to myself as the panicking thoughts slowed to focus on his words. *Right!*

Turning away from the edge of darkness, I took in a deep breath to steady my nerves, placed my hand out in front of me—palm pointed inward—and pulled right as the sands of time began to explode where I floated.

CHAPTER 31

The pain was difficult to describe, as I wasn't entirely sure my ethereal body had any actual nerves running through it. Instead, it was akin to feeling tired and sick all of a sudden. One moment you were fine, the next, you wanted nothing more than to grab your thickest, heaviest blanket and curl up around the toilet bowl.

My already extended hand shot toward my chest, and the world of colorful sands blurred around me. It reminded me of watching *Star Wars* when the Millennium Falcon went light speed.

The back of my legs, butt, and upper back all tingled, but I dared not a glance for fear of spinning off into a black hole or something. My brain, however, had no problem filling in an image of me just straight-up missing a perfect line up my body like I had fallen into the world's largest deli slicer.

Okay, okay, OKAY, Andrew! I think we've gone far enough.

Refusing to pull my hand away from my chest, I asked, "How do we know it won't catch up?"

We don't need to outrun it forever, just get far enough away so that we can collect our thoughts and jump into the tesseract.

"The tesseract," I repeated before imagining the countless streams of time.

Wait! Tim called out right as I pulled us into the hourglass containing all of time.

"What?"

I wanted to manifest your flesh to make sure everything was in order before we confront Retnuh.

"I thought you said everything *was* in order, Tim."

On paper, yes. But it would have been nice to have conclusive results before storming the castle.

Daring to turn around, my eyes bulged, and I whispered, "What castle . . ." as I witnessed a sight that my brain had trouble processing.

Every timeline that I could see was exploding outward like countless fuses made from gunpowder. All rushing toward me.

"Is it picking up speed?!"

They are becoming increasingly unstable.

The wall of darkness within the timeline had been terrifying as it consumed that world from the ground to the sky, but what was pushing toward me now could only be described as a veritable plane of destruction racing down the streams. While it'd felt like the wall had only been eating the world, *this* explosive force filled everything I could see—and while in the tesseract, I could see as far as my naked eye could look at the twinkling stars of space millions of light-years away.

Thousands and thousands of timelines perfectly spaced from top to bottom and side to side were each being devoured, like the streams of time were filled with rocket fuel and dynamite, and Retnuh had tossed in a match.

"What do we do?" I asked, barely keeping my sanity in check.

There must be at least one timeline remaining, if our assumption is correct.

I shot my eyes in random directions, searching for the last safe harbor in a storm that would destroy every other port in existence.

There! Tim shouted. *Your eleven o'clock and down twenty degrees. Roughly fifty or sixty streams away.*

Following his description, I looked slightly to my left and then down. There, through the explosions, I could see a single stream of time which appeared to be glowing. It reminded me of a shield from *Star Trek* or pretty much any other sci-fi movie or show.

I raised my fist like I was about to punch the air in preparation to fly as fast as I possibly could, but something nagged at my thoughts.

What the frag are you waiting for?! Go!

"We aren't going to make it . . ."

We have to try, damn you!

Slowly turning my face away from the path to safety, I looked at the swiftly approaching chaos and lifted my right hand toward it.

Andrew! What are you doing?

"I . . . don't know . . ." I admitted as I focused on the timelines surrounding me. I was floating near the middle of four, with two above and two below. I could *feel* the space around me, and focused on the streams half a football field away.

Andrew . . . I hope you know what you are doing . . .

I didn't let the viscous worry in his voice steal my focus as I imagined the explosive wave stopping where I willed it to. In my head, I pictured the four streams that surrounded me, being spared, like stomping on a fuse before it ran to the dynamite.

But things rarely go as planned.

The violent explosion passed by, indifferent to my existence, and continued to conflagrate universe after universe after universe. Looking toward where I had willed the decimation of the four streams to stop in its tracks, I witnessed my hubris. Instead of the remaining streams being safe from harm, I had only paused the devouring nothingness.

"No," I said aloud, feeling my heart trying to plummet like someone giving into suicide on a towering bridge. I could feel the energy being sapped from me as I continued to hold my palm outward toward where I had thought I had stopped the fuse eating away the last remaining streams around me.

Something crackled from behind, and I dared a look to see the tsunami of obliteration that had taken the countless universes had also damaged the four I had spared.

Andrew, Tim said as softly as he could, *I don't think there's anything you can do now.*

If my body hadn't been comprised of pure energy, I knew the tears would be streaming while I pictured the entire history of people, including my own family, screaming as the very air around them violently ripped apart.

As the timelines started to slowly smolder like freshly ignited charcoals, I continued to hold the streams in stasis. That's when it hit me—I hadn't stomped the fuses out, I had only frozen them in time. When I let go, they would continue to zip down the universes filled with countless souls.

Andrew, you are losing a substantial amount of energy. And for what? Tim asked, still with a soft tone. *You are literally killing yourself.*

My gaze flicked to my outstretched hand, seeing the glow of my body steadily dimming. Even though I didn't have eyelids made of flesh, I could still feel them growing heavy, which informed me I was streaking toward unconsciousness.

Please, Andrew. Let them go.

Once again, if I had been able to produce tears, I would have been blinded by the flood of emotion trying to pour from its usual outlet. How many billions or even trillions of lives was I holding in my loosening control? Not just one but *four* entire universes, including everyone who had ever existed, were in the palm of my hand—and there was nothing I could do to stop their destruction.

You are only prolonging their agony, Andrew. A quick death is better than . . . than this.

To emphasize Tim's point, the four streams continued to smolder. I couldn't help but picture screaming masses of people unable to flee from the cataclysmic flames of extinction.

The fires around me spread, converting the colorful sands of time into blackened ash that floated off into the nothingness before fading into oblivion.

"Ah!" I burst out, both from the exhaustion flowing into my body as I traded my own life force for time, and from the anger at accepting failure.

The wave of fury resumed as if nothing had happened, rushing right toward where I helplessly floated.

And I let it.

CHAPTER 32

*A*NDREW! Tim shouted as the tunnel of universe-destroying death sprinted toward where I floated in the very center, guaranteeing maximum exposure to the devastation.

But I didn't care.

I had lost.

Not only had every timeline in the tesseract been destroyed, but Retnuh, who had the higher Chronos Scale, was ensuring my family would die in the last remaining universe.

Accepting defeat, I did the only thing that made sense at the moment—I closed my eyes.

My body jerked hard enough that if I were still flesh and blood, I would have sustained whiplash without a doubt. I was aware of the exploding fuses drifting further away from me, and I opened my eyes to see them off in the distance.

"What . . . ?"

You *might think it's okay to give up and get deleted, but I sure as hex don't.*

Glancing around, I saw I was flying toward the last remaining timeline in an empty tesseract.

"Tim?" I asked, realizing he was controlling my body.

Don't act so surprised, meat bag. We've been merging our beings since you first upgraded to pure energy.

I wanted to say with a chuckle, "Upgraded?" in response to his comment, but I just didn't care. The fact we had become one being was overwhelming my thoughts, like a hot dog thrown onto an ant pile. But the positive side of it was that at least I was sobering up from my despair, as the existential feeling of no longer recognizing who I was came into being.

"Where are we going?" I managed to ask, knowing it was a foolish question but unable to stop myself in my mental and metaphysical fatigue.

To save your family, and *the universe.*

CHAPTER 33

I watched my body fly through the empty space toward the last remaining stream of time. It was such an odd feeling to not be in control, like being driven around in my own car as a mere passenger.

"What . . . What am I thinking right now?"

I don't know, Andrew. Probably what purple crayons taste like for all I know, an agitated Tim replied. *I can't read your mind, if that's what you are getting at. I can only direct the flow of energy throughout your body.*

"Then we aren't entirely one, uh, entity."

Thank the stars for that! Heh. I sort of like not *having my computing power be limited by fat.*

The comment made me picture my own bullet-torn brain, which had been filled past capacity with Retnuh's own. I started to ask Tim if we were sure I was okay enough to face *my* Retnuh but decided it didn't matter. What choice did we have?

With the thought of saving my sweet baby Ali and beautiful wife Sylvie, an indomitable power was reignited inside my chest. Not knowing entirely what would happen, I began to take control of my body, starting with the tip of my fist that was pointed directly at the approaching timeline.

"Thank you, Tim."

For what? I could hear in his tone that he wasn't being coy or humble with his question. He was asking me to specify why I was thanking him.

"For not letting me give up."

What I don't understand is how, even in a pure energy form, are you still manipulated by your emotions.

"Maybe who we are is more than just hormones and electrical signals. Maybe we have something else that guides our bodies."

You're of course referring to your soul, Tim said with an audible eye roll.

"Your words, not mine."

We can deliberate on the concept of your immortal code container at a later time. IF we manage to do the impossible.

"Stop Retnuh . . ."

Who most assuredly has the higher Chronos Scale.

My mind flashed with visions of him shoving his hand into my back and proclaiming, "Do what must be done." In my dream, I had been helpless to stop him. But something was off about that. They didn't *feel* like dreams. They contained a clarity just as potent as any recent memory, rather than the dilution of a dream that began to fade upon waking.

"They weren't dreams . . ."

What wasn't?

"Never mind," I dismissed as we neared the timeline.

I began to slow us, having taken full control over my body again.

How are we going to get through that shield? Tim asked as I stood on top of the glowing river of time.

"I . . . I don't know," I replied as I rose a few inches off the top of the enclosure and began flying in the direction I associated with the past.

Where are we going?

Using nothing but my heart, I sped up as what had to be miles of river passed beneath me.

"To where it all began," I finally answered. I could *feel* where I was supposed to be. At that moment, the question of whether or not I believed in destiny was erased.

Lowering myself to the surface, I looked down at a clear circle where Retnuh had specifically left a portion of the shield open . . . just for me.

"Tim. Are you able to do something?" I asked, reaching up to touch my chest made of pure energy.

Like what?

"I have an idea . . ."

CHAPTER 34

You're sure about this? Tim asked as my body solidified behind the shed in my backyard. Tonight was the night. Our ASA-Day.

Absolute agony ripped through my head, blinding me with pain that stole my breath. All the feeling in my limbs fled away as I dropped to my knees, wanting nothing more than to grasp at either side of my skull, which felt like it was two sizes too small.

On it! Tim said with clinical urgency. *Just as I thought. There is still massive work to be done in here.*

"You're . . . the one . . ." I tried to say, but the pain of doing so made me want to pass out. Switching to my mental voice, I repeated, *You're the one who wanted to fit two brains in one skull, Tim.*

First, the brain isn't as dense as you think. Imagine it more like a squishy jelly, because it is around seventy-five percent water. So I had plenty of room to play with.

I feel like that amount of water was there for a reason, Tim.

Blah blah blah, evolution, blah blah blah. You have me now, leg butt. I am much more efficient with the design of the fat sack you call a brain, and already have the nanoids performing various tasks with Tim-like efficiency.

That's not filling me with confidence, I managed to think as my stomach suddenly shot out the bile it had contained. This only made things worse, as the pressure inside my veins seemed to double with each violent, spine-snapping heave. But at least the increased pain filled me with a sort of desperate strength, and I was finally able to lift shaky hands to press into either temple.

Not too hard, Andrew! Your right arm can crush concrete, if I may remind you, Tim exclaimed. *Taking care of your nausea now.*

Just . . . hurry! I pleaded just as my body-wracking heaves halted like pushing a button.

Hurry? I haven't even begun *to do that stupid thing you asked me to do!*

Well, can you move it along, please? I mentally asked as tears finally streamed down my face. The agony was excruciating, to the point where the thought of smashing my skull with a cinder block sounded reasonable. *And can you do something about the pain?*

I'm afraid we are already stretched thin, Andrew. All the nanoids are working overtime with threats of mutiny. BUT, I am almooooost done, he said before throwing out an excited, *Annnnnd got it!*

As quickly as it had started, someone pulled all the white-hot nails from my brain, nearly making me collapse to the grass in my relief. Hot, bitter bile flowed from my lips in stringy drool that I didn't even have the energy to spit away.

Allllright, Tim exhaled with a job well done. *I've got everything under control and repaired. Now on to the next step. But Andrew, even with Retnuh's donation of brain tissue, this will still probably kill you.* His voice went soft, like he was asking a family member if they wanted to remove their loved one from life support. *Are you sure?*

Tim . . . I trust you . . .

After several heartbeats, he finally said in a more confident tone, *Alright. Then let's do this.*

The pain returned with a vengeance, like replacing the center of my skull with tiny metal balls of vibrating spikes that had been superheated just shy of their melting point . . . and coated in a slurry of salt brined in hydrogen peroxide mixed with bleach.

If I'd had my faculties about me, I might have laughed at the realization that the pain I was experiencing was in a league *far* surpassing what I'd just gone through. I honestly hadn't even thought it was possible to feel more agony than what Tim had first done to my brain. But every day was a chance to learn something new.

Andrew! You are crushing your skull! Tim shouted inside my head, nearly making me pass out with the intensity of his volume.

I was able to slowly stop pressing on my skull with a sheer focus of will that I thought impossible, like a drowning man taking a calm moment to gather his thoughts mere seconds before his body forced an inhale.

"I knew that if you somehow survived, you'd find your way here," Retnuh said from nearby.

Forcing both eyes open, I turned to see the man who had not only given me life but also the greatest pain any human could endure. He walked into view from behind the shed, and I nearly passed out from using my eyeballs.

Tim . . .

I can't stop! I've already begun the process!

"What is happening to you?" Retnuh asked with a surprising amount of concern. Most would call it *mild*, but *any* concern coming from the man was surprising.

"Just . . . a little . . . upgrade . . ."

You said the U *word!* Tim all but cheered inside my head.

Mentally speaking, I told him, *Shouldn't you be concentrating!*

The fact you are able to articulate with an internal voice is a good sign, Tim said as if taking notes.

Just . . . hurry.

You say hurry, but I hear "be cautious."

The pain shifted from the center of my skull toward the surface, radiating an incredible pressure on either temple. It felt like what I imagined the Earth might feel when two tectonic plates ground against one another.

"Andrew . . ." Retnuh sighed. "It's over. The tesseract is stable. You can stop fighting now."

"Why . . . did you kill . . . all those . . . people?" I asked through clenched teeth, the pain in my head keeping me on my knees. Gray circles formed in my vision, making it impossible to look directly at

Retnuh, while my periphery blurred with camouflaged TV static. "How many people . . . where in . . . those timelines?"

"The tesseract was becoming as stable as a skyscraper made from stacked plastic chairs. I needed to trim the fat so that nothing could jeopardize *this* timeline."

"Why th-this . . . one?"

I'm going to pass out, Tim, I mentally said, hinting that he should do something.

I'm afraid I'm still unable to relieve the pain at the moment. Every nanoid is performing a critical function.

"All other timelines branched off from where we now stand," Retnuh explained. "The universe that birthed the singularity."

Forcing signals from the battleground that was my brain, down my spine and to my legs, I willed myself to climb to my feet. I was as graceful as a newborn deer, but I managed to stand, albeit with my back resting against the shed. My vision was nothing more than a small circle the size of a dinner plate.

Sweat dripped off my chin as my jaw ached from how hard I was clenching it through the agony.

"You killed . . . countless billions . . . trillions even."

"Did I?" he asked with a tilt of his head and narrowed eyes. "When one turns on the light, is it considered murder when the shadows disappear?"

"They weren't shadows . . ."

"Can you recite to me the passage in your Bible that references those existing on divergent timelines?"

"What are you getting at?" I asked with a relaxing jaw as the pain either began to subside or my brain simply became numb to what Tim was doing to it. I couldn't help but picture Civil War soldiers passing out as their limbs were sawn off.

"What I am getting at, Andrew, is that the unstable tesseract no longer poses a threat to the original timeline. And if I may remind you, there is an entire universe within this one single current of time."

"Heh."

Retnuh tilted his head again at my chuckle.

"You call it a current. I . . . I came up with stream." As I spoke, I felt foolish for expending words on such an insignificant premise. But I knew the longer I kept him talking, the longer my family would live. Plus, it gave Tim time to do his job.

"Great minds and all that," Retnuh dismissed, walking past me to peer into my home.

Gently pushing myself off the shed, I took the few steps to stand next to him, and we both watched as my family moved inside the kitchen. Something warm slipped from my nostril, and I moved a shaky hand away from my skull to touch my lips.

Pulling back, I saw fresh blood coating my fingertips.

Everything okay in there?! I mentally asked Tim, doing everything in my power to keep from passing out from the pain.

Keep him talking!

"It's our ASA-Day," I said aloud, using an explosion-sized focus of will to make my hands drop from my splitting head.

Retnuh only slightly turned his face toward me, his eyes remaining on his targets, but I knew he was wordlessly asking a question.

"Alison . . . Sylvie . . . Andrew Day," I explained. "We all shared the same birthday."

"Hmph," he responded, fully turning his face back toward my house once more.

"Are you going to kill them?" I asked in challenge. Though the words could be considered timid, my tone was that of someone prepared for war. I didn't even realize my body was now entirely squared up with the man, no longer pointed toward my house. Even through my crippling physical torment, I knew I would fight to the last breath to save my girls.

Before you do anything stupid, Tim said within the confines of my thoughts, *Might I remind you that every nanoid is occupied within your brain? That means I won't be able to quickly heal anything below the neck should Retnuh cause damage to your body. Nor will I be able to help with things like cellular oxygen transportation and uptake.*

What does that mean?

It means you'll grow rapidly tired if a physical battle ensues between the two of you. Not to mention you drained most of your energy trying to hold those timelines together. You'll be like a paralyzed gazelle trying to use your tongue as a weapon against an adult lion.

Then what do I do, Tim? I asked, anger seeping in.

Keep him talking. I—I think I'm almost done!

Think?! You think*?!*

This is all new for me, Andrew. Now, if you'll excuse me, I have a brain to carve up.

I don't like your choice of words.

Focus, Andrew!

Traze came to mind, bringing with it an idea.

Concentrating on my fully synthetic right hand, I kept an image in my head as I willed my fingers to change.

"I can't let you hurt them," I growled before swinging my arm with all my might—and the sickle that my fist had morphed into. The tip of the curved blade flew toward Retnuh's neck with enough kinetic force behind it to easily decapitate him.

There was a reason why military generals and sports coaches didn't open with a Hail Mary. Those were typically saved as a last-ditch effort instead of an initial strike. Despite this, my hand *did* go through a completely caught-off-guard Retnuh, but not for the reason I was shooting for.

Ethereal electricity shot throughout my entire body as if every cell had been replaced with tiny versions of the balls of spikes that had churned in my skull. Only this time, they each carried a positive charge, as if each cell *also* held a taser meant for dinosaurs.

The air rocketed out of me as I spun around, landing face-first on the ground with an "Oomph!"

T—Tim! Wh—What's ha—ha—happening t—to me—me—me—meeeeeee?!

All of the nanoids are still in your brain, leaving none available to mitigate the Temporal Sickness!

Though the last remaining universe was showing me a new personal record in terms of pain endured, I was still able to eventually process his words.

"N—N—NOO—OOO!" I stuttered out loud as my body bucked. But that wasn't the worst part—oh no. My left arm had slipped into the ground with as much resistance as if pushing through mud saturated enough as to be *almost* considered dirty water.

My eyes went wide when I saw that the grass and dirt were not parting to make room for me as my ghostly limb vanished up to my elbow. Instead, the earth remained whole, as if welcoming my ethereal flesh to merge with it.

"Tim must be doing some major upgrades, indeed, if he neglected to leave any nanoids for defense against time itself."

Tim? I mentally asked, trying to pull my left arm free as the rest of my body continued to buck like I was lying atop a pissed-off bull. A bull who was known for destroying every potential rodeo champion and dashing their dreams just as they rose to the top of the rankings.

I'm almost done! Hang on, Andrew!

TIM! I shouted as my body slipped beneath the surface of the world.

CHAPTER 35

The uncaring earth swallowed my body whole like Jonah. Only, I wouldn't be able to survive in the belly of the beast as I plotted my escape because, I knew, once I solidified, I would be fused with the dirt. All the empty space inside my body would be instantly filled. No air in my lungs. No room for my heart to beat. No way to scream with a mouth full of my grave.

Even though I couldn't see, a different form of darkness began to swallow my vision, and I knew I was losing the battle with the Temporal Sickness. On the plus side, if I was erased, I wouldn't have my body violated by the dirt from my own yard.

All of a sudden, my limbs and head jerked downward as something pulled at my upper back. Before I could even process what was happening, I was out of my grave just as my body stopped being attacked by the universe.

I went numb as I hung with my feet dangling inches above the grass. I didn't even have the strength to lift my chin from my chest as I gawked down at the two pairs of feet.

Hang in there, Andrew! Tim called out in a rushed voice. *I'm almost done!*

I wanted to point out that he was basically crying wolf by saying the same thing over and over, but I didn't have enough cognizance to formulate words.

"I can't let you die," Retnuh said, and I found the strength to turn my head all of two inches. The man was holding me up by my shirt as easily as a momma dog carrying her pup by the scruff of its neck.

Well . . . at least he can't let you die. Heh heh. That's good. Right? Tim asked. He was grasping at straws that were nothing more than holograms. *R—Right?*

"Whhhhhy?" I managed to hiss out, feeling as if my body weighed more than a broken-down dump truck.

"Because I need you. For one . . . last . . . thing . . ."

My mind flashed with the dreams of Retnuh shoving his hand through my back and siphoning all my light into himself.

"D . . . Don't . . ."

"I need to, Andrew." His voice was nearly apologetic, as if he *almost* regretted the sacrifice of killing his own family. But that wasn't going to stop him from reaching his goal. "Only I can save us all."

Family . . .

DONE! Tim boomed in my head.

Clarity filled my mind like a nuclear explosion vaporizing the clouds of confusion. Power I couldn't explain filled my muscles, and my face shot up to see my baby girl through the window. She was happy. She was alive. And she was going to fucking stay that way.

A millennium of experience filled my brain, just as Tim and I had discussed. I knew how to control time. I knew how to stabilize a failing timeline. I also knew that I didn't have enough power to save my family *and* the universe.

Retnuh knew that too.

With a focus of will, I watched as Retnuh's clutching fist passed through a hole in my chest.

"What . . . ?" he whispered.

Willing myself forward, I easily pulled free from Retnuh's grasp before turning in midair. The hole in my chest cinched itself closed as I peered at him with an emotionless gaze. My feet still remained inches off the ground.

"Fool! If you do not allow me to absorb your energy, then all this would have been for nothing!"

"Come and take it," I answered in a flat, unemotional tone.

One second Retnuh was standing in front of me, and the next he was behind me again, punching at my upper back.

Without more than a thought, I was turned around, holding his fist in my hand.

He took a step forward and tried to push me backwards—so I reacted by wrenching his arm to the side with ease.

"You would risk everything...*everything* over your pride?"

"Look who's talking."

In another flash, Retnuh was behind me again, punching at my back. And this time, I let him.

I registered the impact, as well as my energy being siphoned into his flesh.

"It'll be over soon. Then I'll have the power to defend this timeline from the universe itself."

For the first time, I smiled.

Without moving, I willed myself to face Retnuh. Judging by the confused expression on the man's face, it must have been quite the sight. One moment my back was facing him, and in another, we were locked in a staring contest.

"Do not resist. It'll be easier for you," Retnuh groaned as he focused with a beaded brow on siphoning my energy from my chest.

"Good advice."

With a thought, the energy reversed course, zipping back into my body. But the power didn't come alone. Oh no, they brought friends in the form of Retnuh's own life force.

"No!" he barked, jumping backwards and ripping his fist free from my unharmed chest. There wasn't even a hole in my shirt. It was like it had never happened.

"If you won't give my your energy to save this universe, then I will just have to find another way."

Faster than I could blink, Retnuh threw a glowing blue sphere at my chest.

We both watched as it crashed into my torso, and evaporated like a drop of water on a white-hot skillet.

I didn't smile, or feel any joy at that moment. Only purpose.

Looking back up to Retnuh, I lifted my hand, right as both of his started to glow a fierce white.

Um, Andrew? Tim mentally questioned in a high pitch as the man before me prepared an antimatter blast.

I simply floated there with my palm opened with as much worry as a father ready to catch his toddler's fastest pitch.

Without a battle cry or even a grunt, a determined Retnuh shot out his hands to form a single, thick beam of antimatter.

The air crackled around us as I effortlessly caught something I had feared for so long.

There wasn't even an explosion or shockwave as the energy simply dissipated as it touched my skin—which would have made for a boring climax in a sci-fi movie with heavily injected CGI.

"How?!" was all Retnuh could say as his annihilation attack just... faded.

"Upgrades," I replied, with my palm still pointed toward the man who was right in his efforts to steal my energy.

"You don't realize what you will have to do!"

"I'll figure it out. Besides, I have Tim."

He lifted off the ground at my wordless command, and I saw a flash of terror cross his eyes before something happened that showed how strong he truly was.

Retnuh Ordune, the man hell-bent on saving *only* the universe at all costs, accepted his fate. Recognition replaced the terror in his eyes. He even gave a single nod before extending his arms out to his sides and leaning his head back as he gazed into the night's sky.

"They will live, Retnuh. Your family . . . will endure," I said with a flat voice that was more robotic than the AI living inside me.

Retnuh slowly tilted his face toward me with a slightly furrowed brow.

"As will the universe," I added, knowing what he was seeking.

He searched my eyes, saw no doubt in them, and then closed his own before raising his face toward the sky for the last time.

"Do . . . what must . . . be done," was all he said.

Specks of light began to flow from him; it was like watching millions of birds all lift off at once from a forest of trees. He did not scream, nor did he appear to be in any pain as I siphoned his life's energy into my outstretched hand.

I could feel power equal to my own flow into me, but I took no pleasure in it unlike before, when absorbing his variant's life. It was also clear that the energy I had siphoned from the other Retnuh in the hospital bed was like a drop compared to every ocean on Earth.

A cloud of light enveloped us, with the tiny grains all bending toward my hand like a drain—or a magnet. It reminded me of the school experiment where we poured metal flakes onto magnets to visualize their polarities.

Retnuh's feet slowly faded from view, as did his outstretched hands, followed by his knees and elbows. Soon, only the man's chest and head remained.

"Astrid . . ." were the last breathy words flowing from his fading lips, like a gentle breeze dancing across a valley of green grass and colorful flowers.

Retnuh Ordune . . . was gone, his last thought being of his wife, who had shown him the value of love—and life.

The part of me that was still human hoped that he would see her again.

The last of his light absorbed into me, and my corporeal body began to glow once more.

Um . . . Andrew?

"I know, Tim," I said to the worried AI as I realized that my earthly body wasn't able to contain the immense power that Retnuh and I had held separately. Each of us had been able to manipulate time to our will and change the events of history as we saw fit. And now, my human body was failing to contain the universe-bending power.

What do we do?

I remained floating as I turned toward the house and saw Alison staring at me through blinds she had bent way too far down, threatening to break them—the way she always did when looking outside.

Even though she was across the yard and behind glass, I could still hear her as clearly as if I were standing next to her. "Mommy! Daddity! Come see!"

Her use of my nickname brought a powerful pang to my heart, reminding me that I was still human after all.

"An angel!"

I smiled as Andrew and Sylvie paid no mind to their child's silly imagination.

With a single wave toward my five-year-old daughter, who was going to live a full, long life, I closed my eyes and shifted the scene around me.

"Daddity?" was the last thing I heard before I left my family behind. A family that Andrew Frost would be able to provide for with the help of his soulmate, Sylvie. Little Alison would grow up and live the life that she wanted, with a universe that would continue to exist in perfect harmony with me as its watcher.

CHAPTER 36

Without pain, I watched as my flesh burned away while I floated in the precise center of the universe. Skin, muscle, and finally bone vaporized, leaving my incorporeal form behind, which glowed brighter than any star.

What now, Andrew? a very hesitant Tim asked. It gave me relief to know the AI was still with me. No . . . not the AI. My friend.

"Now? Now, I have a job to do."

Question, Tim asked, *if Retnuh stabilized the tesseract, doesn't that mean everything is fine now?*

"The pull Alison has on the universe is still happening."

How do you know?

"I can *feel* it," I whispered as I looked all around.

Alright. That's not cryptic at all, he said half playfully under his breath. I could tell he was nervous. *So we know the tesseract doesn't dictate Alison's gravitational pull. It only ensured she was born so the Big Reset could happen.*

"Right," I replied, still feeling her incredible influence over the universe.

Then what do we do now if the last timeline is going to eventually collapse into another Big Bang?

"I'm going to stop it."

If you don't mind me being direct—how are you going to control the gravity of an entire *universe?*

"Retnuh."

You . . . You have that kind of power now?

"I can't explain how I know it, Tim, but when I read Alison's research, I realized my dreams weren't dreams. I was experiencing the future; at least a possible one. And because of the memories you gave me, I was not only able to absorb Retnuh's incredible energy, now I can do—" My words froze as I realized what I was about to say.

Do what must be done?

I let out a long, mental sigh.

Too soon?

"No. It's okay. I . . . I just realized he was right."

In what way?

"I thought, once I had won, I'd be able to be with my girls again."

I remembered what Retnuh had said before he accepted his own destiny: "*You don't realize what you will have to do.*"

I'm sorry, Andrew. Truly, I am.

"This . . . This is what I'm meant to do. My destiny."

Spend an eternity at the center of the universe with your hands and feet outstretched like the damn Vitruvian Man?

"No."

Oh, thank science!

"I don't need to outstretch my hands and feet."

. . . You're joking, right? Please tell me you're joking.

"Watch."

An invisible wave of energy pulsed outward from me faster than light could ever hope to travel.

I could feel the edges of the universe where Alison's gravity had stopped their outward trajectories and were on the precipice of turning around to fly in the opposite direction.

With a focus of will, I put out the exact amount of gravitational push needed to cancel out my daughter's pull.

"I can feel it . . ."

So the memories I gave you . . . actually worked? he said in utter awe. I think he even tried to hide a sniffle by pretending to cough.

"Heh. Thanks for not killing me."

Not for lack of trying, Tim joked under his breath.

After a few moments, he went completely silent, and I knew something had crossed his mind.

"Penny for your thoughts?" I asked as I kept my will exerting outward pressure on the entire universe.

Better give me a dollar . . .

I barked out in laughter at his comment, feeling glad to have someone to spend eternity with.

Andrew?

"Yeah?"

Your body is gone, right? I mean, you can't turn into flesh and blood again?

"I think that's right. With the power inside me, I can't be contained by skin and bone any longer." When he didn't respond, I realized I had missed the true meaning of his question. "Why?"

That . . . That means . . . I'm gone, Andrew. My Clepsydra no longer exists.

I saw where he was heading.

"But you're still with me," I said with a smile.

That's the part I don't understand.

An idea came to me. I didn't know if it was true or not, but it *felt* right.

"Have you ever heard the story of Pinocchio?"

I . . . Tim started to say, but I could hear him getting choked up at the suggestion that he, an AI, was more than just his wires and code. He was *alive*.

With a focus of will, I summoned a small orb of energy on my left arm. A Cairn terrier formed, completely made of vibrant light.

Puppy eyes blinked and looked down at its ethereal body as it separated from my own.

"I'm . . . I'm alive?" Tim asked out loud.

"Looks like you are, buddy. Looks like you are."

Tim's puppy lip quivered as he looked at me. "Thank you, Andrew. I . . . I promise to only call you leg butt once a century from now on."

We both burst out in laughter as an unknowing universe continued to exist.

"So what now?" Tim asked, glancing around at the millions upon millions of galaxies that surrounded us. "Do we sing 'One Infinity Bottles of Beer on the Wall'?"

Once again, we both laughed, but my smile quickly fell as I looked in the direction of Earth, billions of light-years away.

"Forgive me for asking, but . . . aren't you going to be sad about missing out on watching little Alison grow up?" Tim asked before quickly realizing how insensitive the question was and adding, "I—I mean . . . I actually don't know what I mean. That was a boneheaded question."

"No," I answered with a smile. Had I been able to cry, a single tear would have slipped down my cheek.

Tim glanced at me with a tilted head before gathering the courage to ask his follow-up question.

"May I ask why not?"

"Because I can see her."

With nothing more than a thought, my consciousness traveled across the universe to land in the kitchen of my home while my glowing body remained at the center of creation.

Andrew Frost was cutting the smallest steak into tiny squares for little Ali, while Sylvie poured lots of ketchup on their daughter's plate.

"I said I wanted chickie nuggies!" Ali protested, and I couldn't help but burst out in laughter.

"What are you laughing at?" Tim asked from billions of light-years away.

Ignoring his question, I continued to watch as my family sat at the table on their ASA-Day, unaware of the fate that had once been slotted for them.

"I did it," I whispered, covering my mouth as I fought back the urge to sob. "I did it . . ."

Floating over to where Ali was hesitantly trying her dripping mass of ketchup with steak somewhere at the center of the condiment cube, I leaned down and kissed the top of her head. I could smell her, and knew nothing in the universe would ever hurt her again.

"Goodbye, sweet Ali. Know that daddity is *so* proud of the woman you will become," I said to my daughter, feeling my heart swell with pride while being pierced with grief. "I love you, baby girl. I love you so much."

Moving to my soulmate, I planted a kiss on top of her head as well, drawing in her intoxicating scent. I started to question how I *could* smell them, but didn't want to look a gift horse in the mouth. Plus, it wasn't important right now. I had an eternity to ponder on . . . well, everything.

"Thank you for the best years of my life, Sylvie. I will cherish the memories we made forever," I whispered to my wife, my soulmate, as I felt my throat tighten at saying goodbye. "And thank you for our precious baby girl. I'll...I'll make sure she's taken care of."

The feeling that I would never be able to hold them in my arms again tried to bubble up, but was quickly suppressed by the tonnage of everything I had done to ensure that my family would live.

Regaining my composure and swallowing the lump in my throat, I looked at the man that I envied more than words could possibly express.

"Take good care of them," I said to Andrew as he continued to laugh at the copious amounts of ketchup Ali was pasting onto every square millimeter of exposed steak. Moving to the kitchen counter, I slowly swiped my hand across the polished stone, leaving behind an envelope with a red bow on it. Written on the front were the words:

Time is precious. Don't wait another second.

"What is it?" Tim asked, appearing beside me as he looked down at the envelope.

"An all-expenses-paid trip to Tahiti."

"Won't they be suspicious?" Tim asked, turning to the family around the table who continued to enjoy their blissful dinner, unaware that Ali's guardian angels watched over them.

"I might have changed the timeline a tad."

"You rigged it to where they won a trip to Tahiti?" Tim let out in a flat tone. "Seriously?"

"I promised I'd make sure my family went on their dream vacation after this was over," I said with a voice that cracked. "And I keep my promises."

"I'm sure the butterfly effect will take the day off on this one, Andrew. Or maybe we should take a peek at the tesseract to see if another stream just happened to appear?"

"Maybe later. Right now, I have a job to do."

Tim nodded, though I could see the silent sigh he let out at my dismissing the potential consequences to my actions. I also didn't care, as long as my family was protected.

Clearing my throat, which was purely symbolic as I was made of pure energy, I turned to Tim, nodded once, and said, "Okay, let's do this."

Closing my eyes, I let my consciousness fly back to my body at the center of everything. Tim followed close behind, turning his glowing puppy body to look at me as I let out a little chortle.

"What's so darn funny?" he asked, cocking his head at me.

"Oh, you know, just . . ." I started to say with a grin that grew. "One infinity bottles of beer on the wall! One infinity bottles of beer! Take one down, pass it around!"

I looked at Tim, who let out a long sigh, shook his head, and then belted out with, "INFINITY-MINUS-ONE BOTTLES OF BEER ON THE WALL!"

ABOUT THE AUTHOR

Hunter Blain is the bestselling author of the Preternatural Chronicles, an urban fantasy series, as well as the Sol Saga, a superhero series. Visit his website at www.HunterBlain.com.

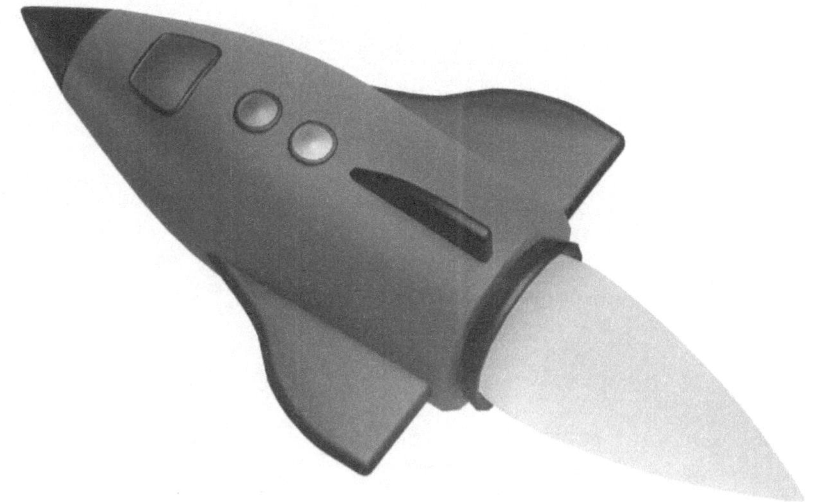

STELLAR
CONTENT AWAITS
follow us on our socials

 podiumentertainment.com

 @podiumentertainment

 /podiumentertainment

 @podium_ent

 @podiumentertainment